RAVENOUS

QUANTUM SERIES, BOOK 5

MARIE FORCE

Donna,
Enjoy Jasper + Ellie!
Marie Force

Ravenous
Quantum Series, Book 5
By: Marie Force
Published by HTJB, Inc.
Copyright 2016. HTJB, Inc.
Cover Design by Moonstruck Cover Design & Photography
Layout: Holly Sullivan
E-book Formatting Fairies
ISBN: 978-1942295525

marieforce.com/quantum

The best way to stay in touch is to subscribe to my newsletter. Go to marieforce.com and subscribe in the box on the top of the screen that asks for your name and email. If you don't hear from me regularly, please check your spam filter and set up your email to allow my messages through to you so you never miss a new book, a chance to win great prizes or a possible appearance in your area.

The Quantum Series

CHAPTER 1

Ellie

While everyone celebrates Hayden and Addie's engagement, I slip out a side door, needing some air after watching the emotional reunion between Addie and her dad and his acceptance, finally, of Hayden. I'm so happy for both of them. I think they're great together, and Hayden needs someone like Addie to keep him grounded and sane. Not to mention that after the shameful way he was raised, he deserves to be someone's true love.

As I walk out to the far end of the pool deck at my brother's gorgeous home in Mexico and look down on the sea below, I can't help but wonder whether I deserve the same. Watching my brother, Flynn, fall madly in love with Natalie, and now Hayden and Addie, who've gone from an unexpected kiss at the Oscars a few weeks ago to engaged, I've begun to question whether I'm ever going to get my turn. Both my sisters have been married for years to great guys I would've hand-chosen for them. For the longest time, Flynn and I were the Godfrey family holdouts, and now he's gone over to the dark side, too.

Though I suppose it's not really the dark side if the perpetually happy, silly grin on his face is any indication of his true feelings about love and marriage. Natalie is the ideal woman for him, and I'm thrilled for them. I used to worry he would never find anyone real or genuine in the Hollywood fishbowl in which he lives. But Natalie is as real as it gets, and I adore her. My whole family does. Everyone is happy.

That leaves me as the only Godfrey still single. At Flynn's wedding, I heard my mother tell someone she's proud of me for focusing on my career. My sisters both have successful careers—Aimee owns a dance studio, and Annie is an attorney—*and* they have beautiful families, too. They make it look easy, when I know it's anything but.

Annie and Hugh have been together since high school, and Aimee met Trent in college. Flynn was married briefly in his early twenties to "Valerie the Hag," as my sisters and I called her back when she nearly ruined our beloved "baby" brother's life with her shenanigans.

Me? I've never come close to getting married. Truth be told, I've never come close to being in love.

Guys are a mystery to me. No matter how great one of them may seem, there's always a downside. I've dated guys who were handsome and charming and said all the right things, only to find out they were saying all the right things to a lot of women—at the same time. Then you have Social Guy's alter ego, who is no less frustrating. You know the type—you have to pull every thought out of his head because God forbid he should share anything voluntarily.

I've dated the bad boys, the ones who make a woman's motor run on full steam, before their "badness" evolves into regular old poor behavior that's an instant turnoff. Then you've got your run-of-the-mill commitment-phobes, the ones who tell you from the outset they aren't looking to settle down—ever. Why should they when they can have a different woman every night?

Recently, I had the misfortune of getting mixed up with a whole new type right when I thought I'd seen it all. You know what that guy was after, other than the obvious? An introduction to my famous brother. Yeah, being used to get to my brother was a real blast, and frankly, he turned me off dating in general. I'd rather be by myself forever than be used to get to my famous family members.

Or so I tell myself... Then I'll see my adorable nieces and nephews, my ovaries exploding from the craving for a child of my own, and I'm reminded that I'm not getting any younger. Soon I'll be thirty-six, which isn't ancient by anyone's standards, but my eggs are definitely on a timer.

Now there's a cheerful thought.

I'm thinking about having a baby on my own. Why not? It's the twenty-first century, after all, and I have friends who've done it. One of my college friends had twins by herself and then met a single dad two years later. They're married now and delighted with their combined family.

Not that I think having a baby would improve my luck on the dating front, but I'm sick of waiting for something that probably isn't going to happen, and I don't want to wake up someday, after that timer has gone off, and realize I missed my opportunity to be a mother.

I've gone so far as to look into what would be involved, and my doctor is willing to work with me to make it happen. I'm due to see her again when I get home from Mexico, and the thought of actually doing it makes my skin tingle with excitement and fear and a million other emotions. I haven't told anyone, even my sisters, who usually know everything, but I suppose I'll have to cue in my parents before I actually go through with it.

I giggle at the thought of showing up at my parents' Beverly Hills home, thirty-six, single and pregnant.

"What's so funny, darling?" a voice asks from behind me. And not just any voice, but the panty-melting voice with the British accent that makes me swoon every time I'm around him. I once talked him into reading *The Night Before Christmas* to my family just so I could listen to the way he said the familiar words. My only regret is that I didn't think to record it.

I turn to face Jasper, my brother's close friend and business partner, who has also become my good friend during my tenure as a production manager at Quantum. Jasper... tall, blond, muscular in a lanky sort of way, handsome as sin, talented as all get-out and a manwhore of the highest order. He's the proverbial pot of honey when it comes to women, attracting them as effortlessly as he breathes. Speaking of a man who will never settle for just one when he can have them all, Jasper Autry fits that bill to a T.

"I was just thinking about something funny that happened at home," I say in response to his question, because I can't very well tell him I was thinking about egg timers and ovulation cycles.

"Care to share the joke?"

"It was one of those had-to-be-there things with the kids."

"Ah, I see." He hands me one of the two mimosas he brought outside with him.

"Thank you."

"You're welcome." His golden-brown eyes are always full of mischief, as if he's got a huge secret he's dying to tell me, or at least that's how it seems. Now is no different. Those amazing eyes are alight with glee. "How about our boy Hayden and our lovely Addie? Got to say I never thought I'd see him so... domesticated."

"He's happy," I say more sharply than I intended. "Nothing wrong with that."

Jasper's brow lifts in response to my tone. He's not used to women speaking sharply to him. He's far more accustomed to them dropping their panties at his feet than talking back to him. "Nothing wrong indeed."

"Sorry. I just mean it's nice to see. That's all."

"Believe it or not, I agree, even if my mates are falling like dominoes these days."

"You might not want to drink the water."

"Drinking the water is never a good idea in Mexico."

I crack up laughing, which doesn't surprise me. He makes me laugh frequently. His endlessly witty take on life is one of many things I enjoy about him.

"I couldn't help but notice you looked awfully pensive out here, staring at the deep blue sea all on your lonesome. What's on your mind, darling?"

God, I want to tell him. I want to tell *someone*, and why not Jasper, my good friend who I trust to keep my confidences confidential? He's not in my family. He's not one of my girlfriends who would try to talk me out of it, certain that my Mr. Right is just around the next corner waiting to be found. In fact, he might be the perfect person to test this idea on.

"If I tell you, do you promise not to breathe a word of it to anyone, especially Flynn?"

"Of course I won't tell anyone. Let's not forget you could fairly ruin me with the secrets you've kept for me over the years."

"That is very true."

He takes me by the arm and leads me to one of the double lounge chairs on the pool deck. "Step into my office. My initial consultation is free of charge, but only for the best of friends."

"You are far too charming for your own good."

"My mother says the same thing. I say I'm just charming *enough* for my own good."

Rolling my eyes at his outrageousness, I curl up on the lounge and take a greedy drink from the glass, seeking some much-needed liquid courage.

"Now tell me this deep dark secret before I expire from curiosity."

With the moment of truth upon me, my nerves go bat-shit crazy. This'll be the first time I've said it out loud to anyone who matters. "I'm thinking about... No, wait, that's not true. I'm not thinking about it anymore. I'm actually going to do it."

His brows lift, and I swear he stops breathing.

"I'm going to have a baby."

"You..." His gaze falls to my flat abdomen. "Like... Are you already... Oh. Well. Okay, then."

I can't help but laugh at his stuttering commentary. "No, I'm not pregnant at the moment, but I hope to be. Soon."

"Forgive me for asking the obvious, but I can't help but notice you seem to be stubbornly single. So who's the lucky guy who gets to father this child of yours?"

"Don't know yet. That's part of what has to be decided when I get back to LA. I've got thousands of men to choose from, and I have to decide whether I want looks over brains, or maybe I'll get lucky and find both in one donor."

He closes his eyes and sighs. "Ellie…" Opening his eyes, he looks directly at me and says, "For the love of God and all that's holy, you do *not* need to resort to a sperm bank to find a father for your child."

That makes me angry. "When you're a single woman who wants to have a baby, you *do* need to 'resort' to a sperm bank."

"You, my love, could have any man you want."

"That's not true. It's different for women. We can't run around the way you guys do without getting a nasty reputation, especially when our parents and brother are household names. It's not as easy as you think."

"I hadn't really looked at it from that point of view. I can see how fame by osmosis might pose a bit of a challenge. And PS, we don't 'run around,' as you say."

"What would you call it?" I ask in the drollest tone I own.

A charming smile lights up his gorgeous face. "Having fun?"

"I've tried that route. Hasn't been all that fun. I'm done waiting for lightning to strike. I want a baby, and I'm running out of time to make that happen. I'm doing this." At some point during the getaway to Mexico, my plan moved from *maybe* to *definitely*.

"And you're sure you want to do it this way?"

"I'm sure this is the only way to do it in light of my perpetually single status."

"It's not the *only* way."

I'm almost afraid to look at him, and when I do, the calculating look he gives me makes my skin heat with awareness of him. "What do you mean?"

"You could ask an old friend who is both handsome *and* smart, not to mention incredibly charming, to provide the start-up 'capital' you require to get your project off the ground."

I'm flabbergasted by what he's suggesting, but I can't show him that. I can't take the chance he might be joking. "If only I knew someone who fit that bill."

His low chuckle is both sexy and exciting. "You do. You know just the guy."

My heart is beating so hard and so fast, I fear I might hyperventilate. "And this guy would be willing to provide his 'capital' for such a project?"

"Under the right conditions."

After a long pause, I say, "What conditions?"

"It happens the old-fashioned way. No laboratories, turkey basters or test tubes, just hot, sweaty, no-holds-barred *capital infusion*."

My body ignites at the images that scorch my brain in the scope of five seconds. *Holy shit.* Have I gone blind, deaf and dumb, or is Jasper Autry telling me he wants to have sex with me—and make a baby with me? "Are you for real right now?"

"My darling Ellie, I have never been more 'for real' in my entire life than I'm being right now." He leans in closer to me, so close I stop breathing. "Say yes."

I swallow hard. "Are there other conditions?"

"Only a few."

"I'm listening."

"When you're with me, you're with *only* me."

"Same goes."

Nodding, he says, "Same goes. And we do this my way or not at all."

"What does that mean?" I ask, my voice squeaking.

"I'm in charge in bed."

I'm suddenly so turned on that I'm concerned there'll be a wet spot on the lounge chair when I get up. "What if I'm not into that?"

"Then there's no deal."

I take a moment to process what he's saying. He's dominant in bed. Oh. My. *God.* Clearing my throat, I say, "What about custody of the output of your input?"

Smiling, he says, "All yours with occasional visitation for the capital contributor."

"Would he or she know that you're the contributor?"

"If that's what you want."

"And you'd be amenable to legally binding documents that spell out these things in advance?"

With his finger on my chin, he forces me to look directly into his eyes. "I'd be amenable to anything that gets the supremely sexy and endlessly untouchable Ellie Godfrey into my bed."

Now imagine that sentence said in the sexiest fucking British accent you've *ever* heard. I know, *right*?! What the hell else can I say to that but "Okay."

"Okay, what?"

"We have a deal."

He gifts me with the sexy smile that made a cinematographer into a celebrity. "Suddenly, I can't wait to go home."

CHAPTER 2

Ellie

Two days after Jasper and I struck our "deal," it's clear to me that I've gone into "business" with the devil himself. He watches me constantly, making me feel hunted, but not necessarily in a bad way. More in the about-to-be-devoured way that an antelope would experience when in a cheetah's cross hairs. And yes, I just compared myself to an antelope. But they're always the ones who get eaten in the nature shows, so the analogy fits.

Thankfully, none of the friends or family we're vacationing with has noticed that I'm playing the nervous antelope to Jasper's hungry cheetah. I'll confess to being conflicted about his newfound interest in me, but I suppose I shouldn't be. If a reasonably attractive woman offers a man unfettered access to her vagina for the purposes of breeding, she ought to expect a certain level of interest.

But there's interest, and then there's cheetah-level interest, thus my dilemma. In all the years I've known Jasper and secretly lusted after him and his sexy British accent, I've never once suspected he returned the admiration. Sure, he likes me as a buddy, a colleague, as his close friend's sister, as a woman to vent to about other women. But as a romantic partner? Not so much.

Since our conversation the other morning, however, all that has changed, and his interest is such that I find myself in a perpetual state of arousal and heightened anticipation, wishing we could act immediately on our plans. At the thought of my longtime dream of being a mother coming true, I'm a mess of emotions—excitement, anxiety, joy and fear. That's a lot to hide from the perceptive group that surrounds me on lounge chairs by the pool on our last full day in Mexico.

Everyone is still over the moon about Hayden and Addie's engagement, and talk of wedding plans continues unabated forty-eight hours after the big announcement. Addie is incandescent with happiness, and Hayden hasn't stopped smiling for even a minute. I've never seen my brother's best friend look so serene. Normally, he's like a thundercloud looking for a place to explode. That intensity has served him well in his career, but has made for a messy personal life.

Falling for Addie has grounded and centered him, and I couldn't be happier for both of them. Hayden is the second of our group to take the marital plunge, the first being my brother, Flynn, who can't keep his hands off his lovely wife. They've disappeared together so often during this trip that jokes about search parties have been a daily occurrence.

I enjoy being with Flynn and Natalie for the few hours every day that they come up for air. My brother has spent his adult life in the public eye, his life before Natalie a series of high-profile film roles, adoring fans and a brief disastrous marriage that left him determined to stay single—until Natalie came along and changed his mind about a lot of things.

I'll admit to being a tiny bit envious of my brother, who, like our two sisters, has found true love and a life partner. Only recently have I started to take stock of my life and realize I'm going to end up alone if I can't see past my exacting standards where men are concerned and find someone I can stand to spend my life with.

How's that for a pretty low bar? Someone I can *stand* to spend my life with. You've uncovered my big secret—I'm a realist without a romantic bone in my body, and after having dated every form of toad known to mankind, I'm ready to settle for one who doesn't disgust me. I'm under no illusions that my baby-making enterprise with Jasper will be anything more than a DNA exchange with, perhaps, a few satisfying sexual encounters along the way.

In the meantime, I need to get busy finding an actual father for my yet-to-be-conceived child. I like to think of myself as a modern, independent woman, but underneath my contemporary veneer is the heart of a traditionalist. I was raised in a two-parent family, my nieces and nephews are being raised in two-parent families, and I want the same for my child. I want a man who is ready to settle down, who is mature, comfortable in his own skin, confident but not cocky. Someone who works for a living and won't be looking to sponge off me or my famous family members. It would be nice if he's handsome and polite. As you can see, I'm not being unreasonably picky. I know women who won't date a man if he has so much as a crooked tooth, even if he's the nicest, sexiest, most charming man they've ever met. The tooth is a deal breaker.

I'm not that girl. No one is perfect, least of all me, so why would I expect someone else to be? I'm not looking for perfection, but it would be nice to find someone I could talk to about things that interest me, who keeps up-to-date on what's going on in the world, who cares about the things that matter to me—family, friends, my community, the larger world around us.

None of this sounds overly ambitious, right? Well, you'd be hard-pressed to find a man in Los Angeles, or most of Southern California, for that matter, who meets even half of my reasonable criteria. I've found if he's handsome and fairly intelligent, he's already been married three times and comes with several ex-wives, not to mention multiple kids with all different women. In other words: drama. No, thanks. I get enough drama at work, the kind we manufacture on behalf of Quantum Productions.

I get plenty of drama by association from my famous brother and our famous friends. I don't need it in a relationship, too.

Or maybe you find a guy who is mature, never been married, confident but not cocky. Except when the other shoe drops, you discover he can't hold down a job to save his life, or he doesn't speak to his mother or some other highly undesirable quality emerges that negates the good things.

It's *exhausting*. If it were going to be just me, I'd say to hell with finding a nice, normal guy to settle down with. But I can't deny my child a daily father figure in his or her life simply because I'm tired of the dance. That's not fair to my future child, thus my determination to find *someone*.

When I get home to Los Angeles, I'm going to do something I said I'd never, ever, *ever* do, no matter how desperate things got. I'm going to register with an exclusive dating service that's come highly recommended by my dear friend Marlowe Sloane. The service has a reputation for pairing people who aren't able, for whatever reason, to be listed online. I'll still have to use a different name, so I can keep my famous family out of the equation. If I can find a man who falls in love with *me*, Ellie, and not the Godfrey name, that'll be cause to celebrate. If I find one who might also be willing to raise my unborn child as his own, that'll be a flat-out miracle. I'm hoping for a miracle.

Addie spreads a towel on the lounge next to mine and plops down to work on her already impressive tan. I stay huddled under my umbrella with Estelle Flynn's voice in my head, telling me I'll have wrinkles by forty if I keep up my sun-worshipping ways. My gorgeous mom with her porcelain skin is a real buzz-killer on a Mexican vacation.

"You aren't working, are you?" she asks, eyeing my iPad.

"Nah, just taking a quick look at my email." As head of the production logistics team at Quantum, we're always working two or three films ahead of the rest of the group, scouting locations and securing the permits necessary to film in far-flung locations. We also handle travel, lodging and meals for the talent and crew. "My people have things under control, or so it seems."

"The best part about going on vacation with my boss is that my people are on vacation, too," Addie says. "Ahhhh, so relaxing."

"And so unfair," I say. "I'm on vacation with the bosses and still getting slammed."

"Totally unfair, especially since you're the sister of one of the big bosses."

"Right? I need to demand a meeting with my brother."

"Just do it next week. His assistant is on a badly needed vacation."

My laughter morphs into concern when I notice a big bruise on the inside of Addie's wrist. "What happened there?"

Addie shades her eyes from the sun. "Where?"

"Your wrist is all bruised. Is that from when you fell the other night?" She tripped and nearly fell down a sharp embankment during a thunderstorm. Fortunately, Hayden and Flynn were right behind her and managed to help her to safety.

Turning her arm inward, Addie takes a closer look at it, as if seeing it for the first time. "Oh yeah, must be." Keeping her other hand propped over her eyes, she says, "Tell me I'm crazy, but there seems to be an Englishman in our party looking at you like he wants to have you for dinner."

I don't know where to look—at Jasper sitting on the other side of the pool with the guys or anywhere but there. "I... I have no idea what you mean." The one thing I know for certain is that my brother and the other Quantum partners *cannot* know about my deal with Jasper. It's our personal business, and the last thing I want is to make this a group project with everyone asking questions. I shudder at the thought of it.

"You and Jasper... I can really picture that."

I snort out a laugh. "Glad you can, because I can't. Me and the playboy? Right."

"You know better than to believe everything that's said about him. You know *him* better than that."

"I know that he goes through women like you and I go through water."

Since she can't dispute that fact, Addie says, "Hayden and Flynn think the world of him. That ought to count for something."

"Of course it does, and I also think the world of him, but I know him too well to ever picture what you're envisioning." However, I think enough of him to make a baby with him, not that any of our mutual friends and colleagues will *ever* know about that. The idea of actually "making a baby" with Jasper makes me feel overheated. "I'm going in the pool. Want to come?"

"Thanks, but I'll stay here and grab some Zs while Hayden is in the meeting with Flynn and Nat."

I stand and remove my cover-up, revealing the bikini that seemed modest until I have to wear it in front of Jasper. Now I feel overly exposed, and not in a good way. "They're in a meeting? On vacation?"

"It's informal, which is why I'm out here rather than in there. They're talking about the screenplay for Nat's story. Flynn's got a guy lined up to write it, and he wanted Hayden's input before they move forward."

"They're really going to make that film, huh?"

"Flynn is extremely determined, and you know how that goes."

I laugh, because yes, I know how driven my little brother can be when he sets his mind to something. I'm not unlike him in that way. I've decided I want a baby, and less than two weeks after finally making that decision, I've found someone to father my child and I have a plan. It's a Godfrey family trait. We're all Type-A, get-things-done people, and as I take the steps into the pool, I notice that my baby daddy is watching me. He's watching me very closely.

Jasper

She's killing me in that teeny, tiny bikini that leaves *nothing* to my fertile imagination. If I were to create the ideal Southern California girl, Ellie Godfrey would be her—long legs, full breasts, a flat, toned belly and real blonde hair that cascades down her back, nearly reaching her supple arse.

It's all I can do not to drool at the sight of her in a peach bikini as she disappears under the water and resurfaces looking like a sea nymph. She's an actual wet dream, and the thought of making a baby with her grabs the attention of my John Thomas, which is the last bloody thing I need with Emmett and Sebastian sitting on either side of me and Kristian next to Seb. They're reading, sleeping and listening to music, and thankfully paying no mind to my aroused state.

Wouldn't that be something if they were to tell Flynn that I sported wood while watching his sister in the pool? Thank God for sunglasses. If they happened to notice the wood—and why would they be looking anyway?—at least they won't be able to tell what—or *who*—caused said wood.

Since my conversation with her the other day, all I can think about is having sex with Ellie Godfrey. Prior to that life-changing twenty minutes, the possibility of any kind of sex with her was so remote as to have only been considered in passing. Such as, *Damn, Ellie looks hot today*, or *I wonder how she'd be in bed*, or *Cripes, I'd love to know if her breasts are as fantastic as they look*. Check that one off the list. The bikini confirms they're every bit as spectacular as they appear when fully clothed—a thought that does nothing to ease the ache in my groin.

Bloody hell. I'm lusting after the sister of my friend and business partner. If I wasn't half-knackered on sun and tequila, I might tell myself to knock it off. But I haven't been in my right mind since she confessed to wanting a baby and I offered to provide stud services. As I've yet to have a moment alone with her since, I've wondered a few times if perhaps I dreamed the whole thing.

But I wasn't dreaming when the exquisite Ellie Godfrey told me she yearns for a baby. I wasn't dreaming when I told her I'd happily father her child, but only if we make the baby the old-fashioned way. In truth, I never expected her to take me up on my offer, and that she did so willingly tells me a lot about how badly she wants this baby we're going to make together.

In the days that have passed since our momentous conversation, a few other thoughts have come to mind. First and foremost, no one, especially my family back home in England, can *ever* know that I've fathered a child, for reasons Ellie hasn't the first clue about. Second, I need to talk to Emmett about the legalities, and Ellie needs to engage a lawyer of her own. We need to do this completely by the book.

The last bloody thing on God's green earth that I need is legal problems with any member of the Godfrey family. My association with Flynn has been successful and profitable beyond my wildest dreams, not to mention I value his friendship. I won't risk that even if it means finally getting a chance to touch gorgeous Ellie. Regardless of my worries, my relationship with Flynn won't stop me from moving forward with my plans to get into the baby-making business with his sister.

She's a grown woman who can make her own decisions, and she's decided to allow me the supreme honor of fathering her child. I can't and won't take back my offer, nor will I leave her to the impersonal process of sperm banks, and God knows what else is involved with that. I shudder to imagine how that works.

No, I'm more than happy to do this the way God himself intended, and to allow her to raise our offspring as she sees fit. She'll be a marvelous mother. Of that I have no doubt. She *has* a marvelous mother. I'm more than halfway in love with Stella Flynn, as are most of Flynn's friends. I want Ellie to have her fondest desire, and I expect to fully enjoy knocking her up. As much as I like and admire Ellie, though, she and I could never be an actual couple. She's too sweet—and far too vanilla—for the likes of me.

I can do sweet and vanilla to make a baby. But long-term? No way. I'm almost thirty-seven years old, and I found out a long time ago that I'm not capable of nice and sweet as a rule. No, I want hot, dirty, kinky sex. I *need* it the way some people need caffeine to get through a day. A man reaches a point in life where he's not willing to compromise on certain things. My kink is nonnegotiable, and thus my realization quite some time ago that I'm likely to remain single rather than have to settle for a nice, wholesome girl who'd rather be electrocuted than tied up, flogged, spanked and fucked every which way to Tuesday.

No matter how hard I try, I can't picture Ellie Godfrey submitting to me or any other man. She's not a sub, but I *am* a Dom. I'd like to live to celebrate my next birthday, so I won't be dominating Flynn's sister, as much as I'd love to release the beast with her. The beast shall remain chained and under wraps while we make this baby she wants so badly.

How long could it take anyway? A month, maybe two? Once there's a bun in the oven, I can get back to business as usual, and that means lots of different women who are as kinky as I am, if not more so. Far fewer complications in the long run, even if thoughts of more than baby-making with Ellie have crossed my mind a few times in the last few days. It's just not possible, and that makes me unreasonably sad.

I look over to see that Emmett has put down his book, Seb has his eyes closed and his headphones in place, and Kristian is snoring loud enough to wake the dead, the way he always does after getting pissed on whiskey. "Can I have fifteen minutes Monday morning?" I ask Emmett.

"Sure, what's up?"

"A personal matter." Though it would probably make more sense to retain outside counsel for this personal matter, that's a risk I don't want to take since the mother of this child is Flynn Godfrey's sister. I can't risk some outside attorney deciding it would be more profitable to sell that tidbit to the rags than to serve as my counsel. Finding another lawyer would also take time I'm not willing to waste. I'm afraid to give Ellie the opportunity to reconsider our agreement. As a Quantum partner, I pay a portion of Emmett's salary, and he'll respect the attorney-client nature of our conversation. I have no worries about him telling anyone, even if I fear he won't approve of our plans.

"Everything okay?" he asks, as my friend and not as my attorney.

"Yeah, it's all good, mate. Just a detail I need seen to."

"I'm your guy for details."

Ellie emerges from the pool, glistening with drops of water offsetting her tanned skin, her nipples tightening into buds that I can clearly see under her skimpy top. I have to grit my teeth to contain the urge to pounce right here, right now. Since that's not an option, I'll see to the legalities, and then we'll get down to business as fast as bloody possible.

CHAPTER 3

Ellie

A happy, relaxed, tanned group flies back to Los Angeles on Sunday night. We agreed to stay as long as we possibly could, which is why we touch down at LAX at ten after ten. Flynn and Hayden have nine o'clock meetings in the morning, but I'll be at the office by seven to catch up on the two million emails that piled up while we were away. I'm meeting with my team at nine thirty to be looped back into what's going on.

I'm gathering my stuff when I catch Jasper staring at me. He's done a lot of that over the last few days, and I'm beginning to expect that when I glance his way, he'll be looking at me like he can't wait to see me naked. Antelope, meet cheetah. My body hums with awareness of him, especially the girl parts. If he can make me hum just by looking at me, what'll happen when we get down to baby-making?

"El?" Kristian gestures for me to go ahead so he can follow me off the plane.

"Oh. Sorry."

"Still daydreaming that you're in Mexico?" he asks, chuckling.

"Something like that." I can't very well confess to fantasizing about having steamy baby-making sex with Jasper. Ugh, I'm a hot mess over this, and nothing has even happened yet. All he has to do is speak in that deliciously crisp British accent, and my panties melt.

He could read the Chinese menu to me in that accent, and I'd be done. My family still talks about me getting him to read *The Night Before Christmas* to us just because I wanted to hear it read in that accent. What they don't know is that I went home and got myself off with Pete, my biggest vibrator, still hearing that delicious voice read the most innocent of words.

To this day, the words "'twas the night before Christmas" make me wet when I think about him saying them.

Speaking of Pete, I try to remember the status of his batteries and whether they still have some life left in them. I sure hope so, because I need to take the edge off this crazy craving that's been happening ever since we struck our deal. Every part of me is tingling in anticipation, and I wonder, for a brief second as we get into cars to head home, if I'll see Jasper as soon as tonight.

I go into a panic at the thought of him showing up before I'm ready. I need to shave and wax and... polish. I can't just throw open the gates and let him come rolling in. Preparation must be done, and I need proof that he's clean before the gates open for business.

He must sense my panic attack, because the next time I glance his way, he's got his right eyebrow raised in inquiry. He's getting into the passenger seat of Kristian's new silver Tesla while I unlock my red BMW M6 convertible. Jasper points to his phone, and I nod before getting into my car.

Call you in an hour, his text reads.

Ok.

I can deal with a call. I'm not ready to take him on in person. Not yet anyway. I leave the airport and head north on Route 1 to my home in Venice. I'm not sure if Jasper is going to his place in the city or to his Malibu beach house, but what does it matter? When he calls in fifty-seven minutes, I'll tell him I'm not available tonight and we can talk tomorrow.

My skin feels tight, as if it's shrunk in the time we spent away. Probably too much sun. But if that's the case, how do I explain the beaded nipples and the tingling between my legs that occurs every time I think of the plans I made with Jasper? To say his willingness to father my child was unexpected is putting it quite mildly. Never in a million years had I expected to tell him I want a baby, let alone accept his offer to father my future child.

"It happens the old-fashioned way. No laboratories, turkey basters or test tubes, just hot, sweaty, no-holds-barred capital infusion."

Dear God, remembering the way he said that has me pressing on the accelerator, desperate to get home to Pete. I roll into Venice Beach and drive along the famous boardwalk, which is still busy even late on a Sunday night. While my brother and his friends prefer the refined sophistication of Malibu, I dig the edgier, artsy vibe of Venice. I live a block from the beach in a two-bedroom bungalow that I've fully restored myself. I've taken do-it-yourself classes on everything from plumbing to electrical rewiring to refinishing floors to plastering walls.

Every inch of the gleaming beauty I call home has my stamp on it, and I enjoyed it so much that I'm looking for another house to restore. At this point you must be wondering what a Hollywood princess like me is doing in Venice Beach, renovating my own house when I can afford to hire people to do it for me. That's true, I can. My parents are fabulously wealthy thanks to successful careers in show business. The whole world knows who Max Godfrey and Estelle Flynn are, and their crown prince, Flynn Godfrey, is an international superstar.

But I'm just Ellie, daughter of stars, sister of a superstar, and I live off what I make from a job that pays me very nicely. My parents set up trust funds for each of us that matured on our twenty-fifth birthdays. My sisters used some of their money to buy homes for their families, but I've never touched mine, and I don't think Flynn has ever used his either. He doesn't need it, and neither do I.

I have everything I need in this cozy home within walking distance of the Venice Beach boardwalk and the beach itself. I can smell the ocean from my front porch, along with the scents of fried food and sunscreen and occasionally the exhaust from too many cars and motorcycles.

My parents are "babysitting" my dog, Randolph, and tomorrow I'll go to Beverly Hills to pick him up from Grammy and Pappy's house—and yes, that's what they call themselves when they refer to their granddog, Randy. I think they fear they'll never have actual grandchildren from me, so they go all-out in their affection for my fur baby. Have I ever got a surprise in store for them!

The house is strangely quiet without Randy to greet me, and it smells musty from being closed up all week. I throw open the windows to let in the cool ocean breeze that ruffles the curtains. And no, I didn't make them myself, although sewing is on my list of things I still want to learn how to do. At the doorway to the room across the hall, I flip on the light and study the empty space that I hope to soon fill with a crib, changing table and everything else I need for the baby I want so desperately.

My heart beats faster with excitement now that I have a plan in place to make my dream come true. Jasper and I will make a beautiful baby. I have no doubt about that. I'm just not sure how I'll stand to wait nearly a year to meet my little one. Sighing with impatience, I turn off the light and go into my room.

Though I thought about Pete all the way home, I hold off on our reunion, knowing Jasper is going to call. I unpack the clothes I washed before we left Mexico, change into comfortable pajamas, wash my face and brush my teeth before getting into bed with my phone plugged into the charger. My skin is sensitive and tingly, as if something is about to happen. If he can wind me up like this in anticipation of a phone call—

The phone rings, ten minutes ahead of when he said he would call, and I nearly jump out of my tingling skin.

"For Christ's sakes," I mutter before taking the call and forcing a cheerful, this-is-no-big-deal-when-it's-the-biggest-deal-ever tone. "Hi there."

"Hello, darling." The word sounds like *dahling* in his yummy accent, and the endearment has me melting into the pillows.

"Hi." Wow, how exciting does my *hi* sound after his oh-so-sexy *dahling*?

"Well," he says, "you've put me into a right state the last few days. I hope you know that."

"Wait. What? What did I do?"

"Um, shall we start with the show in the pool yesterday?"

"What show in the pool?" I ask, genuinely baffled.

"The peach bikini, the wet skin, the hard nipples, the endless legs, the hair. Need I continue?"

"I... You..."

His deep, rich laughter makes me hot all over. "All I've thought about since the other morning is how long I have to wait to make good on our plan."

"Oh. You... You have?" That last word sounds more like a squeak than a word from a usually articulate woman. It's the accent. It's my kryptonite. I could die happy if I could go listening to him talk.

"I have indeed. What about you?"

"It's crossed my mind. A time or ten thousand."

That laugh is quickly becoming my second-favorite thing about him.

"So you're excited, then?" he asks in a low, intimate tone that I've never heard from him before. Of course I haven't heard it. I've never been intimate with him before.

I press my legs together, as if that alone can stop the insistent throb between them. "About the baby? Very much so."

"How about the making of the baby? That, too?"

"Um, yes, that, too."

"Ouch."

"Oh no! That's not what I meant! You don't know how relieved I am to not have to go the clinical route to have a baby. You're doing me a huge favor, and I appreciate it."

"Well, I'm sure it'll be a dreadful hardship," he says, sounding so terribly British I would've swooned had I not been in bed, "but somehow I'll get through it."

"You're joking, right?"

"Yes, darling. I'm joking."

"Oh." I release a nervous twitter that sounds nothing like my usual laugh. "Good."

"However, I'm not joking when I say we need to see to the practicalities of our arrangement before we proceed."

"What practicalities do you mean?" Is he thinking your-place-or-mine type of stuff?

"The legal kind, for one. Due to our friendship and as well as my friendship and partnership with your brother, I think we need to tend to the legal business before the fun stuff. Just so there can be no misunderstandings later."

"I can live with that."

"Do you have a lawyer you can ask to represent you?"

I immediately think of my childhood friend Cecily St. James, who's in private practice in LA. "I do."

"If you shoot me his or her info, I'll have Emmett set up a meeting."

"Emmett? As in *Emmett Burke*, who we *work* with?"

"As in Emmett Burke, the general counsel who works for me as one of the Quantum principals."

"But... He's Flynn's friend, his lawyer, his..."

"Ellie, take a breath. I trust him implicitly, and I'm using him as much for your protection as mine."

"How will he protect me if he's your lawyer?"

"He cares about all of us. He'd never breathe a word of what we're planning to do to anyone. I can't be that certain about another lawyer, and I want to be certain. Don't you?"

Well, when he puts it like that... "Yes, of course I do. I'll get you my lawyer's contact information."

"Excellent. We'll get it sewed up right quick and move forward. Yes?"

"You said for one thing. What were the other things?"

"I figured you might have some conditions."

"This may seem somewhat insulting, but I wondered how I'll know that you're, you know... clean."

"You're wise to ask. I'm happy to provide documentation. I assume you'll do the same?"

I tell myself I shouldn't be insulted that he would ask, but the question stings nonetheless. "Absolutely." I was due to see Dr. Breslow on Tuesday and could take care of it then. And since I hadn't had sex since my last exam, I'd be able to easily prove I was STD free.

"Well, very good, then. Soon enough we'll have ourselves sorted and can get down to it."

"Is that a euphemism where you're from?"

"I think it's a euphemism everywhere for what I'm referring to."

His dirty laugh sets off a wildfire that warms me from the inside and makes my face—and other important parts—feel overheated. "I'll see you tomorrow?"

"Yes, see you then." I press the big red button on my phone to end the call and put it aside to reach for the bedside table, where Pete is waiting to take the edge off. That's when I remember I forgot to get batteries. Hopefully, he still has some life left, because I need him tonight.

Jasper

Though I arrive at the office early, eager to see to the details of my arrangement with Ellie, Emmett's first opening isn't until eleven. I'm useless as my morning passes with an unusual lack of productivity. All I can think about is getting Ellie into bed, which is perplexing more than anything. I've known her for years, worked closely with her and hung out in our tight group of friends regularly. Over the years, she's become somewhat of a sounding board for my trials with other women. But until that morning in Mexico, I never allowed my overly active imagination to seriously *go there* with her, because of who she is to Flynn, more than anything. Now she's all I think about. How does that happen so quickly?

I want the details sorted as quickly as possible so we can get on with it. With that goal in mind, I make an appointment with my doctor for tomorrow. Legal, medical and logistical. Two down, one to go. Where will we meet to make our baby? Her place or mine or somewhere neutral, such as a hotel room? I need to ask her what she prefers.

I have shit I need to get accomplished on this first day back to work, but with most of the blood in my body hanging out with J.T., my concentration is crap. By the time eleven rolls around, I'm a useless bag of nerves and hormones, not to mention anxiety. What a potent combination.

Right about now, I should probably make a confession. While I never allowed my imagination to run in Ellie's direction, more than once I wished she wasn't off-limits to me. I've harbored a low-burning, what-if, wouldn't-it-be-nice-if-we-could-but-we-never-will sort of crush on her. Not that I *ever* would've acted on it, for reasons you know by now. But she intrigues me. I can't deny that if I were to seek out an actual relationship, she's someone who could make me reexamine the way I live my life.

However, my life is set up the way it is for reasons I've kept to myself all these years, and I'm not at liberty to reexamine anything. That's why I need to be very, *very* careful with how I approach this baby-making project so no one, especially Ellie, gets hurt.

Emmett buzzes my extension to let me know he's free. When I stand, I experience a moment of dizziness that reminds me of where most of the blood in my body is currently located. "Give me five," I say in reply to him.

"See you then."

The line goes dead, and I force myself to think of the most unsexy things in the world—the smell of liver cooking at my grandma's house on Sundays, smoking, facial tattoos, people who are rude to waiters in restaurants. That last one does the trick. I abhor rudeness.

Now that I've got J.T. under control—for the moment anyway—I head down the hall to Emmett's office, entering after a quick knock.

He's on a tense-sounding call, so I take a seat and feign an interest in my phone to give him some privacy.

He ends the call, slamming the receiver onto the desktop phone.

I raise a brow in his direction.

"I despise the first day back after vacation."

"That bad, huh?"

Emmett waves off the aggravation and forces a smile. "What can I do for you?"

I choose to go for shock value since his day has been shitty so far. "It seems I've decided to have a baby."

Emmett's mouth falls open. "You... You wanna run that by me one more time?"

"You heard me right the first time."

"And you... Have you..." He clears his throat. "Is a baby already on the way?"

"Not yet." Suffice to assume he's no longer thinking about his frustration. I'm amused by the uncharacteristic stammer in his voice. He's usually so cool and collected. It's funny to experience Emmett shocked nearly speechless.

"Oh, so..."

"I've agreed to father a friend's child." I can almost see his brain working overtime to wrap itself around what I'm telling him.

"This friend... She's someone you know well?"

"She's someone we all know well."

Emmett stares at me, waiting for me to fill in the blanks for him.

"Ellie."

His eyes nearly bug out of his head. Yep, definitely not thinking about whatever was stressing him out earlier. "As in *Ellie Godfrey*?" he asks, blanching.

"The one and only."

"Pardon me for asking, but *are you out of your fucking mind*?"

I can't help myself. I laugh. Hard.

Nowhere near as amused as I am, Emmett sits back in his chair, arms crossed, glaring at me.

When I get myself under control, I say, "First off, she's the one who wants a baby. Second, I offered to help her out so she's not stuck messing with a sperm bank. Third, the baby will be hers and hers alone. And fourth, that's where you come in—making sure it's clean and legal and all sewn up."

"So you and Ellie are going to—"

"Make a baby. Right." I stick out my chin for effect. "I imagine he'll be a cute little chap, don't you think?"

"I, uh, yeah, of course. But Jesus, Jasper, it's *Ellie*."

"Yes, I know."

"And do you also know Flynn will fucking kill you for touching his sister?"

"No, he won't. She won't let him. This is what she wants, Em. She wants it more than anything, and if we have our way, no one other than our lawyers will need to know who the baby's father is."

"You really think you can keep something like this a secret?"

"We aren't going to tell anyone. Are you?"

Emmett scowls. "Don't ask me that. You know better."

"I do, and that's why I trust you to handle it for me. I'm giving her full custody and anything else that has to happen to make the baby entirely hers."

He picks up a pen and balances it between his fingers as he eyes me with trepidation in his expression. "As your attorney and your friend, I feel I have to warn you against signing away your rights before the baby is even conceived or born. You may feel differently once you meet your son or daughter."

"I won't feel differently, and Ellie has agreed to liberal visitation, which is all I'm interested in. I have no desire to change nappies or have my beauty sleep interrupted for months." An ache in the center of my chest makes a big, fat liar out of me, but my reality is what it is, and no child of mine is going to be saddled with the burdensome obligations that have marked my life. I wouldn't do that to my worst enemy, let alone my own child.

"Jasper, I can't, in good conscience, allow you to do this."

"Do I need to get another lawyer?"

"Of course not. I just want you to think about it—*really think*—before you do something that can't be undone."

"You're one of my best mates, Em, as you well know. So is Ellie. I don't expect anything to change between her and me once we conceive this child. We'll still be friends, and she'll have what she most wants. I'll get to have some hot sex with a beautiful woman. It's a win-win." And I... I'll be able to look on from a safe distance as my child grows and thrives without the weight on his shoulders that's been sitting on mine since the day I was born.

Emmett taps his pen on the desktop as he continues to stare at me. "This hot sex you're going to have with our friend's sister..."

"What about it?"

He leans in, elbows on his desk, gaze intense and focused now that the shock has worn off. "She's not in the lifestyle, Jasper."

"I know that. I have no plans to dominate her, not the usual way anyhow. She wouldn't have it." I wait a beat while trying to gauge his mood. "So, you'll represent me, yes?"

"Yeah, I'll represent you," he says with obvious reluctance. "I just hope you know what you're doing."

"You say that like I'm often off the rails and out of control."

"You never are, which is why I'm concerned. This isn't like you."

"Every so often, we have to step outside our comfort zone to see what's going on in the rest of the world."

"So that's what this is?"

"This is me doing a favor for a dear friend. Nothing more. Nothing less."

"There are ways you can do this favor without ever laying a hand on her."

"I'm well aware of that, as is she. We've agreed that we prefer the time-tested method of conception over the laboratory version."

Emmett pauses for another long moment before he says, "Does she have representation?"

"She's arranging that today. Shall I have her lawyer get in touch?"

"Um, sure, that'd be good."

"You're not bowling me over with your enthusiasm."

After another long pause, Emmett says, "Despite our close friend-ship, you're still one of my bosses, Jasper, and my job is to protect you, the other principals and Quantum itself from exposure. I wouldn't be doing my job as your counsel if I didn't tell you I think this might be a bad idea. As your friend, I fear it won't be as simple as you make it out to be, and I worry you're getting into something that could be disastrous for you on a number of levels, not the least of which is that Flynn will kill you if he ever finds out—and people you consider close friends may offer to help him."

I listen to what he has to say, and even though I don't agree, I appreciate the place it's coming from. Indeed, we pay him to look out for our best interests, and that's all he's doing. But his warnings aren't going to convince me to rescind my offer. I'd never do that to Ellie—and besides, I'm looking forward to it too much to even think about reneging.

"I understand what you're saying and why you're saying it, but I'm set on this. If you're concerned about being put in an odd position with Flynn, I can get someone else—"

"No. You're not getting someone else."

"Very good, then. We'd like to get the details sorted this week. I know you're swamped after vacation, but I'd appreciate a swift resolution."

"No problem," he says, though I can tell he still isn't happy about it.

No matter. He doesn't need to be happy. He just needs to make sure it's all set up the way we want it.

"Once I hear from her attorney, I'll draw up the papers and set up a meeting for all of us on Thursday. Will that work?"

Three days. I suppose I can wait three more days if I have to. "That works. Thank you." I get up to leave, but I feel his gaze on me as I go. If I'm being truthful, I probably would've said the same stuff to him if the roles were reversed.

The hallway is deserted, so I take a chance and knock on Ellie's closed door, and when she calls out to come in, I duck in before anyone can see me. Yes, I'm aware that I'm being somewhat silly, but our plan feels fragile and tenuous. I'm terrified of something messing it up—like her brother catching wind of it and freaking out before we can consummate our plans.

"Hi," she says, giving me a curious, adorable look. "Just dropping in?"

I realize I'm leaning against the back of her door, acting as if I've escaped from something. Reaching for my lapels, I adjust the fit of my bespoke suit coat and try to find some of my legendary cool. I'm so rarely rattled that the emotion catches me off guard. "I saw Emmett."

"And?"

I drop into her visitor chair, my gaze drawn to the photo of her with her parents that sits on the credenza behind her desk. Today, Ellie is wearing a pretty floral silk blouse and her hair is down. She's lightly tanned from the trip, and the dusting of freckles on her nose is so damned sweet.

"Jasper? Are you all right?"

"I'm sorry. I don't mean to stare. You look quite lovely today. Well, every day, but today in particular." I sound like an utter prat. When she asks me what an utter prat is, I realize I've said that out loud. "It's slang for idiot."

"Ahh, well, you're not an idiot, but you are acting sort of strange."

I comb my fingers through my hair, looking for a way to expend some of the energy rattling around inside me. "Emmett threw me for a bit of a loop."

"Why? Does he disapprove?"

"He didn't say so in as many words, but the gist was that I may regret signing away full custody of a baby who hasn't even been conceived yet."

"Oh."

"Don't worry, I haven't changed my mind about that or anything."

"That wasn't the part I most expected him to object to."

"Well, he did mention the possibility of Flynn and others I consider close mates conspiring to murder me."

That makes her laugh, and the husky, sexy sound catches J.T.'s immediate attention. I cross my legs, hoping to squash the blood supply, but J.T. is a persistent bugger when he sets his mind on something—or someone.

"Have your attorney contact him. He promised to get it done this week."

"I'll have her call him today."

"I'd like to take you to dinner tonight." I hadn't planned to say that when I came in here, but I need to see her away from the minefield that is the office. I need more of her, and that need isn't just coming from J.T. It's bigger than that, a thought that makes my heart beat a little faster than usual. What the bloody hell is wrong with me?

"Oh, um, sure. I can do that. I have to get Randy from my parents' house, but I could go after that."

I decide to get out before J.T. blows up into a full-on cock stand that she'll surely notice. "Great. I'll pick you up at your place at eight." I'm out the door before she can reply or see what being around her has done to me. Christ, I'm a wreck, and I haven't even touched her yet.

CHAPTER 4

Ellie

The second Jasper leaves my office, I'm on the phone with the woman who handles all my waxing needs. I've been going to her for years, but she's usually booked solid weeks in advance. This is one of those instances in which the Godfrey name comes in handy. She's done for the day at five thirty, but agrees to see me after hours. I have no idea whether "dinner" is another of Jasper's euphemisms, and I need to be ready just in case.

His invitation demolishes my concentration for the rest of the day. I sit in on several meetings with my team to go over the sort of details I usually wallow in when it comes to my work. Today, I can't be bothered. All I can think about is the way he looked this morning in a navy suit coat that had obviously been handmade for him, his hair brushed back off his forehead the way he wears it to work, his cheekbones prominent, his skin tanned from the vacation and his golden-brown eyes—

"Ellie?" My assistant, Dax, looks at me with raised brows. He's a hipster, from the top of his curly head to his black-framed glasses to the stud earing, formfitting T-shirt hawking a band I've never heard of, and his lanky frame. He's also frighteningly efficient, and I'd be lost without him. "You with us?"

"Yes, sorry, what was the question?"

"We're talking about the location shoot in Helsinki. Kristian and Hayden had a few questions that we're working on getting answered."

"Right, Helsinki. Okay, what've you got?"

The meeting ends a short time later, and my team files out, leaving me alone with Dax.

"Where are you today, boss lady?" he asks. "Still on vacation?"

"Maybe," I reply with a sheepish smile. "It was a good vacation. I have to leave at four today. I'll catch up from home later."

"Sure, no problem. I'll be here late."

"I appreciate the long hours you've been putting in lately. It hasn't gone unnoticed."

"Are you kidding? My friends are so jealous that I work here, and I love it so much it hardly feels like work."

I hired him after he interned with me while attending UCLA's film school, and he's made himself completely indispensable to me over the last two years. I need to talk to the principals about a raise for him. "Appreciate it."

I return to my office, wade through the swamp that is my email box and acknowledge that Jasper has succeeded in ruining me for the rest of the day. At three, I let Dax know I'm leaving and head out to pick up Randy at my parents' house.

On the ride to Beverly Hills, it occurs to me that I need to get my shit together. I can't afford to blow off work to focus on baby-making and sexy Brits. I've got too much to do and too many people counting on me to get flaky. Besides, I'm going to need to support this child I plan to conceive, so screwing up at work isn't on my agenda.

Tomorrow I'll go back with new focus and give the job my usual attention. But today... Today's a bust. I arrive at my parents' place and see my sister Annie's Mercedes SUV parked outside. I hope she's brought the boys. Inside, Ada, our longtime housekeeper, greets me with a kiss.

"Nice to see you," Ada says. "How was the trip?"

"Fantastic. The return to reality, however, is not so great."

"Ah, give yourself a break. You'll get back in the groove. Are you hungry?"

"I could go for a little snack."

"Coming right up, honey."

"You're the best, Ada." She's worked for our family since we were kids, and we adore her.

"You all say that when you show up hungry," she says, laughing as she heads for the kitchen, calling over her shoulder, "They're out back."

Though it's only in the low seventies today, my nephews are in the pool that my dad keeps heated year-round for his grandkids. Connor, Annie's oldest at seven, is jumping into the deep end with his mom and my dad standing watch as Mason, age four, and Garrett, age two, splash around the stairs in the shallow end with my mom watching them.

Connor lets out a yell when he sees me. "Auntie El, watch this!" He performs a perfect cannonball that soaks my father, who laughs.

"That was a ten," I tell my grinning nephew when he resurfaces. His blond hair is plastered to his head, and his missing front teeth are adorable.

"Watch me spit through the hole in my head!"

"I'm watching." I laugh when he shoots the water through the gap. "Enjoy that while it lasts."

Mom holds out a hand to me. "Welcome home, honey."

I take her hand and bend to kiss her cheek, which is hidden under a huge straw hat. The scent of Joy, the perfume she's worn all my life, tells me I'm home. I kick off my shoes and sit next to her, feet in the pool.

"How was the trip?" Dad asks.

"Horrible. We hated it."

"Don't say 'hate,' Aunt El," Mason says. "It's a bad word."

"You're absolutely right, and I'm only teasing. We loved it."

"I'm so jealous," Annie says from her perch, seated at the center of the pool with her feet in the water. "Our unencumbered siblings jetting off for fun in the sun while Aimee and I are stuck at home. No fair."

A sharp stab of pain in the vicinity of my heart takes me by surprise. If only my sister knew how badly I want to be encumbered. "Don't give me that baloney. Flynn told me you and Aimee are using the house over spring break."

"That's more than a month and a half from now," Annie says, sighing.

"That's what you get for enrolling your kids in school," Dad says with a teasing grin. "I told you you'd regret that."

"You also told us we should homeschool, as if that'd ever happen," Annie replies.

"Are you off today?" I ask her.

"I worked this morning while the monkeys were in school and preschool. I've given up on working afternoons." She runs a small law practice from her home, working around the boys' schedules.

"She brought them here to burn off excess energy," Mom adds. "Which is just fine with us." Garrett comes up the stairs on chubby little toddler legs that I want to bite. He's so damned cute. Mom removes his swim vest and wraps him up in a big beach towel, mindless of the fact that he's probably getting her wet. My parents are magnificent, hands-on grandparents, and I can't wait to see them with my child.

Garrett pops his thumb in his mouth, his eyes heavy as he stares at me.

I lean over to kiss his soft cheek, and he giggles.

"Are you still good for Saturday night?" Annie asks me.

"I can't wait." The boys are sleeping over at my house while their parents go to a wedding in Santa Barbara.

"You're the best aunt ever," Annie says.

Though I know she's sucking up to me because I'm going to watch her kids, the compliment goes straight to my heart. Being the best aunt ever to all my nieces and nephews is very important to me. "I invited Ivy and India to come help me," I say of Aimee's daughters, who are seven and nine.

"Good call," Annie says. "You'll need crowd control."

"Tell the girls your news, Stel," Dad says. He's got his arms propped behind him, his demeanor casual, but I pick up on some unusual tension between my parents, who are, without a doubt, the happiest married people I've ever known.

"What news?" Annie asks. Even though she's wearing sunglasses, I can see her brows narrow into what we call her lawyer mode.

Mom adjusts the towel to protect Garrett from the late-afternoon sun. "I've been offered a residency at Caesars Palace in Las Vegas."

"What does that mean?" Annie asks for both of us.

"Your mom would have her own show, five nights a week, for two years," Dad says. "It's a huge honor."

You're moving to Vegas? The words are out of my mouth before I can take a second to contemplate what I'm saying or how I'm saying it. How can my parents be moving when I'm about to have a baby?

"Nothing has been decided yet," Mom says. "I've received the offer, and your father and I are talking it over. There's a lot to consider." She snuggles Garrett in closer to her as Mason works his way onto her lap, too. Even Connor has gone quiet as he swims in the shallow end. Life without Grammy and Pappy here whenever we need them? Unimaginable! "I can't fathom living away from my family for six months a year."

Six months a year? I can see Annie's what-the-fuck expression even with her sunglasses covering her eyes. They can't live in Vegas for six months a year! No way. And yes, I realize I'm nearly thirty-six, but I see my parents a couple of times a week. Our family is close. We always have been. The thought of them living out of state for *half the year* makes me slightly nauseated, especially in light of my plans. How can I have a baby without my mom nearby to talk me through every aspect of pregnancy, childbirth and motherhood?

"What do you think, Dad?" Annie asks.

"It's an incredible opportunity for Mom, and she's sacrificed many opportunities to raise kids and support my career. Even though neither of us is super eager to live in Vegas, I'm leaving it totally up to her. I'll go where she goes."

Underneath the perfect-husband response, I sense his tension. He doesn't want to go, and I can't blame him. His kids and grandkids are in LA. He doesn't want to be away from us, but he's being supportive of her.

"When do you have to decide?" I ask.

"Not for a couple of weeks yet, so don't fret. We'll figure it out."

Don't fret. Right. How will I think about anything else until she decides?

The sliding door opens, and Ada comes out with snacks and Randy, who bolts toward me the second he sees me, smothering me with dog love and the wet, sloppy kisses that I adore. He's a mixed breed of unknown age and origin who I rescued from a local shelter. His head is white, his body is brown and black and his paws are almost as huge as his heart, which belongs entirely to me—and my dad, who spoils him rotten when I'm away.

"Hey, sweet boy." Hugging him close, I kiss his cute face. "Did you miss your mama?"

He responds with a sharp bark that makes the boys laugh. We swear he understands every word I say.

With the weight of my mother's news hanging over us, I help Annie get the boys changed, and we enjoy cheese, crackers and fruit along with Ada's special homemade lemonade that I've loved all my life. She makes it for me to take home, and I spike it with vodka, not that I tell her that. I bet she suspects, though. Not much gets by the beloved housekeeper who helped to raise the Godfrey kids. She's just back from an extended trip to Puerto Rico to visit her family. It's the first real vacation she's taken in years. My parents insisted she go for two months, which is how she managed to miss Flynn's wedding.

Randy and I head home in the late-afternoon Los Angeles traffic, my thoughts racing with the possibility of my parents splitting their time between LA and Vegas. I didn't think anything could get my mind off baby-making with Jasper, but my mom's news has me reeling. And of course that makes me feel selfish. Dad is right. Mom sacrificed a lot to raise us and support his career. She put her own successful singing career on hold when Annie was born and didn't go back to performing until Flynn was in high school.

Surely she deserves this opportunity to headline her own show. I vow to support whatever decision she makes, no matter how it might affect me, but the thought of them being so far away from us for months on end leaves me with a sick feeling in my belly.

Randy bounds into the house and heads straight for his water bowl, parched after hanging his head out the window all the way home. I get him settled and then head out to my appointment, which is a couple of blocks from my house, so I walk.

They know me at the salon and spa I've frequented for years, and the receptionist waves me through to the waxing area, where Bryn, my longtime friend, greets me with a hug. In her mid-twenties, Bryn is petite with hot pink hair, multiple studs in her ears and one in her nose, and sleeve tattoos on both arms. She's one of the coolest girls I know.

"Look at how tan you are!"

"I'm not tan. I have a few more freckles."

"Well, for you that's tan. Come on in."

Bryn talks to me like we're out for drinks while she waxes my legs and bikini area. In deference to my plans, I go for a full Brazilian.

"Got a hot date?" she asks when we're finished.

"Something like that." I'm not sure what you'd call what I have planned with Jasper, but "date" doesn't seem like the right word.

"The rags are reporting that Flynn's wife is already knocked up. Their words, not mine."

"Well, she's not. They're waiting awhile to have kids."

"You know how I *love* having the inside scoop. Were you there when Hayden and his fiancée got engaged?"

"I wasn't in the room, but they were with us in Mexico. It was very exciting."

"I can't believe he's engaged," Bryn says of a man she's never actually met. I'm endlessly amused, as someone on the periphery of fame, at how people think they know celebrities when all they actually know about them is what's reported. And most of that is pure garbage. "I figured he'd still be a single playboy at fifty."

"He and Addie are amazing together. He's very happy."

"That's incredibly sweet," she says with a sigh. "He's *sooooo* hot. I mean, like crazy, wild, sexy hot."

"Tell me how you really feel," I reply dryly.

She laughs and sends me on my way to my "date" with Jasper, ready for whatever might happen.

By the time eight o'clock rolls around, I'm a hot mess of nerves and anxiety and stress. I want to zip back in time to the morning of Hayden and Addie's engagement and not tell Jasper how badly I want a baby. I want to undo our verbal agreement and put a stop to this before we do something that can't be undone.

My phone chimes with a text from Marlowe Sloane, movie star, Quantum principal and one of my closest friends.

I've got a name for that exclusive dating service I told you about in Mexico.

In another weak vacation moment, I confessed to Marlowe my plan to sign on with an agency to find my Mr. Right. I vow right here and now never to touch tequila again. That's the only excuse I have for all the secrets I spilled in Mexico—secrets that can't be put back in the bottle now that they're out.

I'm going to send Serenity's contact info. She's expecting your call.

Thanks. What's the name of the agency?

It doesn't have one. She keeps it very low-key and off the radar to protect the privacy of her clients. You'll be in good hands with her.

Have you used her?

Nah. You know me. No interest in dating. At all. Let me know what you think of her.

I will, thanks again.

No prob.

I find it humorous that Marlowe, who could have any man she

wants, can't be bothered with dating. Not that I blame her. How would she ever know if a man wanted her or access to her celebrity lifestyle? It's much easier for me as the daughter and sister of stars and the friend of stars to manage my life outside the limelight that's always shining nearby but doesn't quite touch me. I like it that way, especially after watching the paparazzi relentlessly pursue my brother. They nearly ruined his relationship with Natalie before it even got started. I'd never want to live the way he does.

No, I'm totally fine with my off-the-grid existence in Venice Beach. I'd just like to find a nice guy to share that low-key existence with. Tomorrow morning, I'll reach out to Marlowe's friend to get that ball rolling. In the meantime, I've got dinner with a sexy Brit to look forward to.

I contemplate my closet, trying to find the right thing to wear to dinner with the friend who will father my child. Haven't seen that particular scenario in any of the fashion magazines. I settle on an outfit that makes me feel sexy and feminine—a flirty skirt and matching top that reveals more of my breasts than I normally show.

I want to be pretty for him, which makes me feel silly. But that doesn't matter. I want to knock his socks off. It occurs to me as I'm putting some long spiral curls into my hair that he has never been to my house, and I didn't tell him where I live. A burst of panic has me checking my phone to see if he's texted, but there's nothing since Marlowe's last message.

Hopefully, he'll find me. We never hang out at my house because everyone else has much bigger places than I do. I'm putting on mascara when I hear Randy start to bark. Glancing at my phone, I see that Jasper is right on time. I take a deep breath, check the mirror one last time and head for the front door, telling my roommate to pipe down.

I open the door, and there he is, handsome, sexy, amused. Did I mention sexy? He's wearing a dress shirt with the sleeves rolled up on his forearms and black pants. No jeans or T-shirts for this guy. No, he always looks like he stepped off the pages of a men's fashion magazine.

"Come in. You found me. I was wondering if you had the address."

"I had to do a little detective work, but I found you."

The voice, the accent, the entire enticing package has the usual effect on me. It won't take much effort on his part to put me in the mood for baby-making when the time comes. I only have to *think* about getting naked with Jasper for my body to feel electrified with desire. I can't imagine what the reality will be like.

CHAPTER 5

Ellie

"You look smashing, darling."

"Thank you." I appreciate that he approves and that he says so. Most of the guys I've dated fail to notice the effort put into date preparation, and it's always a disappointment when they don't seem to care that I at least tried.

"And your home is beautiful, too. What a gem."

"I've restored every inch of it myself."

"Is that so? I'll need to hear more about these hidden talents of yours."

The most mundane things take on dirty overtones when said in that accent, but the words "hidden talents" are positively filthy. "Where're we going? Do I need a sweater?"

"Wouldn't hurt to bring one. It got chilly after the sun set."

As I go into my bedroom to grab a sweater, I realize he didn't say where we're going. When I return, he's down on one knee giving Randy some much-appreciated love.

"What a lovely boy you are." Yes, even that—a compliment intended for my dog—sounds sexy coming from him.

"That's Randolph, also known as Randy."

"Pleasure to meet you, Randolph." Randy laps up the attention, snuggling into Jasper's neck. He laughs at the dog's shamelessness. "Any port in a storm, huh, buddy?"

"He gives his heart to anyone who wants it."

Jasper looks up at me with gorgeous golden-brown eyes filled with delight. "You want to bring him with us?"

"Oh, um, that would be okay?"

"Absolutely." He gives Randy one more pat on the head and then stands to his full height. "I thought we could use some privacy for the things we need to discuss, so I'm having dinner delivered to my place in Malibu. I hope that's okay."

His place. By ourselves. Well, with Randy if I choose to bring him, and why wouldn't I if we're not going out? "Sure, that's fine."

"Shall we?" He ushers me and Randy on his leash out the door to a low-slung gunmetal-gray sports coupe that I haven't seen before.

"This car is far too nice for Randy," I say, admiring the sleek lines.

"He's fine." Jasper produces a blanket out of the trunk that he lays across the well behind the two seats for Randy. "Up you go, Randolph."

My dog responds to Jasper as if he's the one who feeds him. Once he has the dog settled, he holds the door for me, waiting until I'm belted in to close the door. It smells like leather and cologne and man. I want to breathe in that scent until I have it committed to memory. The aroma only gets better when the man himself gets into the driver's side and starts the car.

"What kind of car is this?"

"Your brother would be appalled that you have to ask."

"Trust me, I know, but I'm clueless when it comes to cars despite his best efforts to educate me."

Chuckling, Jasper says, "It's a Jaguar." In his accent, that comes out as jag-y-ar.

"It's lovely."

"I like it."

"Is it new? I haven't seen it before."

"A recent acquisition, a little gift-to-self after the Oscar."

"Good for you. You should celebrate winning the Oscar. It's an amazing accomplishment."

"I owe it all to your brother and Hayden. They had an incredible vision for *Camouflage*, and it was an honor to be part of it."

"It's my favorite movie ever—and not just because my brother starred in it. Everything about it was perfection, especially the cinematography."

"You flatterer," he says, laughing.

"No, I mean it. The camera work was exceptional, and you deserved every award you received."

"Thank you, darling. I appreciate that."

My heart does a funny fluttery thing when he calls me that. "How did you get into filmmaking?"

He pauses for a second before he says, "I don't ever recall a time when I wasn't taking pictures and making movies, beginning with a camera my grandfather gave me and an eight-millimeter camera that someone gave my dad for Christmas one year. He never touched it, but I filmed everything. I drove my family mad with it. Captured a few things we'd all rather forget." I notice that he tightens his grip on the wheel and that his jaw pulses with unusual tension. "But it was definitely my calling. Over my father's vociferous objections, I attended film school at USC, did a few well-placed internships, met your brother and Hayden on one of my first films, and the rest, as they say, is history."

"Why did your father object if it was obviously your calling?"

"He thinks anything having to do with Hollywood and the movie business is vulgar, and of course it is, which is why we all love it so much." This is said with the humor I've come to expect from him, but I don't miss the bitter edge to his voice.

"What did he say when you won the Oscar? Nothing vulgar about that."

"That's the very *epitome* of vulgar. Have you seen that statue? It would be stuffed in a closet in my father's home."

Suddenly, I'm angry on his behalf. "He wasn't happy for you?"

"Darling," he says indulgently, patting my knee, "I don't give a rat's arse whether or not he was happy for me. His opinion stopped mattering to me decades ago. He's just the man who spawned me. My mum and sisters were thrilled. That's more than enough for me. And my family, my *real* family these days, is all of you. My Quantum family."

I'm terribly sad to think that he could win his profession's top award and not have a father who was bursting with pride the way mine would be.

"Not everyone gets a Max Godfrey," he says softly.

I send him a rueful smile. "You read my mind." After a pause, I ask, "Are you close to any of them?"

"I talk to my mum and sisters quite regularly. One of them is in New York, and the others are back in England, raising families, doing what's expected of them."

"So you're the black sheep?"

"Something like that." As always, his wry humor comes through, even when discussing what sounds like an estrangement from his father. I'd love to know the details, but I'd never ask for more than he's willing to share—and I sense he's already told me more than he usually tells anyone. Over the years, I've heard him tell hilarious stories from his years at boarding school, but I realize I've never once heard him talk about his father. Now I know why.

"And here I've been pouting all afternoon because my mom told me she's been offered a residency at Caesars Palace in Las Vegas."

"Wow, good for her."

"Absolutely, but what does it say about me at almost thirty-six that the thought of my parents living somewhere else half the year breaks my heart?"

"That you love them and are extremely close to them."

"Yes," I say softly, horrified by a rush of tears. "And how do I have a baby without them to hold both my hands?"

"*Awww*, poor poppet. Your mummy is going away and leaving you."

I try not to laugh and fail. "Don't make fun of me. I'm quite distraught over this unexpected development."

"Correct me if I'm wrong, but knowing Stella as I do, if she were to hear another wee one is on the way, is it possible she might turn down that delicious offer in Vegas?"

"I suppose she probably would, but that makes me feel selfish. It's such a great opportunity for her. I'd hate to see her turn it down because of me."

"So which is it?" he asks, laughing. "You want her to stay or you want her to go?"

"I don't know! I'm an awful daughter."

"That's hardly true. You and your sisters and brother are very devoted to your parents, and I envy the Godfrey family bond. I truly do."

"Well, you're certainly part of the Godfrey family. You know that."

"Thank you, love. That's kind of you to say."

I shiver in my seat and not because the night air is chilly. No, it's the way he calls me "love" and "darling." He's easy to talk to, even when he's poking fun at my dithering. "It's true. Everyone at Quantum is part of our family. That's the way my parents have always been. They collect people. Their friends, our friends, everyone is always welcome. I want to be like that with my child. I want mine to be the house they all come to because we've got the best snacks and a mom who's genuinely interested in them the way my mom was."

"That sounds lovely," he says with a wistful sigh.

"I'm sorry. You just said you had a difficult time with your father, and here I am going on—"

His hand covers mine, warm and solid and delicious. "No apologies needed. Your vision of motherhood is truly lovely, and our child will be very lucky to have you for a mum."

I think my fallopian tubes just melted. At the rate at which he makes important parts of me melt, I won't have a reproductive system worth a damn when I need it. Turning my hand up so we are palm to palm, I give his a squeeze.

"I get all fluttery inside when you talk of our child," I confess. "I still can't believe this is actually happening."

"No post-vacation regrets?"

Alarmed, I look over to find him watching the road with no hint of amusement in his expression. "N-no. Do you? Have regrets, I mean?" I die ten thousand deaths as I wait for him to reply.

He squeezes my hand, setting off fireworks in my bloodstream. "I have no regrets, and I can't wait to get started."

My sigh of relief is audible.

Glancing over at me, he frowns ever so slightly. "You didn't actually think I'd back out, did you?"

"I don't know. I've been all over the place about this for days. I'm an emotional disaster area, which is why my mom's news hit me so hard today."

"I would never do that to you, Ellie. Ever."

"Thank you for understanding how much this means to me."

"I do understand, and I'm fully committed to infusing my capital."

I laugh, but only because spontaneous combustion isn't an option. I'd hate to make a mess in his new car. Every part of me is awake and alive and filled with anticipation.

We arrive at his gorgeous but cozy contemporary-style house in Malibu, where I've been a guest many times in the past. Randy goes bounding in ahead of us, giving the new place a thorough sniffing. He's fully trained, so I'm not concerned about him lifting his leg, but I keep an eye on him anyway.

"Don't worry," Jasper says from behind me. "There's nothing he can hurt here. Let him have his fun."

His hand lands on my shoulder, and I startle from the unexpected contact.

"Whoa." He has both hands on my shoulders now. "What's this?"

"I'm nervous." The confession seems to relieve some of the anxiety that has knotted in my belly.

"To be with me?" he asks, sounding incredulous. The whisper of his breath against my neck sets off a chain reaction of sensation that ends in a throb between my legs. I've been on edge all day, and I had blamed that on Pete because his batteries died before he could finish the job last night. But now I know it wasn't Pete's fault. It's Jasper.

"No, it's not that." I'm so glad he's behind me and can't see the scarlet hue that has overtaken my face.

Naturally, he turns me, forcing me to reveal my embarrassment to him. "Then what?" He runs a finger over my right cheek. "What's wrong?"

I force myself to look up at him. "Are you worried that it'll be weird?"

"That what will be weird?"

God, is he really going to make me say it? "This. You, me, *us*."

"The sex part, you mean?"

"Ah, yeah," I say with a nervous laugh.

With both hands now framing my face, he shakes his head slowly. It takes a second for me to realize he's getting closer, and my breath catches in my throat in the second before his lips brush up against mine. "I don't think it'll be weird." His voice is a gruff whisper that sets off more fireworks inside me. "I don't think it'll be weird at all." He draws me in closer, until our bodies are pressed together. The unmistakable shape of his erection against my belly lets me know he's equally affected.

I should do something, but I can't seem to move, even to put my arms around him to encourage him to keep kissing me. A slight whimper escapes from my lips, which draws a groan from him. As if someone has thrown a switch, the kiss goes from innocent to filthy in the scope of a single heartbeat. His tongue slips between my parted lips, and suddenly, I'm no longer paralyzed with indecision.

My hands move from his chest to his shoulders to the back of his head, where I bury my fingers in his hair to keep him from getting away.

One of his hands moves from my face to my back, sliding down until he's cupping my ass and pulling me in even tighter against him. This is, without a shadow of a doubt, the most erotically charged kiss of my life, and I can't get enough of his tongue and his lips and the scent of expensive, sexy cologne.

It all comes to a crashing, sudden halt when Randy jumps up, nearly knocking us over as he breaks us apart. Only Jasper's hand on my arm keeps me from falling. My legs wobble under me as Randy looks up at me with his cute, smiling dog face. He's damned proud of himself for protecting me.

"No, no, Randy," I say when I've recovered the ability to speak. "No jumping."

He drops into his playful puppy pose and barks.

Jasper laughs at his antics. "Whose idea was it to invite you, spoilsport?"

"Yours. All yours."

Randy barks again, looking for someone to play with him.

Jasper runs a fingertip over my cheek and once again has my full attention. "See? Not weird. Not weird at all. In fact, hotter than bloody hell, just as I always suspected it might be."

Wait, what? He always suspected it might be? "You... You thought about me that way, before Mexico?"

"Darling, I've thought about you that way since the day we met."

CHAPTER 6

Jasper

I'm so hard, I can barely function. That kiss, that bloody kiss... It blew the top right off my head and left me dying for more. Next time, Randy-the-mood-killer stays home. When I think about what might've happened if we hadn't been so rudely interrupted, I get even harder, if that's possible.

"How about a drink?" I ask, desperate for a distraction, anything to calm the wildfire that burns inside me. One taste. That's all it took to turn my world upside down. Since I confessed to having had a thing for her for a while now, she hasn't had much to say. And why exactly did I feel the need to blurt that out?

Blame it on the overload of testosterone that's currently addling my brain.

"Um, sure. I could use one."

Smiling, I take her by the hand and tow her behind me into the kitchen. "What's your pleasure?"

"Vodka would do the trick."

I pour her a Grey Goose and soda and add a twist of lime, just the way she likes it.

"Someone has been paying attention."

Shrugging, I pour Bushmills Irish whiskey for myself, straight up.

"We've certainly shared a few cocktails together. Cheers." As she touches her glass to mine, I note the rosy glow of her skin and her swollen lips. I can't resist leaning in for another taste.

"Still not weird."

Her shy smile makes me feel curiously off balance.

"It occurs to me," I say between sips of liquid courage, "that it might behoove us to partake in a dry run. Well, not a *dry* run, terrible choice of words, but more of a *rehearsal*, if you will."

Her eyes widen as my suggestion registers. "Like, now?"

J.T. stands up and cheers in support of now. Right fucking now. "After dinner, perhaps?" I reach across the annoying expanse of the kitchen counter that now separates us to take hold of her hand. "We could get the awkward preliminaries, if there are any, out of the way before we get down to business." I fear I may appear shamelessly opportunistic, but I can't be bothered to care. After the hottest bloody kiss of my life, I want more, and I can't wait days to have it. Or her.

"Awkward preliminaries," she says, touching her bottom lip in a way that has me zeroing in on her mouth. "Is that what we're calling it?"

"After that kiss, I think we can safely drop the awkward part and just call it preliminaries. Or rehearsal for the main event."

Before she can reply, the doorbell rings, breaking the spell that lingers between us. "That'll be dinner," I say, cursing the timing of the delivery. Now I have to get through dinner without her answer to my question. With Randy hot on my heels, I go to the door to accept the delivery, pressing a twenty into the hand of the young delivery guy.

"Thanks, man."

In deference to Ellie's well-documented love of all things Mexican, I've ordered from one of the best restaurants in Malibu, hoping she's still excited for Mexican cuisine after the trip. Maybe I should've gotten something different, since we gorged on authentic Mexican for a whole week. I'm so rarely uncertain when it comes to women, and here I am again off balance where she's concerned.

"That smells amazing," she says, putting me immediately at ease.

"I know it's your favorite. I just hope you haven't had enough of it recently."

"I will never, ever, for the rest of my life, have enough Mexican."

"Oh, good." I'm inordinately relieved to have gotten it right.

She helps me unpack the bag, oohing and ahhing over my choices. "Flynn loves this restaurant."

"He's the one who told me about it."

I'd planned to set the dining room table, but we end up on stools in the kitchen, which is utterly perfect. Despite the kiss that rocked us both, the conversation is easy and unencumbered by the weight of expectations—or anticipation. I'm full of both, but I make an effort to keep things light while we devour fish tacos, shrimp ceviche, tortilla salad and delicious rice.

"This is so good," Ellie says between bites. "I've been going through withdrawals since we got home."

"Glad you like it." I surreptitiously pass corn chips to Randy, who's already figured out I'm a soft touch. If the way to a woman's heart is through her dog, I'm well on my way. Like a needle dragging across a vinyl record, that thought brings me up short. Am I trying to get to Ellie's heart? Of course not. This is about sex and making a baby. Nothing more.

Except that kiss...

Was just a kiss. Making it into something more would be a mistake of epic proportions.

"I've made a decision," Ellie announces after polishing off a second taco.

"What's that?"

"I'm going to join an elite dating service to find someone who can be an everyday father to my child."

Again, the needle drags across the vinyl. W-what did she say? "You're going to..."

"Find a man to settle down with. It's time, wouldn't you say?"

"Oh. Well, I suppose so." I'm definitely going to need some more whiskey for this conversation. I stand up to refill my glass, aware of an ache in the vicinity of my chest that hadn't been there a minute ago.

The thought of Ellie, beautiful, sweet, vivacious Ellie, with another man suddenly appalls me. Yes, I'm well aware that I have no right to be appalled by anything she does, but I am nonetheless.

"I need someone to filter out the frogs for me," she continues, apparently unaware that she has stuck a knife in my chest with this news. "Marlowe knows someone who runs an agency for high-profile people. Not that I'm high-profile, but I'm related to people who are. I'm trying to come up with a different last name so no one will know who I am. Maybe Ellie Flynn? They wouldn't connect me to my brother because that's his first name. What do you think?"

What do I think? First and foremost, I want to strangle Marlowe, my close friend and partner, for hooking Ellie up with a dating service. Second, I want to murder every man she goes out with, and while I'm feeling felonious, maybe I'll take out the friend of Marlowe's who runs the bleeding service.

"You don't think it's presumptuous of me to consider myself high-profile, do you?"

"Um, no, of course not." Why are my hands trembling as I cap the bottle?

"The last guy I dated wanted me to introduce him to Flynn. I'm a little burned after that. I don't want anyone to know who I really am until I decide I want to keep him, you know?"

The bottle lands a little harder than expected on the counter, the sound drawing a bark from Randy, who'd been sleeping on the kitchen floor.

"Jasper? Are you okay?"

No, I am not okay. I force a blank expression when I return to my seat. "I, uh, I thought we were going to be, you know, exclusive during the capital-infusion portion of the program."

Her face lights up with laughter and embarrassment. "I'm not going to *sleep* with any of them! What do you take me for?"

"Oh, um, uh..." Christ, she's turned me into a babbling prat!

"No, this is all about dating, not sex. Not now anyway."

"And how do you plan to explain the child you hope to soon be expecting?"

She ponders that for a moment. "I'll say the baby belongs to my ex, who's not interested in being a father. That's kind of the truth, right?"

Every single thing in me rejects that statement. Everything. I want to rage and roar and rail against the absolute unfairness of it all. In any life other than the one I was born into, I'd want to marry a girl like Ellie and give her as many babies as she wants. But in my life, that's simply not possible, and I fucking hate that reality.

"Jasper? Are you okay? Why are you sweating? Oh, it's the jalapeños!" She jumps up, finds the glasses, pours me a tall glass of ice water and puts it down in front of me. "Drink that. It'll help."

Looking to buy myself some time to explain my odd reaction to myself so I can explain it to her, I down most of the water in one big drink.

"Better?" she asks, watching me carefully.

"Yeah, thanks." I say what she wants to hear, but nothing is better. No, everything is seriously screwed up, and I have only myself to blame. I'm the one who told her I'd happily help her make a baby but that our offspring was all hers to raise as she saw fit. So how can I object to her plan to find a real father for the baby, someone who will be there for him or her every day when I can't be?

If I know it's the best thing for her and our child, why does my heart feel like it's been put through a paper shredder? My stomach turns, the satisfying meal souring in my gut.

"Do you want to go outside and get some air?" she asks, looking at me with concern.

That sounds like a bloody good idea. Maybe I'll be able to breathe out there. "Yes, let's."

Randy tags along as we go out onto the deck that overlooks the Pacific. Usually it's my favorite place in the whole world, but tonight I'm too out of sorts to properly enjoy the stunning view. We settle on a double lounge chair, sharing a blanket. It's chilly, so she snuggles up to me while Randy settles on the other side of her. The cool air helps to calm me, but having her snug against me puts J.T. on full alert.

"Will you help me decide which guy would be good for me and the baby?"

That question drives the dagger deeper into my chest, making breathing a difficult proposition.

"I mean, it'll be your child, too, and you ought to have a say in who helps to raise him. Or her. I'm not sure why I always picture myself with a boy," she says with a laugh.

I can see him so clearly—a blond little boy who looks just like his mother. The ache is nearly unbearable. What the hell is wrong with me? Why does the thought of her choosing another man to raise my child make me feel like I'm having a heart attack? It's what I said I wanted when we struck our deal, but now...

Fuck. Fuck, fuck, fuck, *fuck*.

"You're quiet. Are you okay?" She looks up at me with those clear blue eyes that are always so open and honest.

I don't want to talk about the other guys she's going to date. I don't want to think about her with anyone else but me. At least not while she's snuggled up to me, warm and soft and endlessly appealing. "I'm thinking about that kiss."

"Oh."

"Are you thinking about it?"

"It's crossed my mind a time or maybe two." She looks up at me at the same second I look down at her, and everything goes still. I'm no longer aware of the breeze or the sound of the waves roaring toward the shore. I can't smell the ocean. I only see her. I only hear her. I only smell her unmistakable scent. And then I'm kissing her again, this time skipping over the preliminaries and going right to the tongue-twisting good stuff. I want to fuck the thought of other men right out of her, and yes, I'm well aware that I sound like a savage even thinking such a thing. But there it is anyway.

Without breaking the kiss, I pull her on top of me, dropping my half of the lounge down a few notches to get the angle I want.

Randy whimpers in his sleep but doesn't wake up. Just as well, he'd probably tear my throat out if he knew what I plan to do to his mother. And what exactly do I plan to do?

Everything.

Ellie

I'm on top of Jasper, who's kissing me wildly, with a sort of desperation I didn't expect from him. He cups my breasts and runs his thumbs over my nipples, making me squirm from the need for more. Something happened earlier when I told him my plans to find a full-time father for our child. Did he not like hearing that? Should I not have told him?

We've always talked about our dating exploits. Is everything different now that we're fooling around?

"Let's go inside," he says in a raspy tone between kisses.

With his hands on my hips, he helps me up and takes my hand. We leave Randy snoring on the lounge. I expect him to lead me to the sofa, but we go directly to the stairs. Am I ready for this? Am I prepared to actually have sex with Jasper? Watching his tight, muscular ass proceed up the stairs ahead of me, I decide that hell, yes, I'm ready.

My legs feel rubbery and uncooperative as I scramble to keep up with him. He's in a rush all of a sudden.

"Jasper..."

"Yeah?"

"What, I mean... You... You're in a rush."

"A rush," he says with a dry, ironic laugh. "You've had me on the edge of madness for *days*, and you say I'm in a rush." Taking hold of my hand, he places it over the rigid flesh of his cock, which is long and thick and very hard. My mouth waters in anticipation. "I've been dealing with *him* since that morning in Mexico, so you'll pardon me if it doesn't feel like a rush to *us*."

Is he really referring to his cock as a person? The thought of that makes me giggle.

His brows narrow in annoyance. "You think that's funny?"

"A little bit."

"I need to fuck you."

The blunt statement takes me completely by surprise and sends my already overheated body into the red zone.

"Is that okay?"

I'm so aroused and surprised by this unexpected alpha side of him that I can barely think, let alone formulate a reply.

"Ellie, focus," he says sternly. "I won't touch you until you say it's okay."

"It's... It's okay."

He forgoes the buttons on my blouse and pulls it up and over my head. Groaning, he buries his face in my cleavage, kissing and licking and nibbling on the tops of my breasts.

I hold on to his shoulders because I might topple over if I don't hold on to something. My bra disappears, my skirt falls to the floor, and I'm left standing in a skimpy pair of bikini panties and wedge heels.

"So fucking sexy," he says in that low growl that's made even more insanely hot by his accent. "I almost came in my pants watching you swim the other day. I wanted to put my hands on you right there in front of everyone. It almost killed me that I couldn't."

Before I can process the things he's saying, he takes my left nipple into his mouth, stroking it with his tongue and sucking on it at the same. I cry out in surprise as a sharp spike of desire registers between my legs.

"You have no idea how many times I wished I could take you by the hand and drag you off somewhere to do this to you." He cups my mound, pressing two fingers into my core with only the silk of my panties blocking the way.

"While we were in Mexico?" I ask breathlessly while grinding against his fingers, seeking relief.

"As long as I've known you." He pays homage to my other breast while continuing to stroke my pussy.

The edge that Pete left me on last night can't be compared to the one Jasper has me on now, as years of fantasy become reality one stroke at a time. God, he's going to make me come, and he's barely touched me. I'm nearly there when he changes the game, withdrawing his fingers from my core and turning me so my back is against his bed.

"Sit on the edge," He never takes his eyes off me as he unbuttons his shirt and whips it off, discarding it along with shoes that go flying. "Lie back." He unbuckles his belt and sheds his pants, kicking them to the side with his shoes.

I do as he asks, propping myself on my elbows so I don't miss anything. I've seen his chest a hundred times, at the beach, on vacation, at pool parties here and in Mexico, but I've never had the luxury of staring that I have now. He's lean and muscular, finely built with golden chest hair that trails down his well-muscled belly and disappears into silk boxers that are currently tented.

His hands find my knees and urge my legs apart.

The muscles in my thighs are liquid, quivering with anticipation and need like I've never known before. This is the man who will father my child. He insisted on doing it the old-fashioned way, a detail I'm now exceedingly grateful for since I've never had sex as hot as this promises to be.

He leans over me, his lips soft on my belly as his fingers press against my clit.

I can't help squirming as I try to find the perfect angle.

"Don't move," he says in that authoritative tone that sends spikes of heat spearing through me. "Do you remember what I said that morning in Mexico? About who's in charge when we're in bed?"

Holding my breath, I nod.

"I own your pleasure, sweet Ellie. You come when I say you can, understood?"

Dear God. Do I understand?

"Ellie? I need the words. Tell me you understand." He takes my nipple between his teeth and bites down just hard enough to draw a keening cry from me.

"Yes," I say on a gasp, "I understand."

"If you come before I say you can, I'll spank you. Do you understand that, too?"

"You'll..."

"Spank you, and I'll make it hurt. Tell me you understand."

I swallow hard, mortified that the thought of his hand crashing down on my ass nearly makes me come. "Y-yes, I understand."

"If you want me to stop, you only have to say so, okay?"

"Okay." At this point, I want to beg him to get on with it, to please relieve the awful ache that's taken me over.

His expression changes then from tension to relief. He's relieved that I've agreed to his terms. "Relax. I don't bite. Not hard anyway."

CHAPTER 7

Ellie

I'm a quivering, trembling wreck as his lips move over my abdomen, working their way down to my pussy.

Reaching under me, he tugs on my panties, and I raise my hips to help him remove them.

"Oh God," he mutters. "You're so smooth and bare."

His reaction makes me thankful I took the time to see Bryn earlier.

My legs are forced farther apart by the broad expanse of his shoulders as he dives face-first into the core of my desire. He knows exactly where I need him, and he focuses on my clit, licking and sucking and driving me insane. I'm already on the verge of explosive release when he drives two fingers into me and curls them until he finds the spot that makes me detonate.

I'm completely lost to the earth-shattering orgasm when I remember that I wasn't supposed to let that happen without his permission.

"Mmm," he says, his lips and tongue soft against my sensitive flesh, "someone is in *big* trouble."

That's all it takes to restart the climb.

"Did you forget the rules you agreed to five minutes ago?"

"I... I... You... That was your fault!"

"That's not how it works. You have to learn to control yourself."

I can hear the amusement in his voice as he continues to stroke me, building the fire all over again. "Don't. I can't. I can't stop it."

"Yes, you can. Focus."

"I need something to focus on besides what you're doing to me."

"I can help you there." He withdraws from me and climbs onto the bed, shedding his briefs as he goes. Then he is leaning over me, his hard, thick cock over my face, and his intention becomes very clear.

Jesus. I haven't done this since I was twenty-something and trying everything once. Grasping his hard length, I begin to stroke him as he leans forward to pick up where he left off, albeit from a different angle. I quickly discover he's no less effective from this side, and decide I need to distract him before he can milk another orgasm from me.

Fitting my lips around the broad head of his cock, I take him into my mouth, sucking and licking as I go.

His low growl vibrates against my clit, making me startle.

Six days after I agreed to allow Jasper to father my child, we're in full-on sixty-nine position, and I'm trying to hold off another orgasm so I won't have to be punished twice. Holding off is easier said than done, especially when the man in charge of your pleasure is a sneaky devil.

His finger slips from my pussy and slides down to press against my anus, just as he sucks on my clit. The combination is overwhelming, and even the press of his cock against the back of my throat can't draw my attention away from the finger demanding entry.

Once again, I erupt in an orgasm that comes from the deepest part of me. I come so hard, it takes a concerted effort not to clamp down on the dick in my mouth. Floating back down from the incredible high, I feel his tongue stroking me and his finger buried deep inside me.

We haven't even had actual sex yet, and already this is the best sex of my life. I should've known that would be the case with the man who could nearly make me come just by reading about the night before Christmas.

"Big, *big* trouble," he whispers against my still-quivering flesh. Removing his finger and wiping his mouth with the back of his other hand, he raises himself up. "Let me go."

I release my hold on his cock, and he pulls free of my mouth.

"Turn over on all fours and spread your legs." After issuing the directive, he gets up and goes into the adjoining bathroom. I hear water running before he returns to get something out of his bedside table. Turning to me, I watch as he rolls on a condom.

Then he's back on the bed behind me, his hands on my cheeks, squeezing and shaping them. "I love your sweet arse, love. I've had so many fantasies about this ripe, supple bottom." His hand comes down on my right cheek, the sound echoing through the room and the pleasurable pain reverberating through my backside to my over-stimulated clit. He follows the spank with a soothing caress that fans the flame. "Tell me to stop."

"No."

"No? Does that mean you like being spanked?"

Before I can reply, his hand comes down on the left side, under the curve, in the space above my leg. I've never been spanked in my life. I had no idea I'd like it so much.

"Had enough?"

"No."

His low growl is filled with approval and what sounds like desire. The blows rain down upon my bottom until I'm reduced to nothing more than the pleasure and pain and unbearable heat. "Your arse looks so hot with my handprints all over it." He presses against my anus again. "Has anyone ever fucked you here, darling?"

"N-no. I've never wanted that."

"I want to make you love it. I want to make you beg me for it." He teases my back entrance with his fingers but aligns his cock with my pussy, pressing into me slowly but surely, grasping my hip with his free hand and holding me still for his possession.

I experience a slight burn as my flesh stretches to accommodate his girth, but then he slides home, filling me completely, and taking me to the edge once again. "Jasper..."

"What is it?"

"I need to... I'm going to come again."

"Not yet." He pulls out abruptly, leaving me desperate as well as needy. "Turn over, darling. I want to see your lovely face."

Moving gingerly, I do as he asks, gasping when my bottom makes contact with the sheets. The sensation travels directly to my clit, like it's attached to a live wire.

"There you are," he whispers, brushing the hair back from my face and leaning in to kiss me. "So sweet and so sexy at the same time, and so permanently out of reach."

"Have you thought that? That I was out of reach?"

"Entirely out of reach for so many reasons."

"Flynn wouldn't care. He's not like that."

"Trust me, darling, with the things I want to do to you, your brother would care."

"He'd never have to know. I'm not going to tell him. Are you?"

"Ah, no, but at some point, your family might want to know who fathered your child. What'll you say to them?"

As he speaks, he presses his cock against my clit without entering me. My hands move down his back to cup his tight ass, hoping to direct him where I want him.

"I'll tell them I went through a clinic."

"So we can do this and other stuff as much as we want, and I never have to worry about losing the respect of the Godfrey family?" He pushes into me hard and fast, stealing the breath from my lungs and nearly triggering the orgasm that's been hovering just beneath the surface.

I can't think about the Godfrey family when he's moving in me and filling me so perfectly. God, all this time, I could've been doing this with Jasper rather than the many frogs who've crossed my path. I've wasted so much time with men who couldn't find a woman's clitoris with a map and magnifying glass. I'm swept away on a sea of pleasure when he stops, withdrawing and leaving me bereft.

He grasps my legs and props them on his shoulders before entering me again at a whole new angle. He's touching me in places no one else has ever been, and rocking my world one deep stroke at a time. How will I ever do this again and not think of the way *he* did it?

"Talk to me," he rasps in that sexy-as-all-fuck accent. "Tell me how it feels."

"Amazing." I reach for his arms, holding on to him as he hammers into me. "I need..."

"What? Tell me what you need."

"I want to come."

"Not yet." He slows the pace, coming to a complete stop while embedded deep inside me. "Take some deep breaths. Slow it down."

"I don't want to slow it down!"

A smile stretches slowly across his face. "Remember when you agreed to allow me to be in charge in bed?"

"Vaguely."

"Shall I refresh your memory?"

"I'd rather you made me come."

His grunt of laughter sends him deeper, if that's possible. "Put your arms over your head and hang on to the rails."

"Do I have to?"

"If you want to come."

Groaning, I do as I'm told while realizing I've never had this kind of conversation with any man, let alone while in the middle of having mind-altering sex. Of course he has to go and ruin me for everyone else, right when I'm on the cusp of venturing into the dating wilderness once again.

"Don't let go."

He's even sexier than usual when he's barking out orders.

As I grasp the iron slats in his headboard, I realize my hands are damp with perspiration. I'm one big nerve-ending, waiting to see what he has in store for me next.

Bending over me, he takes my nipple into his mouth, tugging and sucking on the tight tip and making me writhe on the bed. He surrounds me so completely, there isn't much room for me to move, but my body is now fully in his command, and he plays me like a maestro.

His cock gets harder, stretching me to my absolute limit.

I cry out, overwhelmed by the onslaught of sensation. "*Please...*"

Pressing his thumb to my tingling clit, he says, "Is this what you want, lovely Ellie?"

"Yes! Please... I have to..."

"Come."

I explode. There's simply no other word for it. Every cell in my body is fully engaged. I come back to life slowly, my scalp tingling, the soles of my feet burning, my legs trembling violently. And Jasper, he's gazing down on me, taking it all in as he continues to move in me, still hard, still filling me to the absolute brink.

"That was astonishing," he says with reverence that moves me profoundly.

I emerge from the stupor to imagine how I must look to him with my arms stretched over my head, breasts moving with every deep thrust, legs on his shoulders, body bent nearly in half. It's almost obscene, and yet nothing about this feels obscene. No, that's not the word I would use to describe it, and as soon as I can think of a word that adequately sums up this experience, I'll let you know.

He picks up the pace, driving into me relentlessly until he comes with a shout, his fingers digging into my ass.

My legs fall like two overcooked noodles as he comes down on top of me, his sweat melding with mine, his chest hair caressing my sensitive nipples. I suppose I'm allowed to release the iron rails of his headboard now. I was holding on so tightly that my fingers are stiff and my arms ache from the strain. I wrap them around him as he relaxes into my embrace.

So much for my worries that it might be awkward to have sex with Jasper. Awkward is the last word I'd use to describe what just happened, but now I wonder how I'll ever look at him again and not think of the best sex of my life.

Jasper

She's ruined me. I've had every sort of wild, crazy sex—kinky sex, group sex, you name it, I've done it. But I've never experienced anything even remotely close to what just happened with Ellie. And now I'm well and truly fucked in more ways than one. In the scope of an hour, the thought of her doing what we just did with any other guy has become completely and absolutely unacceptable to me.

I'm enraged by the very *thought* of her getting naked with someone else. I don't want her even *talking* to other guys, which is an unprecedented reaction for a man who has made a career out of not getting involved. I don't have the luxury of getting involved. I come with far too much baggage. It wouldn't be fair to any woman to expect her to take on me or my luggage.

But one taste of the exquisite Ellie Godfrey has thrown my carefully constructed plans straight out the window.

She doesn't know—none of my friends here in LA know—that I'm living on borrowed time. At any time, I can be called home to England to deal with my birthright. That's the deal I have with my father. I'm free to have my "little adventure" as a filmmaker in Hollywood, but only until I'm needed at home.

Until that day comes, I pretend like it's not happening. I pretend like I was born an ordinary person and not the future tenth Duke of Wethersby, heir to one of the largest fortunes in all of Great Britain and all the responsibilities that come with it—responsibilities I want *nothing* to do with.

Funny thing about the British peerage, no one cares if it's what you want or not. You're stuck with your birthright no matter what other hopes and dreams you might have for yourself, and that's exactly why I'll never publicly acknowledge the child I make with Ellie.

He or she will be my best and only chance to be a parent without the weight of expectation landing on my child's tiny shoulders. I won't have that for him or her. And yes, I'm expected to produce an heir, but that's one thing my father can't actually force me to do.

None of my friends in Hollywood have the first clue about my lineage. I use my mother's maiden name professionally, and all they know is that I come from a wealthy British family. That's all they need to know, for now anyway. The day may come when I have to sell out my shares in Quantum and go home to do my duty. I hope that day is a long, long time in the future. If my father lives as long as Queen Elizabeth has, it won't matter that I'm not interested in being his heir. I'll be too old to care. I pray for his health and longevity every day of my life.

"Are you okay?" Ellie's soft inquiry reminds me to stay focused on the present rather than dreading an uncertain future.

"I'm wrecked. You wrecked me."

"I think it was quite the other way around."

"Are you wrecked, darling?" I raise my head to take a closer look at her lovely face. Her eyes are closed, her lips swollen and her cheeks flushed.

"That's the least of what I am."

"I'm sorry... I was rough—"

She opens her eyes and places a finger over my lips. "You were amazing. That was... Amazing."

"Oh." Women so rarely surprise me anymore, but I'm finding that this woman is one delightful surprise after another. She liked being lightly dominated. Perhaps that means she might like—

No. Don't go there. You can't go there with Flynn's sister. You just can't.

I hate when my conscience pops in to set me straight. He can be such a disloyal pain in the rear. I'm losing all perspective where Ellie is concerned, and that can't happen. Grasping the base of the condom, I withdraw from her, though that's the last bloody thing I want to do. "Be right back, darling."

In the en suite bathroom, I take care of business, clean up and take a minute to get my head together after the most fantastic sex I can recall having in, well, ever. Usually I need a lot more than what we just did to make it fantastic, but with her, it was just... I don't have the words, and I always have the words. Bloody hell.

I splash cold water on my face, as if that might snap me out of this odd free fall I find myself in where she's concerned. The water doesn't work to fix what's been happening to me since that morning on Flynn's pool deck in Mexico when I agreed to father her child. And what we just did certainly isn't going to fix anything. No, it's only going to deepen my growing obsession with her.

Funny, isn't it, that you can know someone for years and go along your merry way as friends until one momentous conversation changes the perspective so dramatically that you begin to worry that nothing will ever be the same afterward. I draw in a couple of deep, calming breaths, trying to recover my upended equilibrium.

I need to get back to her before she suspects something is wrong. Nothing is wrong. In fact, the opposite is true—everything is far too *right* with her. Double bloody hell.

When I emerge from the bathroom, I find Ellie fully dressed and sitting on the edge of my bed, a faraway expression on her lovely face. "I thought you might stay the night." I'm deeply disappointed that she's planning to go.

"Oh, that's nice, but I can't. I've got work in the morning and stuff I need to do at home."

At midnight? The question remains unspoken as I pull on a pair of basketball shorts and a T-shirt to drive her and Randy home in an uneasy silence. I want desperately to know what she's thinking, but I can't bring myself to ask. Maybe it's better if I don't know.

I bring the car to a stop outside her cozy cottage—another in a long line of surprises where she's concerned—and prepare to get out to walk her in.

"No need." She takes hold of Randy's leash. "I'll see you tomorrow. Thanks for a great night."

She's out of the car and on her way up the walk before I can say anything in response. What the actual fuck just happened? How did we go from devouring each other to polite silence? We certainly got the awkward preliminaries out of the way, but the aftermath had been the definition of awkward. Two steps forward, one giant leap back.

I drive home in an unusual state of turmoil. I'm not used to turmoil where women are concerned, probably because I steadfastly refuse to get overly involved. Agreeing to father a close friend's child definitely qualifies as getting overly involved, but it wasn't supposed to ruin a cherished friendship or make things weird between us.

Although, how could it not? We've gone from professional colleagues and personal friends to fuck buddies in a matter of days. Of course it's going to be a little weird before it evens out and things get back to normal. I take an inordinate amount of comfort from that thought, and from remembering there'd been nothing weird between us while we were in bed.

I need to keep her naked in a bed if I want to keep the weirdness out of the equation. With that in mind, I send her a text as soon as I get home.

Wear a skirt to work tomorrow. Leave the panties at home.

I see that the text was delivered and then read, but she doesn't reply. Smiling, I can only imagine her reaction, and I'm excited for tomorrow when I'll get things back on track the best way I know how —with my cock.

CHAPTER 8

Ellie

I toss and turn all night after receiving that salacious text from Jasper. Does he honestly expect me to be ready for sex in the office? The same office we share with my *brother* and our closest friends? And why am I *on fire* at the thought of such a thing?

He's good at this. I have to give him that. He's had me primed and ready for whatever he wants from the second I got that text, and the closer I get to the office, the more intense the throb between my legs becomes. I still haven't recovered—physically or emotionally—from what we did last night, and he's already planning round two.

Between now and then, I have a couple of big meetings and a doctor's appointment to deal with. The latter takes the edge off my out-of-control hormones as it occurs to me that Dr. Breslow will probably be able to tell, with one look, that I had some pretty intense sex last night. Great...

This isn't like me. I don't dither over guys and sex and whether or not to wear panties under my skirt. I don't play games with men. I date them. I screw a select few of them. And most of the time I dump them after a couple of weeks of nothing special. I know, almost immediately on a first date, if there's going to be a second date, a trait my sisters say is maddening.

"You need to give them a chance," Aimee has said repeatedly, with Annie nodding in agreement. I do give them a chance, and nine times out of ten, they blow it within the first hour. I can't help it that most of them are self-centered dickwads who try so hard to bowl me over with how awesome they are that I can't get a word in edgewise. Hashtag one and done.

There's nothing worse than having sex with a guy and feeling dirty the next day because you realize you used him for sex when there's not a single other thing you want from him, including a phone call. Ever. I've done that. More than once. And hated myself for it afterward.

Now, you might be wondering what I did about the panties. I wore them. Of course I did. I can't be all out and proud in the office I share with my brother. I just can't, even if I'm dying of curiosity about what Jasper has planned. I figure panties can be removed if need be, but walking around all day without them simply isn't an option.

The day is frantically busy with one meeting after another. I don't see Jasper until a lunchtime get-together in the conference room to celebrate Leah's twenty-third birthday. She's Natalie's former room-mate in New York who was hired last month to be Marlowe's assistant, and Marlowe has gone all-out with a catered lunch and a delicious cake.

I forget sometimes how young Natalie and Leah actually are. Natalie, in particular, is mature beyond her years due to her trau-matic and tumultuous childhood. Leah has a grittier, street-smart way about her, and I can't help but notice that Emmett rarely takes his eyes off her. Interesting. Very interesting.

"Who's around this weekend?" Natalie asks after the cake is served. "My friend Aileen and her kids are coming out for a visit."

"I am," Kristian immediately replies. Also very interesting.

"Me, too," Marlowe says, her mouth full of cake. I love the way we celebrate every little occasion in our office. We are truly more like family than colleagues, and there's not much we wouldn't do for each other.

"I'm babysitting the nephews Saturday night," I say, "but I'm free the rest of the weekend."

"Lucky you," Flynn says, chuckling. "You drew the short straw, huh?"

"I offered." I know he's teasing, because he's crazy about all our nieces and nephews.

"Bring them over to my place to play with Aileen's kids. The pool will wear them out."

"I might take you up on that. India and Ivy are coming to help me out. Ian has a Boy Scout camp-out."

"That would be awesome if you brought the kids over," Natalie says. "We'll have a cookout and make it a party."

"I'm in," Jasper says, his intense gaze fixed on me.

Never have two words packed a greater wallop, and I'm doubly glad I defied his orders and wore panties to mop up the dampness that look generates. Fiend.

After lunch, I leave Dax in charge and head off to my appointment with Dr. Breslow. The elevator doors are closing when I see Jasper coming, sticking his arm between the doors to force them open to admit him. I watch this unfold with a sense of amused detachment from my post in the back left corner, which is suddenly crowded when he presses against me, running his hand up my leg and under my skirt so quickly I have no time to prepare myself before he's cupping me over the silk that covers me.

"Hmmm, someone is very disobedient."

"Someone is exceptionally bossy."

"I like when my orders are followed."

"Do you now?"

"Mmm-hmm." This is said against my neck as his lips leave a path of fire from my throat to my ear. "I can't stop thinking about last night, how hot and tight you were. I can't wait to be inside you again."

No man has ever said anything like that to me before, and it's a good thing he's leaning against me, because that's the only thing that keeps me from sliding into a puddle on the floor.

"I'd ask if you're thinking about it, too, but I can feel how hot you are."

I've almost forgotten where we are when the elevator dings to indicate we've arrived on the first floor. Though it's the last freaking thing I want to do, I give him a gentle shove that dislodges his hand from under my skirt.

He grunts with laughter as he lands against the back of the elevator. "You're leaving me in a hell of a state, love."

I glance down to find him fully erect, and my mouth waters at the memory of what he's capable of with that lovely cock. "That's your own fault. I was minding my business in the elevator when you jumped in to accost me."

"Where're you going?"

"To the doctor, if you must know."

"Funny," he says, "me, too. Got to get tested so I can fuck my lady bareback and knock her up."

Have I mentioned he has a way with words? And that accent, dear God in heaven, the accent...

"Come to my office when you get back. I'll be waiting. And don't bother to put your panties back on after the doctor." He takes me by the hand to tug me behind him as we leave the elevator. When we encounter Hayden in the lobby, Jasper subtly drops my hand, but I wonder if Hayden saw that he was holding it.

"Hey, guys," Hayden says as he steps into the elevator we've just left.

"Hi, Hayden," Jasper says for both of us.

My tongue is tied in knots.

"Everything all right?" Hayden asks, holding the door open.

"Everything is just dandy," Jasper says as he ushers me through the door to the parking lot with a hand on my lower back. "Words, darling," he mutters. "Use your words unless you want the whole office wondering why you're suddenly speechless."

I shake him off. "You're scrambling my brains!"

The bastard laughs, and I'm sucked right in by the smile, the dimples, the eyes, the whole package. He's absolutely irresistible, and he knows it.

"I'll see you in a couple of hours." He leans in as if he's going to kiss me, but my brain isn't so scrambled that I think it's a good idea for him to kiss me where anyone might see us. I turn away from the kiss, even though that's the last thing I want to do.

"Ouch."

"Out of the way."

He steps aside and holds my car door for me, waiting until I'm settled before he closes it, rolling his finger to tell me to put down the window.

"What?"

"The next time you turn away from my kiss, I'll spank your sweet arse until it's bright, flaming pink. I might just do that anyway the next time I see you." He walks away, hands in pockets, whistling like he hasn't a care in the world.

I'm so rattled by the encounter that I drop my keys on the floor and have to dig around by my feet to find them. What I want to know is where has my calm, cool, collected, oh-so-urbane friend Jasper gone? It's like he's become someone else altogether since we made our deal. Not that I'm complaining about new Jasper because I'm not. It's just that I never had any idea *this* side of him existed.

And how would I know that? I ponder that question as I battle midday traffic on my way to Breslow's office. People are always different with romantic partners than they are with everyone else, but I have to admit that I never expected Jasper to be completely different.

If I'm being truly honest, I half expected our "relations" to be awkward, fumbling, comical misadventures that would hopefully lead to a baby. Think Hugh Grant in *Notting Hill*. Or Hugh Grant in *Four Weddings and a Funeral*. Or Hugh Grant in, well, anything. You get the picture, right?

Jasper Autry is no Hugh Grant. After last night, I can confirm there's absolutely nothing fumbling or bumbling about his moves in the bedroom. In fact, I'm beginning to suspect I haven't seen even a fraction of who sexual Jasper truly is. And I'm completely intrigued by what I've seen so far.

Breslow's office is almost always on schedule, which is one of the reasons she's the go-to doctor for women in Hollywood. She knows our time is as valuable as hers. Thankfully, I don't have to wait long in the skimpy cotton gown they gave me to wear for the exam. This was supposed to be my final checkup before she turns me over to her colleague for fertility treatment. Won't she be surprised to hear there's been a change in plans?

My belly flutters with excitement and nerves. I want to be pregnant more than I've ever wanted anything, and before this thing with Jasper started up, I couldn't have cared less about how that happened. Now, the journey is shaping up to be as exciting as the destination.

Dr. Breslow knocks and comes breezing in a few minutes later, heading straight for the sink to wash her hands. "So sorry to keep you waiting. We had a mom-to-be in distress this morning, and I'm still trying to get my day back on track."

"Is she okay? The mom?" I actively try not to think about the thousands of things that can go wrong between conception and delivery.

"She is, and so is the baby. But we're monitoring them overnight just to make sure." She claps her hands and takes a seat on the stool. "So here we are! Last checkup before you graduate to fertility! Are you excited?"

"There's been a slight change in plan."

"Oh." Her smile fades ever so slightly.

She's well aware of how badly I want this baby, so I quickly set her mind at ease. "It seems I have a friend interested in fathering my child."

"Really? How'd that happen?"

I tell her about being on vacation with my brother and our group of friends and how the conversation with Jasper unfolded, without naming names.

"Wow, so how do you feel about that?"

"I feel good. He's a very close friend, and he's fine with me having full custody of the child. And before you ask, we're working out the details with lawyers."

"That's really great, Ellie. So he's going to donate, then?"

"Ah, not the way you mean. We're doing it the way Mother Nature intended. What I need today is a clean bill of health, and he's at his doctor getting the same."

"Sounds like you've got all your bases covered. Let's do a quick exam and talk about ovulation cycles and other fun stuff."

I'm so comfortable with her after years of going to her that it's no big deal to slide down the table, put my feet in the stirrups and bare myself to her. Except, this time, I'm worried about what she might find "down there" after what we did last night.

"Are you two off to an early start?" she asks.

I laugh nervously, wondering just how bad it is. "You could say that."

"Are you sore?"

"A little."

"I'll be gentle."

In spite of her best efforts, I have to grit my teeth to get through the exam, which hurts more than I'd expected it to. I tell myself this is nothing compared to what childbirth will feel like. Still, I'm glad when it's over and she tells me to go ahead and sit up.

We go over timing and figure out when I'm likely to be ovulating based on the dates of my last period.

"It's looks like this next week will be your sweet spot this month, but we could be off by a few days here or there. So my advice is to have as much sex as you can over the next week, and hope for the best. You know the odds are trickier at your age, and it may not happen right away. There's a lot we can do if it doesn't happen natu-rally, so try to stay positive and focused."

I'm surprisingly emotional as we talk it through. This is really happening. It could happen as soon as this week. She gives me a prescription for prenatal vitamins to start now and an ovulation calendar along with a recommendation for a fairly accurate ovulation kit I can buy at any drugstore to confirm her calculations are on target. I'm told to limit caffeine, to stop drinking alcohol for the foreseeable future, to avoid lubricants that contain spermicide, and to relax and try to enjoy myself.

After I conceive, she continues, we'll talk more about the possible risks and what to watch out for, but there's no need to get into that until we have a baby on board.

"All the tests from your recent physical came back normal." After confirming I haven't had unprotected sex since then, she hands me a slip of paper that she has signed. "A clean bill of health for your baby daddy."

I laugh at the term. I'm almost thirty-six years old, and I have a *baby daddy*! "I can't believe this is actually happening." My eyes fill with tears that I blink back, trying to contain them.

Dr. Breslow hugs me. "I'm so happy for you, Ellie. Call me any time if you need me, but I have a good feeling about this. You're going to do great all on your own."

"I sure hope you're right."

"Just remember to relax. Stress isn't good for you or your body when you're trying to make a baby."

Though I'm still sore and cramping after the exam, I fairly float out of Breslow's office, armed with information and full of my own womanly power to procreate. And the best news of all? I need to have as much sex as possible with Jasper Autry for a full week. I feel like the proverbial kid in a candy store.

Jasper

What the hell is taking her so long at the doctor? She's been gone for two hours, which is a frightfully long time to have an erection. The commercials say to seek medical attention after four hours. I'm halfway to a full-blown crisis by the time she comes breezing into my office, eyes alive with joy, skin flushed with the rose-colored hue that reminds me of the blooms in my mother's garden at home, and wearing a big, goofy smile. I'm struck dumb at the sight of her.

She closes the door behind her and leans against it, fairly vibrating with excitement that can't be contained.

I get up and go to her, harder now that she's in the room than I was while thinking about her. "What has you all lit up, darling?"

"This." She produces a signed piece of paper from her doctor.

"Mine is coming soon."

"How soon?"

"As soon as tomorrow."

"Good, because we need to get going in the next few days."

I must look confused, because she fills in the blanks for me.

"I'm due to ovulate this week, so my doctor said we should have as much sex as we can to better our chances."

I barely let her get the words out and I'm on her, kissing her with the pent-up desire I've had to deny all damned day. I reach around her to lock the door before I push my hand under her skirt to discover she followed my orders to forgo the panties after the doctor, which thrills me. I fill my hands with warm, supple cheeks as I lift her against the door. Though it's the last thing I want to do, I break the kiss, but only because there are things that must be said. "Let's go somewhere. By ourselves for the whole week." I bury my face in her fragrant hair, my lips on her neck.

"We just got back from a week away. I can't. I have too much—"

"You're going to get sick. Very, very sick. Something highly contagious that no one will want to be around. On Sunday, you're going to come down with the plague, and it's going to keep you out of work for a week."

"And no one will be suspicious if you're out at the same time?"

"I'll think of something, but we're spending next week together. In my bed in Malibu. You'll bring Randy, and the two of you will stay with me."

"This is crazy. I have a job, responsibilities—"

I kiss her until I feel her begin to yield to me. I want her powerless to resist me, so I kiss her until I feel her moan of compliance. Fuck, her moans make me crazy. I can't wait to hear them for a whole week. The thought of that makes me shudder from the wave of desire that crashes through me.

What is she doing to me? When was the last time that simply kissing a woman made me shudder? I can't remember. It's been a long time. Suddenly, kissing her isn't enough. I need to possess her. Tightening my grip on her sweet arse, I lift her off the door, absorb her squeak of surprise into my mouth and carry her to the small conference table where I lay her out like my own personal feast.

She wrenches free of the kiss. "J-Jasper, we can't. Not here."

"Yes, we can, but only if you're very, very quiet."

The sound that she makes isn't quite a moan and isn't quite a groan, and it travels straight to my cock via my central nervous system. I'm on fire for her, but before I take what I want, I slowly lift her skirt until she's bare before me. Dropping into one of the executive chairs, I spread her wide open to my tongue and devour her.

She makes incredibly sexy noises that tell me how hard she's trying to stay quiet.

I actually can't believe I've got my face buried in Ellie's sweet pussy in the office. I've never done anything even remotely like this in my office, let alone with my business partner's sister. But right now, I can't be bothered thinking about such mundane things as work or office decorum or my precious partners, two of whom share walls with me, although not her brother. Thank God for small favors.

Driving my fingers into her tight, wet heat, I groan against her clit as I roll it between my teeth. Her legs tremble violently, and her internal muscles clamp down on my fingers. I remove one of them and push it deep into her arse. She explodes. Her entire body goes rigid, and only her hand pressed against her mouth keeps the entire building from sharing in the moment with us.

I can't wait another second to be inside her. Fumbling with my belt, zipper, shirttails and the condom takes thirty seconds longer than I have. Grasping her hips, I plunge into her, and she goes stiff— and not in a good way. Fuck, she's sore, and I hurt her.

"I'm sorry, love." I stroke her face and hair as I give her body a chance to stretch to accommodate me. In tiny increments that have me counting backward from one thousand to keep from imploding, she begins to relax and move restlessly beneath me.

"Jasper," she says in a broken whisper. "I need—"

"Say it."

"I need you to move. Please."

"Mmm, you're awfully polite when you're getting well and truly fucked on a conference table in the middle of the workday."

The scarlet hue that overtakes her face thrills me. I decide to stretch this out a bit. Why, after all, would I let her get off easy a second time? Starting at the top, I begin to unbutton her blouse, letting my fingers drag over her soft skin as I go.

"I, uh…"

"Shhh," I tell her, zeroing in on the front clasp of her bra. That's perfect for what I have in mind. The extension on my desk rings. I ignore it as I peel open her bra, revealing the lovely breasts I've thought about constantly since last night. Thrusting ever so slightly, in case she's forgotten I'm wedged deep inside her, I lean in to take her left nipple into my mouth, sucking and tugging and tonguing it.

She fists two handfuls of my hair, pulling so hard I worry about bald spots.

Without releasing the suction on her nipple, I slide my hands under her, drawing her up and into my arms as I fall back into the chair. She comes down hard on top of me, making me see stars. Fuck, that's hot. With a sweet arse cheek in each hand, I raise and lower her while continuing to torment her nipples.

She's moving instinctively on top of me, chasing her orgasm, when I surprise her again with the finger to the back door. What can I say? I'm a certified arse man, and as I've discovered, that trick sets her off every time. She goes nuts, clamping down so hard on my cock and finger that she makes me come, too.

We sit there for a long time, her impaled on my cock, which is still harder than it should be after that explosion, and me with her nipple in my mouth and my finger stuffed up her arse. God, I fucking love dirty, daytime, conference table sex with Ellie Godfrey.

"You..." She squirms, clearly trying to dislodge my finger.

I drive it in deeper, making her gasp, and I swear she has another little orgasm. My lovely Ellie is an arse girl. She may not be willing to admit it yet, but she's hot for it. Wait until she feels my dick there. The visual of her taking me there makes my cock hard again.

She comes back to her senses all of a sudden, pushing on my chest. "Jasper! Stop! *Enough!*"

Chuckling at her outrage, I remove all parts of me from all parts of her, even though that's the last thing I want to do.

"Come with me." I lead her into my adjoining bathroom, where we clean up.

Ellie looks in the mirror and lets out an inelegant squeal at the state of her hair and face. "How am I going to explain what I was doing in here for half an hour and why I came out with a red face, razor burn and swollen lips?"

"You forgot the situation with your hair."

She glares at me, and I experience the oddest feeling of complete and utter rightness. It's euphoria and joy and, hell, it's a thousand and one things all at the same bloody time, and I can honestly say I've never experienced anything even close to it. I'm reeling.

"I can't even believe we just did that *here* of all places." She yanks on her hair, trying to restore order to it, but only succeeds in making it worse. "We're not doing that again."

I could remind her that she agreed to let me be in charge of when and how we do it, but I refrain, sensing she's not finished with me yet.

"And what's with the finger? For God's sake, Jasper, that's just..."

"Awesome?"

"No! It's weird!"

"So weird that you fucking explode every time I do it?" I wrap my arms around her from behind and press kisses to her neck, gratified when she tilts her head to give me room.

"I do not."

"Um, yeah, you do. I can't believe you've never done that before, darling."

"Why can't you believe it? I'm a good girl. I don't do anal."

That makes me laugh out loud and earns me another scowl. "You do now."

"No, I don't." She tries to get away from me, but I only tighten my arms around her.

"Why do you deny you love it when it's obvious that you do?"

"It's dirty."

"Mmm, that's what makes it so bloody hot. Wait until you feel my cock there, darling. You'll go off like a rocket ship."

"You're *not* putting your cock there. We're working on getting pregnant, not exploring new frontiers."

"Why can't we do both? When you're so sore you can't take anymore here," I say, cupping her pussy and making her gasp, "we can explore new frontiers." I press my cock between her cheeks, working her from both ends.

"Jasper, stop," she says with a pleading edge to her voice that has me fully withdrawing from her. "I have to get back to work." She turns to face me. "This was... It was... fun. I've never done anything like that on a conference table in the middle of a workday, but now I really have to go do the job you guys are paying me to do."

"Very well, but next week, you're all mine." My voice is gruffer and harsher than I intended, but she doesn't seem to mind. "Say it."

"Next week, I'm all yours, but after that, I need to get my life back to normal. I can't be blowing off work and appointments—"

"What appointment did you blow off?"

"I was supposed to have a call with Marlowe's friend from the dating service when I got back from the doctor, but it's so late now that I doubt she's even still there."

"Don't do that." The words are out before I stop to consider what I'm saying.

"Don't do what?"

"Date other guys. Not while you're doing this with me." I pull her in tight against my hard cock to make my point. "I won't be able to stand it."

She stares at me, her lips slightly parted. "But my baby, I want him—or her—to have a *father*, Jasper. I need to find *someone*."

I can't handle the note of desperation I hear in that single word. Someone. The incredibly beautiful, smart, sexy, capable Ellie Godfrey shouldn't have to *settle* for just *someone*. She should have the stars, the moon, the entire bloody *universe* from *someone* who worships her the way she deserves. The very idea of her settling is preposterous to me. And it makes me very sad for what can never be.

"You—"

She kisses me quickly. "We'll talk about it later. I've really got to go."

"I'll pick you up for dinner at eight. We'll talk about it then." I have a racquetball match with Kristian after work that I'll have to postpone, because I can't let this day end without hearing that she's put her plans to use the dating service on hold. For now anyway.

After a brief hesitation, she says, "Okay. I'll see you then."

CHAPTER 9

Ellie

Thank God no one is in the hallway when I sneak out of Jasper's office and head for mine, feeling as if the whole world must know what we just did. I tried like hell to be quiet, but he didn't make it easy. The man is *insane*. That's the only word for the way he makes love or has sex or whatever you want to call *that*.

Here I am, almost thirty-six years old, and this man is making me feel like a newly deflowered virgin in the throes of my sexual awakening. All this time, he's been right down the hall, capable of *that*.

My face is on fire, as if I just had a battery acid wash or something equally awful performed by a hack doctor. And my lower half is still twitching and throbbing and otherwise letting me know it's been thoroughly ravaged in the best possible way.

Someone knocks on my door, and before I can say anything, Addie comes breezing in, smiling from ear to ear the way she does now that she has Hayden's ring on her finger and the man himself in her bed. She stops short, her astute gaze zeroing in on the wreckage that is me.

"What's wrong? Are you sick?"

This, right here, is why I've never been a have-sex-in-the-office kind of girl. Nothing good ever comes of it, other than spectacular, life-changing orgasms...

"I'm not sure. I might be coming down with something." And here I am laying the groundwork for my upcoming sick-out, during which I plan to spend days in bed making a baby with the sexy Brit who makes me come like a Roman candle. I'm a bad, bad person, and I'm getting worse by the second.

She comes over to feel my forehead. "It's going around. My friend Tenley has it. She's been holed up at home for days now. You might be a little warm. Should you go home?"

"No, no. I've got too much to do." Not to mention, the idea of leaving work due to a sex-induced fever makes me feel guilty—and I already feel guilty enough about Jasper convincing me to take a week off to get pregnant. A week of *that*. I can't even let my mind go there or I might implode. "What's up?"

"Flynn's looking for a head count for Saturday night at his house. It's you and five kids, right?"

"That's right."

She types something into her phone. "Got it." Taking another close look at me, she says, "You're sure you're all right?"

"I'm fine. I promise."

"All righty, then. I'm off." She breezes out of the room, passing Dax, who's on his way in. They exchange a few words, and Addie laughs at whatever he said. Per usual, he comes in talking, but stops mid-sentence when he actually looks at me. I'm never allowing Jasper to touch me in the office again. Ever.

"What. The. *Hell*." Dax shuts the door and keeps his hand on the handle, as if he might need to escape quickly.

"Girl troubles," I whisper, clutching my midsection.

His lip curls in horror. "*Ewww*."

"You asked." Eager to get rid of him, I add, "Was there a reason for this visit?"

"We, um, there's an issue in Budapest." Without making eye contact with me, he goes into a rambling explanation of a cultural tradition that is bumping up against our request to film in the city.

My team has been trained not to come to me with a problem or challenge without also having some solutions for me to choose from.

"We can move the dates by two days and avoid the entire fiasco, but that would mean shifting everything back in Rome, too."

We've spent months setting up Rome, and we're not moving anything.

"Can we start two days earlier in Budapest?"

"I can ask."

"Do that, and let me know."

"Right. Um, feel better." He's out the door before I can say thank you.

Groaning, I drop my head into my hands. I should've stuck to the sperm bank. At least then I wouldn't be trying to hide the evidence of a midday office hookup with my colleague who is also, technically, one of my bosses. And one of my brother's closest friends.

"*Ugh!*"

BY THE TIME eight o'clock rolls around, I've built up a head of steam that I unleash on Jasper the second he comes through my door. Randy, that traitor, goes running over to give him enthusiastic dog love.

"*That* is never, ever, *ever* happening again at the office. Do you hear me?"

"I think they heard you in Malibu, darling."

"Don't call me that! I'm not your *darling* or your... your anything. We're having sex and making a baby, and that's all we're doing. And we're *not* doing it in the office. That's not happening again!"

"I understand."

"Do you? Do you really understand what it's like for everyone who isn't a partner? That's my job, my livelihood—"

"Darling..."

My glare doesn't deter him.

He rests his hands on my shoulders. "Let me put your mind at ease. You could never, ever, *ever* be fired from Quantum. You're family —not just Flynn's family. We're all family. We take care of our family. Don't give that worry another thought."

I shake him off. I've learned to be cautious about letting him touch me at all if I don't want to end up spread-eagled under him. "I'm not the kind of girl who has sex in the office and then goes on with her day like nothing happened. I had to tell Dax that I have girl problems so he wouldn't ask any questions. The poor guy is *scarred for life!*"

Jasper runs his hand over his mouth in an obvious attempt not to laugh.

"If you laugh, I'll throat-punch you."

"I'm not laughing!" His dancing eyes betray him. I wonder if he knows how adorable he is when he's trying not to be amused. Of course he does. He's adorable twenty-four-seven, and he absolutely knows it. He comes closer to me, moving cautiously as if he's not entirely sure I won't punch him.

My crossed arms don't deter him. He places his hands on my hips and draws me into him. I want to push him away, but that would be difficult with my arms mashed between our chests. His lips brush against my neck, and my knees go weak. And yes, I hate that's all he has to do to make that happen.

"No more sex in the office. Are we all sorted now?"

"Yes, as long as you know I mean it."

"I know you mean it. Now what do you want for dinner?"

"Wait. There's another thing." I step back from him, needing the space so I won't forget what I want to say. That's another of his super-powers—kissing me or touching me and making my brain go blank.

"What's this other thing of which you speak?"

"We're only having sex to make a baby. No more...extras."

His brow lifts in inquiry, which is also ridiculously adorable. Can I punch him for that, too? "By extras, you mean..."

"You know what I mean!"

"Darling—"

"Don't call me that!"

"Ellie, *sweetheart*, as honored and delighted as I am to be fathering your child, I'm not a robot. Things," he says, gesturing to below his belt, "don't just *happen* without some... inspiration. I can't just *produce* on demand."

I'm definitely going to punch him. When I get done squirming.

"So you see, the extras, as you refer to them, are a necessary part of making this baby you want so badly."

"Fine, but we're only doing what we have to do to make everything work, and then we're done. That's it."

He rubs at his chest. "I'm feeling strangely wounded by your rejection of my extras. Especially since I've had ample evidence of your enthusiastic enjoyment of my repartee."

"Are you making fun of me?"

"Absolutely not. I'm merely pointing out that we've both had fun practicing to make a baby and why can't we continue to have fun making the baby?"

"Because! Your kind of fun leads to sex in the office, which leads to mortification, which leads to mmph—"

He kisses me, and sure enough, I forget what I was going to say, because I'm far too busy wrapping my tongue around his and losing myself to the ridiculous way he kisses me, as if he'll *die* if he can't kiss me right here and now. Have I ever been kissed the way he does it? No, never, and as much as I want to fight him and push him away, I seem to have lost the ability to move my arms along with my wherewithal to manage this "situation."

Jasper kisses me until I'm a malleable pile of putty in his hands. How does he do that? "I hate to remind you, darling, that you did agree to allow me to be in charge of certain things, and I'm afraid I'm going to have to hold you to our original agreement, along with all the extras I can dream up."

Before I can disagree or argue the point, he's kissing me again while backing me up in the direction of my bedroom. Wait, what's he doing? I should stop this before he makes me forget I'm angry with him. And why am I angry with him again? Oh. Right. Sex in the office. Well, he promised that wouldn't happen again. And the extras weren't *bad*, per se...

He kicks the door shut before Randy can follow us, and the dog's pathetic whimper lets me know his thoughts on the matter.

Here I am on my back, spread-eagle while Jasper expertly removes my top and skirt, reminding me with everything he does that not only is he in charge, he's exceptionally good at the extras.

"I think you deserve a punishment for questioning my authority."

Whhhhat did he just say? I open my eyes to find him above me, a fierce, proprietary expression on his face.

"Don't you agree?"

"I most definitely do not agree."

"Well, since you *did* agree to allow me to be in charge in here, and I say you deserve a punishment, I'd say you'd better be on your hands and knees in the time it takes me to get my clothes off, or the punishment will get worse."

I'm stunned speechless, but I can't deny I'm also curious and intensely aroused. I know with the kind of certainty that comes with long friendship that he would never truly hurt me. Because of that and because of the aforementioned insane curiosity, I move into the position he requested.

"Always such a good girl, aren't you?" He lays his hands on my bottom, squeezing and shaping my cheeks. "I think there's a very naughty girl in there, trying to break free. You ought to let her out to play, darling. I think she and I would have a marvelous time together."

Before I can formulate a reply to that audacious statement, his hand connects with my right cheek. The next one comes before I've begun to process the first one. And so it goes, one right after the other, each in a new spot, each followed by a caress that sets me on fire with an urgent need that's all new to me. It's almost painful in its intensity.

"Ah, hell," he whispers when he strokes between my legs and finds proof of how much I enjoyed every minute of his so-called punishment. I'm floating in some sort of oddly detached state, aware of what's happening but unable to participate in any meaningful way. I hear the crinkle of foil in the instant before he enters me from behind. "You're so hot and sexy, love. I can't get enough of this tight pussy."

No man has ever said anything like that to me during sex. Most of them ask things like, "Here?" "Does that feel good?" "More?" Jasper doesn't have to ask questions, because he gets it just right every time, including now. He reaches around to stroke my clit with one hand while he spanks me again with the other, the combination making me come so hard, I taste blood in my mouth after. I think I bit my tongue.

He comes right after me, grasping my hips and groaning as he surges into me one last time.

I collapse onto the bed, a quivering wreck of a woman who used to have control over her life, until she let a sexy, charming Brit into her bed and found out what it's like to completely *lose* control.

He's on top of me, his body warm and heavy, his arms around me, his hands full of my breasts. When he tweaks my nipples, I can't believe the way I contract around his still-hard cock, making him groan again.

We stay like that for a long time. I'm actually on my way to sleep when he withdraws from me and covers me with a blanket I keep at the foot of my bed before going into the bathroom. I vaguely hear water running and the toilet flushing and then he's back, sliding under the blanket and curling up to me. He uses a finger to push the hair back that's covering my face. "Are you alive under there?"

"Barely."

Kissing my cheek and then my lips, he runs a hand over my back to caress my ass.

I gasp with surprise at the myriad sensations his touch sets off, like someone has flipped a switch that brings me back to reality. "Jasper."

"Hmmm?"

"What's all this about?"

"Pardon?"

There's something so incredibly British about the way he says that single word. "You, the spanking, the dirty finger, the bossiness in bed. What's it really about?"

"It's just how I like it."

"Why?"

"I'm not sure exactly. I always have." He continues to run his fingers over my back and bottom as he talks. "I was involved with an older woman while I was at university, and she taught me to be assertive, to get what I want in bed and out. She said there's nothing wrong with being dominant in my sexual relationships as long as I'm always a respectful Dom."

"So you would call yourself an actual Dom."

He pauses, only for a second, before he replies. "Yes."

"Is there more to it than the spanking and the orders and stuff?"

"Yes."

"Like what?"

"I thought you weren't interested in the extras, as you call them."

"I didn't say I wanted to do it. I'm just curious about the rationale behind it, that's all." I can tell he has so much he'd like to say to that, but he curbs the urge.

"It's hard to explain to someone who isn't part of the lifestyle."

"Try."

His stomach lets out a loud growl that makes us laugh. "Apparently, I need to feed the beast."

"I could eat, too."

"Would sharing a shower count as an 'extra'?"

"Of course not. This is Southern California. It would be considered conservationism."

"In that case..." He gets up and offers me a hand.

His growling stomach got him out of the conversation for now. But I still want answers to my questions, even if I'm a little afraid of what I might find out.

Jasper

She wants to know about my life as a Dominant. Bloody hell. Flynn's sister wants to talk about dominant sex. He'd kill me dead if he knew I was even hinting at that conversation with her. Telling her about me doesn't necessarily mean telling her about him and the others. But I need to tread carefully here—very, *very* carefully. Their secrets are not mine to tell, and I'd never betray my friends that way.

Ellie's curiosity is dangerous, but I can handle it. Or so I tell myself as we walk toward the boardwalk with Randy on a leash. She suggested pizza at a nearby restaurant, and that's fine with me. We find a table for two outside, and Randy lies down on the sidewalk next to us as we peruse the menu.

Ellie raves about the cheese pizza here, so we settle on that, an antipasto to share and a glass of red wine for me when she assures me she doesn't mind if I have a drink, even though she's officially off booze while we try to get her pregnant. My stomach is in knots because I know she's not going to forget the conversation we were having before my stomach growl interrupted us.

The young waiter returns with a bottle of cheap red wine and pours me a glass. For some odd reason, I think of my father and what he would have to say about this place. He'd probably complain about the cheap wine, the rushed service, the carnival atmosphere of the boardwalk and anything else he could think of to gripe about. To me, it's the perfect kind of warm Southern California night, and with a beautiful, sexy, intriguing woman across the table, I have no complaints. Well, the wine could be better...

"So," she says, eyeing me expectantly. "You never answered my question earlier."

"No, I didn't." I swish the wine around in my glass, watching the play of the dark liquid because that's better than trying to figure out how to tell her something I never talk about with people outside the lifestyle.

"Are you going to?"

After a slight hesitation, I decide that after the trust she's put in me by allowing me to father her child, I owe her the truth. "The woman I mentioned, the one I was involved with at uni? She's the one who introduced me to the lifestyle. I had no idea it existed prior to meeting her, but I always knew there was something in me that wanted... more, I guess you could say."

"What do you mean by more?"

"To be blunt, basic fucking was fun, but tying up a woman, dominating her, having her willingly submit to me, well, that was bloody *fabulous*."

"So what we've been doing..."

I reach across the table to cover her hands with mine. "Is also bloody *fabulous*."

"But it's not enough for you?" She casts her gaze down at our joined hands, which tells me she's embarrassed to be asking these questions, but that's not stopping her.

"It's not about enough or not enough. It's about *more*."

"What does *more* usually entail for you?"

"You want, like, details?"

She draws her bottom lip into her mouth and nods.

I zero in on her lip between her teeth and forget what I was going to say.

"Jasper?"

"Oh, right, so for me, more usually involves restraints of one sort or another, toys of every kind—I *love* toys—light flogging, spanking, any and all kinds of sex. You name it, I like it."

"You're so matter-of-fact about it. You sound like some people would reciting a grocery list."

I scoot my chair around the table so I'm within inches of her and reach for her hand, placing it over the hard bulge in my pants. "I'm hardly matter-of-fact about it, darling, especially when I'm picturing you trussed up as my willing sub."

She snorts out a nervous laugh. "I've never been submissive a second in my life."

"That doesn't mean you wouldn't enjoy being sexually submissive. The good news is you don't have to check your girl-power card at the door to enjoy being dominated." Still holding her hand, I raise it to my lips and nibble on her knuckles. "It's a common misconception that the sub surrenders all power to the Dom, when it's actually quite the other way around."

Her raised eyebrow conveys a healthy dose of skepticism. "How's that possible?"

"First of all, everything is agreed upon beforehand. There're never any surprises in a Dom/sub encounter. Furthermore, the sub has the power to stop the whole thing with a single word that's also negotiated in advance. So you see, the Dom is, in many ways, at the mercy of his or her sub."

"What if a woman you were interested in or had feelings for wasn't into having a Dom/sub sexual relationship?"

"Truthfully?"

"Of course."

"I don't think I could do without it long-term. It's such a big part of who I am that I'd find it hard to deny that side of myself indefinitely."

I can see that she's mulling it over in that thoughtful way of hers. One of the things I find most attractive about her is her crackling intelligence, and while I'm slightly uncomfortable to be confessing my secrets to Flynn's sister, telling *Ellie* just seems right somehow. I don't want there to be other secrets between us besides the necessary one I'm keeping from her and everyone else in LA, and though I never would've volunteered the information, it's a relief that she knows about the BDSM.

"Do you have a lot of friends in the lifestyle?"

Oh crap. Like, all of them? "A few."

"Anyone I know?"

"Now, darling, I can't tell you that."

"You can't or you won't?"

"Both. It's not my place to 'out' someone else who might not want others to know they're kinky. I can only speak for myself." I can see that she's intrigued by the possibility of other people she knows favoring the lifestyle. What would she think if she knew most of her closest friends, including her brother and now his wife, too, are in the lifestyle? She won't hear that from me.

"So the women you've been with over the years... You've done that with all of them?"

"Not *all*, and there haven't been *that* many."

She gives me a look filled with skepticism. "You've talked to me about most of them."

"It's a case-by-case thing. Sometimes we go there, sometimes we don't. And there're places I can go if I'm looking to hook up with someone who likes what I do. Clubs and whatnot."

"Would you take me to one of these clubs?"

I'm not sure if I blanch or recoil, but the net effect is the same. "*What?* No. I won't take you to one."

"Why not? How will I know if I'm interested in trying it if I've never seen or experienced it?"

Bloody hell, I'm hard as rock at the thought of her wanting to try it, not to mention taking her to one of the local BDSM clubs. Of course I can't take her to the one I own with her brother and the other Quantum principals, but ours is certainly not the only game in town. Our friend Devon Black owns Black Vice, one of the best clubs in LA, especially for people who might be recognized. Discretion is the name of the game at Black Vice, and it would be the perfect place to introduce Ellie to the lifestyle, if I were going to introduce her, which I'm not.

Our food arrives, granting a reprieve in the increasingly uncomfortable conversation as we dive into the pizza and salad.

Randy pops up when he smells the food, and Ellie feeds him a piece of salami. I swear I hear him moan with pleasure. I like that he doesn't beg relentlessly the way some dogs would. He's satisfied with his sample and goes back to his nap, leaving us to eat in peace.

I'm still on edge from talking about my kink, a topic I rarely venture into with women unless I'm about to do a scene with one of them. Then there's a lot of talking and negotiating. This kind of conversation that I'm having with Ellie is highly unusual. But I have to admit that I like that she knows the truth about my sexual preferences and didn't run away in horror.

Quite the opposite, in fact. She seems... intrigued. Is it possible that she might want—

No. Just no. That's not what this is about. I need to keep reminding myself of what we're doing and what we aren't. She wants a baby. I want her. Why does it need to be any more complicated than that?

CHAPTER 10

Jasper

"Would you care if I went to a club with someone else?"

I nearly choke on what had been a rather satisfying bite of pizza.

"Jasper? Are you all right?"

No, I'm not all right. My throat is closed and my eyes are watering, but my raised hand keeps her from getting up. "Christ," I mutter when I can speak again. "Give a guy some warning before you ask something like that."

"It's the new millennium, Jasper, and I'll let you in on a little secret." She leans forward, as do I, desperate to hear all her secrets. "I've even watched porn." As she covers her mouth, her eyes get big, and I can see she's totally mocking me. However, the thought of Ellie watching porn makes me harder than I already was. "So, I'll ask again. What if I went with someone else?"

"Obviously, I can't stop you from doing whatever you want. I can tell you that not all Doms and not all clubs are created equal. I'd hate to see you end up in a situation that frightens or overwhelms you."

"That would be unfortunate. Of course, there'd be no chance of that happening if I took a friend with me, someone who knows the scene and can guide me through my first exposure to it." As she says this, she picks up a hot pepper from the antipasto, holds the stem between two fingers as she dips the end of the pepper into her mouth. I'm riveted by the movement of her lips and tongue, jealous of a hot pepper for the first time in my life.

J.T. isn't immune either. He's pulsing against my fly, like an inmate in solitary confinement, banging on the door, begging to be released.

"Right?" She draws me back to the conversation. What were we talking about again?

"Um, right, yes, I suppose so."

"You'll take me, then?"

Oh, I'll take you, love. I'll take you every which way to next Tuesday and then back again.

"What club should we go to? I want to look it up online."

Wait. What? When did I agree to take her to a sex club? Rarely do I find myself outmatched by a woman, but Ellie Godfrey isn't just any woman. No, if my life was different and I had the options regular guys have, she'd be *the* woman. I wouldn't hesitate to go all in with her, but since that's not possible, I have to settle for whatever I'm able to get, and I'll be damned if she'll be visiting any sex club without me.

"I'll talk to my friend Devon Black, the owner of Black Vice, about taking you in for a visit."

"Really? Like when? Soon?"

Rolling my eyes, I nod. "As soon as he's available. Now, can we please talk about something else?"

"You don't like talking about sex? I thought that was every guy's favorite topic."

"I like talking about it."

"Just not with me?"

I take her hand and once again place it on the hard column of my cock. "Any questions?"

She giggles like a schoolgirl, and I'm absolutely smitten with the sound of her infectious laughter, but I can't let her know that. She'll be completely unmanageable, rather than just mostly unmanageable.

"It's not funny. You think it feels good to sit around with an angry beast inside my pants while you go on about visiting sex clubs and wanting to know more about BDSM?"

"Angry beast?"

"Is that all you heard?"

"Did you say something else?"

Shaking my head with amusement, I signal for the check. Time to get out of here before I do something embarrassing like take her right on the table. When the beast is angry, he tends to lose his decorum.

We stop for ice cream on the way back to her place, and as I try not to stare while she licks her cone, it occurs to me that I haven't been on a sweet, innocent romantic date like this one in years. What's the point of "dating" when there's no hope of an actual relationship?

"Why haven't you ever gotten married or had a girlfriend?" she asks between licks. Is she capable of reading my mind now, too?

"That's sort of a long story."

"I've got time."

Why did I know she would say that? I rub the late-day whiskers on my jaw, trying to decide what I should say. Tell the truth or a portion of it? "I haven't met anyone I cared about enough to marry." That's true. That's absolutely true. But it's not the whole truth. Not even close.

"And why would you want just one when you can have them all?"

God, it kills me to know she thinks of me as a total gadabout, even if the label suits me. I'm exactly what she thinks I am, even if it's not necessarily who I'd choose to be. The opportunity to decide that for myself was taken from me before I was born.

"True enough, darling," I reply with a lighthearted tone and the charming smile that's become my trademark over the years. You can hide a lot of heartache behind the right sort of smile. I'm oddly and strangely disappointed in myself at this moment, which is a rare and hopefully fleeting feeling. I made peace with my lot in life ages ago. There's no sense whatsoever in wishing for things that can never be at this point.

Except, being around Ellie, helping her make a baby while knowing I can't ever be a real father to her child has forced me to confront a reality I thought I had accepted decades ago. The baby isn't even conceived yet, and I already want more of him—or her—than I'll ever be able to have. The very *idea* of a baby with my eyes and her golden hair has unlocked a sense of yearning that can't be tamped down no matter how hard I try.

Ellie curls her hand into the crook of my elbow and leans her head against my shoulder. "I feel like you're out of sorts since I asked about the BDSM."

"Not out of sorts."

"What, then?"

"Maybe a tad off-kilter. I'm not accustomed to talking so openly about something I've gone to enormous lengths to keep private."

"Why do you care what people think of you?"

So many reasons. "You know how it is in this town. If something like that were to become public, I'd be on the front page of every tabloid and the lead story on every gossip show. Plus, it's none of anyone's damn business how I like to get it on."

"That's true."

We arrive back at her house, and I wonder if she'll invite me in or send me packing. After all, we aren't about extras such as sleeping together or anything that would smack of an actual relationship.

My phone rings before we can work out the logistics of what comes next. I withdraw it from my pocket and see Emmett's name on the screen. "I need to take this."

"Sure, come in when you're done." She leads Randy into the house, leaving me to take the call in private on the porch. I've been with many a woman who would've hovered nearby, wanting to overhear the conversation. Ellie is not that woman.

"Hey, Em, what's up?"

"I heard from Ellie's attorney, and we're set for a meeting Thursday at two to go over the details. Does that work for you?"

It doesn't, but I'll move things around to make it work. "I'll be there." He gives me the address for Ellie's lawyer's office.

"The attorney requested that you bring evidence of a clean bill of health."

"I'll have it."

"Jasper... You're really sure about signing away your rights to a child who hasn't even been conceived yet?"

No, I'm not sure, but it's what I have to do. "Yes."

"I really hope you won't regret this."

Of course I will. I already do, and it hasn't even happened yet. But this is the way it has to be. That's all there is to it. "I'll see you Thursday at two, Em, if not before. Thanks again for your help with this."

I hear his sigh before he says, "Sure, no problem."

As I stash the phone back in my pocket, I'm filled with the kind of rage that marked my younger years and caused me huge problems with my father. It's been a long time since I've given the rage free rein to overtake me the way it does now.

Duty.

Obligation.

Responsibility.

The words of my youth, pounded into my head by my father, the ninth Duke of Wethersby, one of the most prosperous, historically significant dukedoms in all of England, and someday, in the not-too-distant future, it'll all be mine. I've chafed against those three words my entire life, and I'll be damned to hell before any child of mine will be saddled with *obligations* on the day he or she is born.

So when Emmett asks me if I'm sure I want to sign away my rights to the child Ellie and I will make together, you better believe I'm sure. Even if it breaks my heart to know I won't be able to acknowledge my own child. I'll give him every possible thing I can, but the one thing I won't give him is my name.

Thus the heartache, the overwhelming rage and despair unlike anything I've experienced before, even during the horrible years I spent fighting my father's plan for my life that most certainly did not include a career in the film business. I won that battle, but I've always known he would eventually win the war. The life I've made for myself in LA is on a timer, sand slipping through an hourglass in a morbid sort of countdown toward my inevitable destiny. As my father gets older, I can almost hear the tick-tock of time going by far too quickly. I live in fear of the phone call that will one day tell me my time is up.

"Jasper?"

I turn to her, captivated by the sight of her framed by the screen door, the lighting behind her outlining the subtle curves of her body. I'd like to capture her on film the way she looks right now.

"You want to come in?"

I want to be with her so badly. I want her in ways I've never allowed myself to want anyone. And that's exactly why I can't stay. "I should get out of your hair and let you get some sleep."

Though her face is shadowed, I can see that my reply has disappointed her.

The ache in my chest intensifies. The last thing I ever want to do is disappoint her, and I fear that's all I'm going to do. But since I'd never renege on our deal, I'll have to contend with my own heartache without letting it spill onto her. I'll do what I've done my entire life and push through it, my British stiff upper lip never wavering. When I agreed to help with her project, I had no idea it would resurrect the rage the way it has. Still, I wouldn't change a thing if it means helping her to have what she most desires.

She comes outside, closing the screen door so Randy can't escape. When she's standing right in front of me, she looks up, and I feel like she can see right through to the heart of me. "Are you all right?"

"I'm fine, love." I kiss her lightly. "Did you hear from your attorney about the meeting?"

"She texted just now."

"You ready to make it official?"

"I am if you are."

I smile down on her even as the ache in my chest continues unabated.

"If you're having second thoughts or—"

I kiss the words off her lips. "No second thoughts, no third thoughts. I'm all in, darling."

She releases a deep breath that I realize she was holding while she waited for me to say I'd changed my mind. "Okay, then. I'll see you tomorrow."

"Yes, you will." And because I need it more than she'll ever know, I kiss her properly, cradling her face in my hands and giving her the tenderness she deserves. When I finally withdraw from her, I'm pleased to see that she's every bit as affected by the kiss as I am. "Sleep well."

I walk away while I still can, knowing there'll be little sleep for me tonight. I have until two o'clock Thursday to figure out a way to give her the baby she desperately wants without sacrificing my own sanity in the process.

Ellie

On Thursday, I arrive early at Cecily's office in Brentwood, the area of LA best known for being the scene of the Simpson-Goldman murders in 1994. I had just finished my freshman year of high school when that happened, but I vividly remember the circus-like atmosphere that overtook the entire city that summer. Thinking about OJ Simpson gives me something to do other than obsess about why I'm here and what's about to happen.

Cecily's assistant shows me into her spacious office, and my friend jumps up to greet me with a big hug. She's tall and strikingly pretty with long auburn hair and a flawless complexion. Her green eyes sparkle with excitement as she takes a good long look at me.

"You look fantastic!" she declares, leading me to a seating area that overlooks the street below.

"So do you." I haven't seen her in a couple of years, but she hasn't changed at all. "And thank you so much for taking care of this for me."

"Trust me when I tell you it's a refreshing change from brokering divorces, child-custody disputes and other fun family meltdowns."

"I don't know how you do it."

"Sometimes, I can't bear it, but hey, it's a living, and every so often I get to help someone amazing get exactly what she wants."

Her heartfelt words bring tears to my eyes. I'm really about to get exactly what I want, and part of me still can't believe this is actually happening.

Cecily reaches for me, and I gladly accept her hug. "I'm so happy for you."

"Thank you."

"So tell me about this guy who's going to be the father. What's he like?"

How to adequately describe Jasper... "He's a very good friend of mine and Flynn's."

"And..." She rolls her hand, obviously looking for the dirty details.

"He's incredibly handsome, charming and very sweet. And he's British."

Cecily fans her face. "The accent..."

"Is to *die* for."

"You lucky bitch. You get to make a baby with a hot guy without having to deal with all the relationship nonsense. Leave it to you to get it just right."

Yes, I got it just right, except over the last couple of days, I'm finding it harder to ignore the hollowed-out feeling I've had since Jasper left the other night. What possible reason could I have for the achy, disjointed sense that something is... off? I can't think of another word to describe it. I haven't seen him yet today, because he wasn't in the office this morning, and I saw him only in passing yesterday. I'm hoping that when he arrives for our meeting, he'll somehow put my mind at ease. Until then, I'm a hot mess of anxiety, hoping this whole thing isn't going to blow up in my face at the last minute.

I'm not sure how I'll manage the disappointment if that happens.

Cecily and I catch up on each other's lives, and she regales me with a series of dating misadventures that have me laughing and forgetting, albeit briefly, about my worries where Jasper is concerned.

Then Cecily's assistant shows Jasper and Emmett into her office, and my heart skips a beat at the sight of him. *No, no, no!* That's not supposed to happen. He's Jasper, my friend, the future father of my child. He's not supposed to make my heart do funny things.

I somehow manage to introduce Jasper and Emmett to Cecily while dealing with my own mortification at seeing Emmett for the first time since Jasper clued him into our plans. To his credit, he greets me the way he always does, as if this meeting is no different from the hundreds of others we've had at work and outside of work.

"We've got everything set up in the conference room across the hall." Cecily gestures for them to go ahead of us. When their backs are turned, she fans her face dramatically. In a whisper that only I can hear, she says, "Shut the fuck *up*. Just shut the fuck up. These guys are right out of central casting, especially your Brit."

I giggle at her befuddled expression and try to imagine seeing Jasper and Emmett through the eyes of a woman who has never met them before. They do make one hell of an impression, especially Jasper. It's the accent. Of course that's what it is. What else could it be?

By the time we're seated on opposite sides of the conference table, Cecily has recovered her professional demeanor, but I notice her stealing glances at both men, as if she still can't believe what she's seeing. I get why she's undone by them. They make for quite an appealing pair—Jasper with his thick blond hair and golden-brown eyes, and Emmett's wavy brown hair and intense gaze. I'd like to think I'm immune to both of them after spending so much time in their company, but judging by my reaction to Jasper, I'm far from immune to him.

Cecily goes over the paperwork that outlines the terms of our agreement in legalese that's somewhat easy to understand. I'll have full custody of the child with everything that goes along with that. For the first time, however, I discover that Jasper has offered a generous monthly amount for child support.

"That's not necessary." I look at him across the table, and the expression I see on his face has me wondering once again if this is what he really wants.

"It is necessary. To me." He looks so sad that my heart begins to ache in ways it never has before.

I pause for a long moment before I say, "Could we... Um, could we have a minute, please?"

"Of course." Cecily stands and says to Emmett, "May I buy you a coffee?"

"That sounds good."

They leave the room, and the conference door clicks shut behind them with a loud echo.

"What's wrong?" I ask, forcing myself to breathe over the rapid beat of my heart.

"Nothing's wrong."

"You don't look right in the eyes."

His lips quirk with the amusement that's so much a part of his charm, but I won't let myself be drawn in by that. "Darling, I'm totally fine, and completely on board with our plans. There's nothing at all to worry about."

"Would you tell me if there was something to worry about?"

He hesitates, ever so slightly, but just long enough to tell me I've hit a bull's-eye. "Of course I would."

"No, I don't actually think you would. I think you're such a good and loyal friend that you'd go through with this before you'd ever disappoint me, even if you'd changed your mind."

After taking a deep breath and expelling it, he gets up and walks around to my side of the table.

My mouth goes dry and my hands are suddenly sweaty as I watch him come toward me.

He places a hand on each of the armrests on my chair and leans in, stopping when his lips are a heartbeat away from touching mine.

I've all but stopped breathing.

"I can't wait to father your child, to watch you blossom with preg- nancy, to see you flushed with excitement and wonder and anticipation. I can't wait to meet the child we'll make together and to watch him or her grow up. I haven't changed my mind. Okay?"

I'm expected to say something after that? The whoosh of my breath escaping from my throat sounds like a sob. Until that exact second, until I was all but certain he was going to back out, I hadn't actually allowed myself to acknowledge how excited I really am to make my dream come true with him. "Okay," I whisper.

Raising one hand to my chin, he forces me to look up at him as he brings his lips down on mine. I swear to God, right in this moment, if he lifted me onto the conference table and stepped between my spread legs, I wouldn't say no to him. I wouldn't be able to.

Thankfully, he reins it in before I end up on my back in another office.

As he starts to withdraw from me, I flatten my hand on his face. "In case I forget to say so, thank you. Thank you so much for this. You'll never know what it means to me."

"I think I know." He kisses me again, fleetingly, and stands up straight.

I try not to notice that he's hard, but my gaze is naturally drawn to the evidence of his arousal, visible proof that he wants me as much as I want him.

"Shall we call the lawyers back and get this sorted?"

For a man with a boner in a Brentwood conference room, his British decorum is in full force.

"Yes, please."

CHAPTER 11

Ellie

*H*e goes back around the table, sticks his head into the hallway and says a few words that get Emmett and Cecily back into the room.

When the four of us are seated once again, I notice Jasper shifting in his seat, as if to find a comfortable position. I hold back a desperate need to giggle madly at his *predicament*.

He sees my struggle and quirks a brow in my direction, and suddenly the need to laugh becomes a whole other kind of need— the kind that directly involves him.

Cecily continues her review of the agreement, noting that each party has produced recent evidence of perfect health, that each party is entering into this agreement willingly and without reservation, that each party has agreed that the child's paternity shall remain confidential except in instances when both parties agree to share the information.

Jasper watches me intently the entire time. His gaze is hungry and sexy and tinged with what could be emotion. I hadn't expected that from him. He's never been the type to wear his emotions on his face or his sleeve or anywhere else. Jasper is all about the lighthearted fun in life. He works hard and plays harder. He doesn't get involved. So why does he seem so invested in this process even as he signs away his rights to our future child?

The papers come across the table to me, and at first I think I must be reading them wrong, because why has he signed everything Jasper Kingsley? Who in the heck is that?

He catches me eyeing him and looks away, his jaw pulsing with the kind of tension I often see in Hayden, not Jasper. Tension isn't his thing, or at least it isn't usually his thing.

When we're done signing, Cecily gathers up the paperwork. "I'll have my assistant get everything together for you to pick up on your way out."

"Thanks very much," Emmett says, shaking hands with her.

She leaves the room to see to the paperwork.

Emmett turns to Jasper. "Ready to go?"

He continues to stare at me across the table. "I'm going to ride back to the office with Ellie."

Oh, he is?

"Great," Emmett says, "I'll see you both back at the ranch."

"Emmett."

He turns to me. "Yes?"

"You won't... I mean I know you're bound by attorney-client privilege and all that, but you won't say anything about this to anyone, right?"

"Never."

"I'm sorry to even ask, but—"

"No worries. I understand that it's a big deal. No one will hear about it from me. I wish you all the luck in the world, Ellie."

His kindness brings a lump to my throat. "Thank you so much."

After he leaves the room, I look over at Jasper, who's still staring at me intently. I lick my lips and watch his gaze move to my mouth, which is an instant turn-on.

"Who's Jasper Kingsley?"

"That's my given name. I use my mother's maiden name professionally."

"Why?"

"That, my darling, is a very long story for another day. We've got far better things to do today."

"Like go back to work?"

"That wasn't what I had in mind." This is said in a way that leaves no doubt as to what he has in mind.

"I have a meeting at four. I can't miss it, especially if you're still expecting me to take next week off to make a baby."

"I'm still expecting."

I get up from my seat, surprised to discover my legs are far from steady as I make my way around the table to him.

He continues to watch me in that sexy, proprietary way that has my motor running on overdrive.

"Why are you staring at me?"

"Because you're so very lovely to look at."

"Do you ever think that it's weird the way this has happened sort of all of a sudden between us?"

He stands and comes to me, placing his hands on my hips and resting his forehead on mine. "It's hardly all of a sudden, darling. For quite some time now, if you're in the room, I've found it difficult to look anywhere but where you are."

All the breath exits my lungs in another big whoosh that leaves me feeling light-headed and off balance. "Th-that's not true. Don't say that."

"It is true."

It takes all the courage I can muster to ask, "Why haven't you ever done anything about it, then?"

"Because of who you are to me, who Flynn is to me, who the Godfreys are to me. Until that morning in Mexico when you gave me the perfect opportunity to have more with you without sacrificing our lovely friendship."

"I feel like there're things you aren't telling me, things I should probably know before this goes any further."

"You're very astute and perceptive."

"So?"

"Suffice to say you know everything you need to know about me for what we're about to do."

"You're just not going to tell me?"

"No, love, I'm not. It doesn't matter."

I wonder if he knows how the sadness in his eyes tells me that despite what he says, whatever it is matters very much to him. I choose not to pursue it any further now when I have a meeting I need to be at in just over an hour. I head for the door, but Jasper stops me from leaving the room by placing his hand flat against the closed door, his body firm against my back, his arm around my waist.

"I'm sorry I can't tell you everything you want to know. If I were going to tell anyone, I'd tell you, darling. I swear I would."

"It's okay." I say what he needs to hear so we can get out of here, but he's already given me the one thing I need to find the answers he won't give me—his real name.

THE FOUR O'CLOCK meeting is torturous, jammed with details that require my full and undivided attention, especially because my team has no idea I'm about to invent an illness so I can work on getting pregnant with my hot-as-fuck kinky lover, who also happens to be one of their bosses. Yes, this is now my life, and it's as exciting a life as I've ever had.

Every time I think about the baby we're going to make, my skin tingles with the kind of excitement that reminds me of being a kid on Christmas and my birthday at Disneyland with all the ice cream I can eat without ever feeling sick rolled up into one amazing day. Only even that description doesn't quite capture the full extent of my excitement.

I find myself daydreaming about cribs and changing tables and nursery designs and onesies and tiny socks when I'm supposed to be thinking about permits and permissions and local customs and production schedules.

It's probably a good thing I'm planning to use some of the weeks of sick time I've accumulated during my ten years at Quantum, because I'm not much good to anyone in my current frame of mind.

Thank God for Dax, who seems to have tuned in to the fact that I'm insanely distracted and takes the helm for me when I fumble over the details. I don't think anyone else notices my unusual lack of focus, but he certainly does. And because he's the best assistant I've ever had, I decide to take him into my confidence.

After the meeting ends, I ask him to remain in my office while the others file out, each of them with a to-do list a mile long.

"I owe you an explanation for my scattered brain lately."

"It's post-vacation blues. I get it."

"It's more than that. If I tell you the truth, can I trust you to keep it between us?"

He gives me a withering "what do you take me for" look. "If you can't trust me by now, Ellie, when will you trust me?"

"You're right, but it's such a big deal that I felt the need to preface it by asking for your discretion."

"You have it."

"I'm planning to have a baby."

His mouth falls open with the kind of shock that can't be faked. Clearly, he didn't see that coming. "You... you're... A baby. Well, that's great. I'm happy for you."

"It hasn't happened yet, but it's in the works, and I wanted to let you know that I'll be taking next week off to, um, undergo some, ah, treatments."

His entire face turns bright red. Even the tips of his ears are scarlet.

"I was hoping you might cover for me again. I'll see about getting you an extra week off this year to make it up to you."

"That's not necessary. I don't mind covering for you."

"Thank you so much. I really appreciate it, and I'll remember it at bonus time."

"Okay, then. I'd better get back to it." I can't imagine he could've moved any faster to leave the room if his ass had been on fire.

I drop my head into my hands, mortified by what I just did to poor Dax. Treatments... *Oh my God*, I'm becoming such a bad person. But it's not like I could tell him I'm going to have mad, crazy, possibly kinky monkey sex with Jasper Autry—or whatever his name is—to make my baby.

Speaking of Jasper... I reach for my phone because I don't dare do this on the company network. Calling up the browser, I type in the name Jasper Kingsley and UK, hesitating before pressing the Search button. What will I find out? What will it mean? How will it change things? He said it was a long story, too long to tell me in a few minutes.

What if he's wanted for some horrible crime in the UK? Or on the sex offender registry or—

"Stop it, Ellie. He's not wanted or on the registry. For God's sake, stop making things up." Now he's got me talking to myself, too. Before I can make up any more fiction, I press the Search button and hold my breath, waiting for the results to pop up.

At first I'm not sure what I'm seeing. There's all this stuff about the Kingsley family, their vast financial holdings, their historically significant place in the British aristocracy. Wait. What? I click on a link to a story in the *International Times* about Henry Kingsley, the ninth Duke of Wethersby, thought to be the wealthiest man in England, and not only because of his inherited fortune.

No, Henry has quadrupled the family's already enormous wealth through a series of shrewd investments and financial acumen that's often compared to that of American business magnate Warren Buffett. His is one of the few dukedoms in all of England to remain intact in modern times, thanks almost entirely to the brillance of Henry and his father before him. In addition to his business wizardry, Henry is known for his love of extreme adventure. He's summited Mount Everest twice and holds several records for piloting experimental aircraft on long jaunts.

"Holy shit," I whisper as it occurs to me that Jasper is a freaking billionaire. I scroll through the story until it mentions that Henry's son and heir, Jasper, is also known as the Marquess of Andover, one of his father's lesser titles. His heir. A *marquess*. Like the guy Edith married on *Downton Abbey*, the one who outranked her father, the earl!

How is it possible that the Hollywood press hasn't picked up on this? Probably because Jasper doesn't use his family name and apparently hasn't told even his closest friends and partners about his aristocratic pedigree... Does Flynn know? I wish I could ask him without giving away what I've uncovered. I do a search for Jasper Autry and find the version of him that I know—an Academy Award-winning cinematographer, a principal in the highly successful Quantum Production Company founded by Academy Award-winning actor Flynn Godfrey and Academy Award-winning director Hayden Roth. The article also notes that Jasper is a notorious playboy known for a series of brief relationships with some of the most beautiful women in the world.

There are photos of him with women—lots and lots of women, many of them actresses, supermodels and a few who are famous merely for being famous. He's smiling in every photo, and why wouldn't he be? He's an Academy Award-winning billionaire. No wonder he's more than happy to sign away his rights to our child. He's got much better things to do than change nappies.

I knew about the women. I've always known about the women, because he's talked to me about them, often sharing in the drama, hilarity, outrageousness and sheer insanity he's experienced with many of them. We'd laugh about it, and the next thing I'd know, the Hollywood press would report he'd parted ways with the flavor of the month. They'd follow him relentlessly until he appeared somewhere with his newest conquest, restarting the feeding frenzy all over again.

That level of attention is unusual for someone who works behind the scenes in the film industry, but a man who looks like Jasper gets noticed in this town, especially when he hobnobs with the likes of Flynn, Hayden, Marlowe and Kristian, four of the heaviest hitters in Hollywood.

I clear the search history on my phone and set it on my desk, unreasonably saddened by what I've learned. What did I think was going to happen? Did I honestly expect that someone like me, a no one compared to the women he usually dates, would be the one to bring Jasper up to scratch? Who would convince him to put his manwhoring ways behind him?

I admit to myself—and only myself—that his eager willingness to father my child had me wondering if maybe he feels more for me than he's let on. He basically told me that he's had a thing for me for as long as he's known me. But how can I possibly compete with the kind of women he normally dates?

Ugh, and how much do I despise myself for even having that thought? Any man would be lucky to have me. In addition to my above-average looks, I wield a mean power screwdriver and drill. I can fix anything. I can install my own blinds, paint my own walls and finish my own floors. I don't need Jasper—or any man—for anything other than his DNA.

Resigned to keeping my heart out of the equation with him, I gather my belongings to leave the office. I need to hit the grocery store, take Randy for a run, do some laundry and go over my notes for tomorrow's meetings. And, it's time to return Serenity's call about the dating service. I've got stuff to do and no time for the man who's turning my usually productive brain to mush.

OH MY GOD... Holy, holy, *holy* God... My entire body seizes as I come harder than I ever have in my entire life with Jasper's fingers deep inside me and his mouth attached to my clit while I grasp the rails of my headboard, per his orders.

Remember that to-do list I had for tonight? Yeah, well, things didn't exactly go as planned after Jasper showed up and backed me into my bedroom, dropped me onto my back and delivered not one but two stupendous orgasms before I could remember that I've forbidden "extras" from our "relationship." He's just proven how utterly powerless I am to resist him when he goes all alpha on me.

He withdraws from me, wipes his mouth with the back of his hand and frees his cock from his pants. "Don't let go of the rails, and keep your eyes on me. I want your eyes." Watching me closely, he strokes himself, making his intentions clear. "No more condoms, right?"

The magnitude of that statement finds its way through the muddled mess he's made of my brain. We're doing this. We're actually going to make a baby, and I could get pregnant any time we have unprotected sex. I've never had unprotected sex, so this is a big moment in more ways than one.

"Darling? Are you with me?"

"Yes, sorry. I'm with you, and no more condoms."

Those words seem to spark something primal in him, and he drives into me, his body shuddering and his eyes blinking closed for a second before he opens them to lock his gaze with mine. "So hot. So tight." Once again, he lifts my legs onto his shoulders, putting me into a position I'd never been in before him. It allows him to go deeper into me than anyone has ever been.

And his eyes never leave mine as he presses the pad of his thumb to my clit and keeps up a relentless pace. I'm coming again before I've caught my breath from the last time, and he's right there with me, coming with a groan that starts deep inside him.

He pulls back enough to settle my legs back onto the mattress, but stays buried deep inside me as we pulse with aftershocks.

"The last time I did that without a condom, I was fifteen and praying the pullout method would work."

Laughing, I say, "And did it?"

"Thank Christ it did. The chances we take when we are young and dumb."

"And full of cum," we say together, laughing as we quote one of Hayden's favorite sayings.

His lips brush softly against my neck, setting off a chain reaction of goose bumps and sensation that coalesces in the place where we're still joined. "I can't get enough of you, Ellie Godfrey. I don't know what sort of spell you've cast upon me, but all I think about lately is being naked with you."

I swallow hard, trying to mask my emotional reaction to his confession. "Then why are we still wearing most of our clothes?"

"Because I couldn't wait another second to have you after you fired me up in that meeting today."

I want to believe he has it that bad for me, but I can't stop thinking about all the things I read about him earlier. Will he ever tell me, for instance, that he's the heir to a vast fortune? Will he ever tell me that he's a marquess, a future duke or anything about the secrets he has kept from the rest of our group or what he plans to do about the vast empire he will one day inherit? What, for example, will it mean for his partnership in Quantum? I have so many questions, none of which I feel I have the right to ask.

That's not what we're about. We're about making a baby, not exchanging deep, dark secrets. Although, he'd probably argue that admitting his kinky tendencies would equate to a deep, dark secret.

I'm having the best sex of my life with him, so why do I feel dissatisfied? Because I want more from him, and I can't have it. That's why. He's made it very clear that he's not a relationship kind of guy. He's proven that by going from one bimbo to another for as long as I've known him, not to mention signing away all rights to a child we haven't even conceived yet. Why would I ever expect to be "different" from the many women who came before me?

"We need to get going," he says, interrupting a long period of silence.

"Going where?"

"Black Vice. My friend Devon Black is expecting us at ten."

"*Tonight?*"

"Is that a problem, darling?"

When he calls me that, I tend to lose my train of thought, and this time is no different. Then I remember he probably calls all his many women that, and it loses some of its luster. "It's... I have to work tomorrow, and it's..." And I need more time to prepare myself for this...

He's watching me in that knowing way of his, as if he understands my heart better than anyone. It's disconcerting, especially since I'm all too aware that he wants nothing to do with my heart.

"It's fine. We can go."

"Are you sure?"

No, I'm not sure. I'm not sure of anything when it comes to you, but I'm incredibly curious. I nod in agreement. "I need a shower after that workout."

A crooked smile works its way across his face. "Worked up a sweat, did you, love?"

Suddenly I want to cry for what can never be. I want to wail and rant and scream at the injustice of it all. He's perfect for me in every possible way. He's gorgeous and sexy, and that accent... But he's also funny and sweet and incredibly kind to his friends, who are like family to him. And none of that even takes into consideration his staggering talent as a filmmaker. He's the whole package, and he's slowly but surely ruining me for all other men.

I can't let that happen. I'm still determined that my child will have a father in his or her life. I'd never want him to grow up without the kind of father I had, and even if it means settling for someone who doesn't exactly make my heart pound with joy, I want to find someone who will be there for my child. I know he's out there somewhere, and as I drag myself into the shower, I'm more determined than ever to find him.

While I wait for the water to heat up, I reach for my phone and send a text to Serenity, asking if she can get together tomorrow. I'll find a way to tell Jasper that I'm going to move forward with my plans to meet new people, and as soon as we've conceived the child I want so badly, I'll let him go to resume his real life already in progress.

CHAPTER 12

Jasper

*H*ow will I stand to know that she and my child are tucked away in this charming little house, living and loving and growing together while I'm always somewhere other than with them? How will I satisfy myself with occasional visits? How will I ever again touch another woman after having known the exquisite pleasure to be found with her?

Listening to the shower running in the next room, I lie in her bed, looking up at the ceiling fan as it spins round and round, a metaphor for the thoughts cycling through my mind.

The supreme unfairness of it all is hard to fathom at times like this, when I'm unable to have what I want most in the world, all because of whom I was born to. Some might think, oh, poor little rich boy, born with a silver spoon in his mouth. What in the world does he have to bitch and moan about? But imagine your fate being decided for you before you're even born. Then all the riches in the world might not look quite so appealing.

I think about the last, bitter argument my father and I had before I left to attend film school at USC. I'd gone around him and applied behind his back, thrilled and elated to have gotten in but sick at heart to know a draining battle would take place before I left.

I declined offers to attend business school at Oxford, Harvard, Yale, UPenn and Dartmouth. I did that before I told him I was going to USC so there would be no other options remaining by the time I broke the news to him. The blowup was every bit as cataclysmic as I expected it to be. He was so furious, his face turned purple, and for a brief, horrible moment, I wondered if he was having a heart attack.

Wouldn't that have been ironic? If he'd dropped dead right in front of me and because of me, he would've gotten what he wanted after all—me as his prisoner. But he didn't drop dead. No, he recovered and managed to say and do some things that I still recall in vivid detail nearly twenty years later. He called me an ungrateful, disgraceful, arrogant waste of his DNA, among other choice words. All because I had a dream that differed from the plan he made for my life before I was born. And that was the least of what happened that day, but I can't allow myself to go back there, to be sucked into that rabbit hole of despair that I've worked so hard to escape.

I left for LA the next day and have rarely been home in the ensuing years. I see my mother and sisters at least once a year, but I haven't seen my father in eight years, not since the funeral for my maternal grandfather. I don't think we exchanged more than ten words during the two days I was home. I'm dead to him in every way except for one—he hasn't gone so far as to actually disinherit me, much to my dismay. I used to pray every night that he would.

My womanizing stemmed initially from my desire to disgust him to the point that he didn't want me as his heir anymore. But nothing I've done, and I've tried a lot of things, has had the desired effect. And that's my own fault. It was my idea to use my mother's maiden name as my surname in my new life, lest I ever be somehow connected to him. So while I'm sure my father is suitably appalled at the way I live my life, the rest of the world has no earthly idea that Academy Award-winning cinematographer and world-class skirt chaser Jasper Autry is actually the heir to the Kingsley billions, in line to be the tenth Duke of Wethersby.

Naturally, it's never occurred to my father that my sister Gwendolyn, the Wall Street financier, would actually be much better at running the family empire than I ever could be, but God forbid his heir be a *woman*. That's not the way of things in his world. If I hadn't been born, finally, after four daughters, he would've left everything to his brother's son before he turned his dynasty over to a mere *girl*.

Gwen is a Harvard MBA with the same head for finance my father has and his father before him had, but she's never worked a day for the family business. She's a bigwig at an investment bank on Wall Street where she's made a name for herself in the same financial circles in which my father is a living legend.

The hairdryer goes on in the bathroom, a signal to me that the shower is free. I run the palm of my right hand over the stubble on my jaw, unnerved by the trip down memory lane that takes me back to some of the most difficult days of my life. I have no regrets about making a stand for the life I wanted rather than having the life he intended to force upon me, but I've always known I'm living on borrowed time.

That's especially true lately as my father spends less time in the office and more time pursuing passions that regularly put his life at risk. Last May, when he climbed Everest for the second time, I don't think I took a deep breath for an entire week while I waited to hear he had successfully descended from the summit.

His latest thing, according to the media, is flying solo around the world in an experimental solar-powered plane, because that's not dangerous or anything. Sometimes I swear he's gotten into extreme challenges just to torment me. I have no doubt he takes a perverse pleasure in knowing I'm constantly on edge, waiting to hear he's managed to kill himself.

The whole world will be watching his latest exploit. If his greatest skill is making money, his second-greatest skill is courting publicity. I'd have to hide under a rock to avoid the coverage. Luckily, my baby-making week with Ellie coincides with my father's latest circus, so I'll stay offline and out of his loop, which is where I'm happiest anyway.

"Jasper?" Ellie emerges from the bathroom. She's wearing a robe, but her hair is dry and she's put on some makeup. Not a lot, but just enough to emphasize her eyes and lips. She looks fantastic, as always. "Are you all right?"

"Of course, darling. I dozed off for a few minutes after you wore me out."

Smiling, she rolls her eyes at me. "What do I wear to a sex club?"

"Something sexy."

"That narrows it right down."

I get out of bed and go to her, putting my arms around her waist. "You could wear that robe, and you'd stand out like the perfect rose that you are. Anything you want to wear will be smashing, I'm sure." I kiss her and step around her into the bathroom.

"You sure you're okay?"

"Why do you ask?"

"You were a million miles away when I came out of the bathroom."

Unfortunately, a million miles wouldn't be far enough to free me from the shackle around my ankle. "I'm fine, darling. I'll be quick." I close the door, unnerved by how completely she "sees" me. She always has, even when we were "just" friends, but since we've become lovers, she's become more attuned to me, and God, I love being *seen* by her. I love being *known* by her. I love everything with her, even if I shouldn't.

I get in the shower and stare up at the water raining down upon me, determined to enjoy every bloody minute I get to have with her before I'm forced to set her free.

We ride to Black Vice in Jasper's car. He's been unusually quiet since he came out of the shower and got dressed. I assume it's because he's not thrilled to be taking me to the club, but I have no way to know that for sure. I'm too excited to experience the club to risk asking him what's wrong. I don't want him to change his mind about taking me there.

Growing up in LA, I was always aware of the city's sexual undercurrents. There are stores devoted to pleasure, basic strip clubs and higher-end "gentlemen's" clubs, not to mention the adult film business that operates on the fringes of Hollywood. There was no avoiding the influences that surrounded me, but I've never had an urge to delve any deeper into the various lifestyles. Until now. Until Jasper confessed his kinky tendencies and made me obsessed with knowing more.

We climb into the Hollywood Hills, far too close to Flynn's house for comfort. Jasper navigates the winding road, pulling into a driveway I would've missed. The driveway bends and twists a few times before revealing what looks like a private home.

Young sexy men in tuxedo shirts and bow ties are working the well-lit entrance, valet-parking cars and greeting guests.

Jasper gets out of the car, takes a ticket from one of the valets and comes around to help me out. Wordlessly, he tucks my hand into the crook of his elbow and walks me inside where I have to blink several times before my eyes adjust to the much darker lighting.

A handsome dark-haired man with dark eyes and the sort of intensity not often seen in men so young comes over to us. Wearing black pants and a dress shirt rolled up at the sleeves, he greets Jasper with a warm smile and the half bro-hug that guys are into these days.

"This is my friend Ellie. Ellie, meet Devon Black, our host this evening."

Devon takes my offered hand and kisses the back of it. "Lovely to meet you, Ellie. Jasper tells me this is your first time at a club like ours. Welcome."

"Thank you so much for having me."

"I'd say the pleasure was all mine, but I hope it'll be all yours."

The statement is so bold that it sends a flash of heat rippling through my veins as I try to imagine what I might be in for.

"Before we go any further, I'll need you to sign our standard nondisclosure form that basically says we'll take aggressive legal action against anyone who speaks of who or what they see here. I trust that Jasper has told you that our club is a place where people are made to feel safe to be themselves. Everything that happens here is anonymous. I can almost guarantee you'll recognize someone you see here tonight. By signing this form, you promise not to disclose that information to anyone."

"That's no problem." I take the form from him and sign it.

Devon takes the signed form, hands it to the woman working the reception desk and gestures for us to follow him. "Come along. Let's take a tour."

"Don't you have to sign the form?" I ask Jasper.

"Jasper is a longtime member of our club," Devon replies.

"I appreciate your time tonight, Devon," Jasper says.

"Not a problem. My lady has been down with the flu. I find myself with some rare free time, so your call was well timed."

"Give Tenley my regards," Jasper says.

"Tenley, the stylist Flynn and Natalie work with?" I ask, making an effort to keep the surprise out of my voice. "Addie's friend?"

"The one and only," Devon says with a soft smile that conveys his affection for her.

So Tenley is part of the lifestyle, too? This just gets more interesting all the time. And I haven't seen anything yet.

We're taken into a huge room with a variety of stages where couples and groups of people are engaged in a variety of activities. On one stage, a woman is bent over an apparatus as her lover flogs her with a device that resembles a mop made of leather. Next to that stage, a man is being dominated by a woman dressed all in black leather and wearing the highest, spikiest heels I've ever seen. I wince when she stands on his chest and drives those spike heels into his skin. He groans with unmistakable pleasure.

Another stage has a woman surrounded by a group of four men, each of whom tends to a different part of her body. I try to imagine what it would be like to have so many hands, mouths and tongues working me over at the same time, and my clit tingles with unexpected interest.

"That sub is acting out a gang-rape fantasy tonight," Devon tells me. Music is blasting through the room in a sexy, urgent sort of beat, but I can easily hear Devon's voice over the noise.

"People have rape fantasies?" I ask in a small voice.

"People have all kinds of fantasies," Devon explains, "and in clubs such as this, they're free to explore them in a safe, sane, consensual environment. Those three themes form the core of our lifestyle, and they should always be at the forefront of your involvement, whatever it may be."

"Darling, are you all right?" Jasper asks.

I realize I'm staring at the woman surrounded by men as I wonder how her fantasy will unfold. Will they all take turns? Will they have her at the same time? What would I want if I were her? I wouldn't ever fantasize about rape. That much I'm certain of. Multiple guys tending to my pleasure? I could possibly live with that, but it's not at the top of the list of things I want to try.

"Ellie?"

"Yes, sorry, I'm fine."

I'm a one-guy-at-a-time kind of girl, and the only reason I'm curious about what goes on here is because it interests Jasper. And he interests me. His hand on my lower back keeps me focused on the here and now, which requires my full attention.

I note that the waitresses and waiters are all wearing butt plugs with tails attached to them and only enough other clothing to cover their genitals. The women are all but topless with their nipples covered by tassels and other ornaments. I try to imagine what it would be like to land a new job and be told, *Oh, by the way, you're required to wear butt plugs on the floor and nipple pasties as you serve our clientele.*

"Are they told during the interview that they're required to wear butt plugs as part of the uniform?"

Devon chuckles at the question. "They're not mandatory."

"So they wear them because they like them?"

He shrugs. "You'd have to ask them. We require only that they dress provocatively, in keeping with the theme of the club. Anything else they choose to do is entirely up to them."

"And I assume your staff is required to also be ridiculously hot?"

"Again, not a requirement."

We walk up a flight of stairs to an open gallery area where Devon gestures to side-by-side closed doors. "Behind those doors, you'll find a variety of scenes unfolding between consenting partners. Left side is the playroom, right side is observation, and intercourse is allowed up here but not on the main floor."

"Do you want to take a look?" Jasper asks.

I'm trying to decide how far I want to take this quest for information, when one of the left-side doors opens and a couple emerges. They are so wrapped up in each other that they don't notice us until I gasp and draw their attention to us. Hayden and Addie.

They do a simultaneous double take when they see us standing there with Devon.

Hayden's happy, satisfied expression turns stormy. "What the hell are you doing here, Ellie?"

"She's here with me," Jasper says, putting an arm around my shoulders.

Hayden looks from him to me and then to him again. "You wanna run that by me one more time?"

"You heard me."

"I asked him to bring me," I say.

He stares down Jasper. "What the hell for?"

Before Jasper can answer, I say, "I'm not planning to ask what you're doing here, Hayden, so maybe you should afford me the same courtesy."

His eyes narrow, and I can tell there's a lot more he wants to say.

"Hayden." Addie tugs on his hand. "Let's go home."

After a long pause, he says to Jasper, "You'd better hope Flynn doesn't hear you brought her here."

That makes me mad. "Newsflash, Hayden. I'm thirty-five years old. I don't ask my little brother for permission to do anything. It's none of his business that I'm here, and it's none of yours."

"She's right, Hayden." Addie pulls harder on his hand. "Let's go."

He lets her lead him away, but not before he directs another stormy scowl at Jasper.

"Well," Jasper says cheerfully after they walk away, "always a treat to run into Hayden."

"My apologies," Devon says. "I was upstairs with Tenley earlier and hadn't heard they were here tonight. I would've given you a heads-up."

"No worries, mate."

One of Devon's employees approaches us and confers privately with him. "If you'll excuse me, I have something I need to see to. Feel free to wander at your leisure. I'll meet you back at the bar to answer any questions you might have, Ellie."

"Thank you." I realize that though I revealed myself as Flynn's sister during the encounter with Hayden and Addie, Devon doesn't seem particularly concerned about my brother's potential ire.

"I'm sorry about that, love," Jasper says when we're alone. "I had no idea they were members here."

"But you knew they were part of the lifestyle."

"Yes."

"I can totally see it for him, but Addie..."

"She's new to it."

"Ah, I see. Since she got together with him, and he just willingly introduced her to his lifestyle?"

"Um, I don't think it went quite like that, but you'd have to ask her."

I'm struck by the memory of the bruise I saw on Addie's arm in Mexico. Is it possible that was caused by shackles of some sort? Well, I'll be damned... "I feel like I'm back in high school, and all the cool kids know something I don't."

He smiles down at me, his eyes alight with amusement. "It's not like that. Most people don't go around talking about how they like to get off. For example, I've never once heard you tell anyone you like to be spanked."

I reach up and squish his lips shut. "I didn't know I liked that until I did it with you."

"Exactly," he says, the word muffled by my fingers. He reaches up to remove my hand, kissing my fingers before wrapping his hand around mine. "You never know until you try, and that's one of the central tenets of our lifestyle. Everything once. Twice if you like it. There's no shame in experimenting or stepping outside the lines to see what's possible."

"I'm trying to understand, as a feminist, the attraction to being submissive. I feel like I'm setting all of womankind back decades by allowing a man to control me in bed in an actual relationship."

"I can understand why it seems like you'd be giving up your hard-earned power, but it's not like that. You retain all the power by dictating in advance what you want and don't want." He pauses before he adds, "How many decisions do you make in the course of an average day?"

I have to think about that for a moment. "Hundreds?"

"Right, so imagine a scenario where you let someone else do the thinking for you, and the only thing you need to be worried about is your own pleasure."

"Isn't that kind of selfish?"

"Not at all, darling. To me, seeing to my partner's pleasure is the ultimate turn-on. I'd go so far as to say that turning over your pleasure to your partner is the ultimate use of your power as a woman."

"You make a compelling case. I'll give you that."

"Don't just take it from me. Let's go see, shall we?"

I'm nervous about actually watching other people have sex, but I allow him to lead me into the nearest observation room because I'm too curious to turn back now. We're the only people watching as a couple in the adjoining room acts out what appears to be a hard-core bondage scene. The guy is huge, easily six foot four, with muscles on top of muscles, broad shoulders, a narrow waist and a tight, muscular butt. His back is to me, so I can't immediately tell if he's big all over, but I can't wait to find out.

His submissive is bound at the wrists, which are attached to a hook over her head that leaves her suspended.

"Does that hurt her arms?" I whisper even though Jasper tells me they can't hear us. We can hear every word they say, however.

"He won't let her stay that way long enough for it to hurt."

Sure enough, he raises her legs to counterbalance the weight on her arms. He tweaks the bindings until she is partially reclined, her legs open and attached to another set of hooks that hang from the ceiling. "Does anything hurt?" he asks.

She shakes her head, and that's when I realize she's also gagged. I'd never go for that. The very idea of it is repulsive to me. She's tiny compared to him, and when he walks around her to inspect his work, I gasp when I see that he's indeed *huge* all over.

Jasper chuckles at my reaction.

"He'll cripple her."

"And she'll love every second of it. Watch."

I have no idea how long we're there, but we watch as he affixes clamps to her nipples and clitoris. Even over the gag, we can hear her high-pitched shrieks of pain as the teeth of the devices clamp down on her flesh. He soothes and comforts her, but he doesn't remove the clamps.

My own nipples and clit stand up to take a closer look at what's happening in the other room. I cross my arms, looking for some relief.

Jasper moves behind me, sliding his arms around my waist and bringing his hands up to cup my breasts, running his thumbs over my nipples as he presses his hard cock into my back. "I've got you, love. Just relax and enjoy. It turns them on to know we're watching."

I can't imagine being watched by strangers during such an intimate moment, but I'm finding that people enjoy a lot of things I've never imagined doing.

The man reaches for an object on the table next to him and holds it up for her to see. Her eyes get big and round, and she shakes her head.

"How does she use her safe word if she's gagged?"

"They'll have worked out a signal that stops everything if she does it. Such as blinking twice in rapid succession or rolling her eyes or something that tells him it's game off."

"So shaking her head to say no doesn't do it."

"Nope. The only thing that stops everything is the signal they've worked out in advance."

"What is that thing?"

"It's a butt plug."

"*That* is going in her *butt*? Jesus. It's huge!"

His body shakes with silent laughter.

I elbow him. "It's not funny! She'll never sit down again."

"Sure she will. He's probably getting her ready to take *him* there."

"No way. There's no way in hell he'd ever fit."

"Not only would he fit, he'd make her love it."

I can't believe I'm standing here watching him work that enormous plug into her ass while she writhes and grunts and screams as much as she can over the gag. Her body glistens with perspiration, and tears run down her cheeks. Part of me wants to rush in there and rescue her. I have to keep reminding myself that she knew ahead of time what he was going to do and agreed to it. Though I find it hard to believe she agreed to have that *thing* jammed up her ass. By the time the object is fully seated, she's trembling madly. He runs his hands over her legs before dipping his head to lick her pussy. Whatever he does to her has her screaming again, this time in obvious pleasure.

She's still coming when he drives his big cock into her, making her go stiff with what appears to be shock and pain and pleasure all mixed together. My knees buckle under me, and only Jasper's arm around me keeps me upright as the man hammers into his sub, his pace relentless and merciless.

"He's going to hurt her," I whisper.

"No, he won't. He's watching over her very closely to make sure she's enjoying it as much as he is."

I have to force myself to keep watching, to remain present when all I want to do is duck my head and look anywhere but at what's happening right in front of me. Then he moves his hands to her breasts, toying with her until he releases the nipple clamps and she screams again, thrashing in agony when he also releases the clit clamp.

"Watch her face," Jasper says softly against my ear.

I zero in on her face and can't deny that something has changed. She's slipped into a Zen-like trance as he continues to plow into her, his pace unrelenting.

"That's called subspace," Jasper says. "It's when the endorphins kick in and take the sub right out of the present into a state of blissful acceptance. It's one of the most transcendent sexual experiences a person can have."

His description reminds me an awful lot of the way I felt after the first time we made love.

We watch as the man finally climaxes, surging into her repeatedly. Then he immediately gets to work tending to her, removing the plug and the gag and then releasing her from the restraints. He gathers her into his arms and holds her close to him, whispering words that I can't quite make out.

Though her eyes remain closed, her small, satisfied smile tells me she's more than fine.

"Come." With his arm around my waist, Jasper escorts me from the room on legs that are less than steady. He leads me to a seating arrangement in the hallway and sits next to me on a love seat. "Talk to me. Tell me how you're feeling."

"Overwhelmed, turned on, more curious than I was before."

"Do you want to see more?"

"I want to see everything."

His eyes blaze with heat as he leans in to capture my mouth in a kiss that has me wanting to rip his clothes off and have him right there, to hell with who might see us. "You're so bloody perfect," he whispers when we come up for air. "When you first told me you wanted a baby, all I could think about was having the chance to finally touch you. But now, there're so many other things I want to do with you besides make a baby."

"You want to do this stuff with me?"

"Hell, yes. I want to do everything with you, but only if it's what you want, too."

"I... I think I'd like to try some of it, but only with you. I couldn't do it with anyone but you."

"You'd better not do it with anyone but me, or I won't be responsible for my actions."

"You're sounding awfully possessive for a man who prides himself on not getting involved."

"You noticed that, did you?"

"Mmm." I nod as I let my gaze drop to his lips, which are still wet from our kisses.

"I want you to do something for me."

At that moment, I think I'd give him anything he wanted. "What's that?"

"Don't join that dating service."

"Jasper—"

"Give me some time to figure out some things before you date other guys."

"How much time?"

"I don't know yet, but please... All I know is the thought of you with other guys makes me crazy."

"This wasn't supposed to be serious. It was about making a baby. And now..."

"And now... I'm asking you not to see anyone but me."

"Aren't you asking for more than that? Isn't that why we're here?"

"If I could have anything I wanted, I'd be asking for everything with you. This," he says, gesturing to the club, "the baby, your whole damned life if you'd give it to me. But I'm not at liberty to ask for that. Not now anyway."

"How can you feel that way about me when only a week ago we were just friends?"

"We were never *just* friends. Not in my mind anyway. And when you told me you wanted a baby, I saw an opportunity to have more with you. I wasn't strong enough to walk away from that opportunity, even if I probably should have." He runs his finger over my cheek, setting off chain reactions I feel everywhere, especially between my legs. Brushing his lips against mine, he says, "Do you want to watch some more, or do you want to play?"

"Here?"

"Uh-huh. Devon made a room available to us if we're interested."

I swallow hard. "Would other people be watching us?"

"Not the first time. That would be just for us."

"I..."

"No pressure, Ellie. It's totally up to you." He drops soft, open-mouthed kisses on my neck, driving me wild with the touch of his tongue on my skin. "Whatever you want, whenever you want it."

"I want it." I want it so badly, I don't even know quite how to ask for what I want.

"Tell me."

"What he did to her. I want that."

"How much of it?"

"All of it, except for the gag and the clit clamp. That's not at all appealing to me."

"To be clear, you want to be restrained, you want your nipples clamped and your ass plugged while I fuck you. Is that right?"

I swallow hard. Part of me can't believe I'm even here, let alone agreeing to a laundry list like that one. "Yes."

"What would you like your safe word to be?"

"How about 'baby'?"

He smiles. "That's a good one." Squeezing my hand, he says, "You're sure about this?"

"Yes, Jasper, I'm sure."

"And you won't join the dating service?"

"I won't join the dating service. If that's what you want."

"That's what I want."

CHAPTER 13

Jasper

It's possible I've died and gone straight to heaven. Ellie is naked and bound, her legs spread as far apart as I could get them. Because this is her first time, I didn't suspend her. Rather, her arms are stretched over her head and attached to the iron rails of the bed, and her knees are bound to clips above the bed. The position is nothing less than obscene, and I love it. I can't wait to feast on her, but first I have to put her at ease. She's trembling madly, and her eyes are darting around the room, a sign of impending panic.

"Take a deep breath, love."

She does as she's told, drawing in a shaking deep breath.

"Now let it out." I walk her through a series of deep breaths until I see her begin to relax ever so slightly. "Keep breathing, and tell me your safe word again."

"Baby."

"You know if you say that word, everything comes to a halt, right?"

"Y-yes."

"You look so beautiful. Do you have any idea how amazing I think you are, how fearless and sexy?"

"I'm not fearless."

"You have no reason to fear me. Ever. I'd rather die than ever hurt you. Tell me you know that, too."

"I do. I know that."

"And you trust me to make this amazing for you?"

"I trust you."

"That means so much to me, my love. You'll never know how much." I kiss her softly and sweetly, sensing she needs both right now. "Now you don't say another word except your safe word and only if you need it. Are we clear?"

She nods, and I brush the hair back from her face as I withdraw from her to prepare for the scene. First, I remove my clothes and then I choose from a wide array of objects in the closet Devon keeps supplied for his members. I take my time getting ready, knowing the anticipation will ramp up her excitement and her anxiety, both of which will feed her pleasure.

I return to her, overwhelmed with gratitude for her bravery and more aroused than I can ever recall being before a scene. I'll admit that some of this has become rote and routine after so many years in the lifestyle, but there is nothing rote or routine about it with Ellie, especially knowing this is the first time she's ever done anything like this.

I start off with soft kisses on her neck and throat, working my way down to her breasts. Her nipples are already hard and tight, and I spend long minutes licking and sucking them until she's writhing under me, looking for more. I place the first clamp on her left nipple, and she screams from the pain of the teeth sinking into her sensitive flesh. I lick the clamped nipple, and she whimpers. I notice her pulse hammering in her throat, and I lick her there, too.

I kiss down to her belly, dragging my tongue in circles around her belly button and then down to her sweet pussy, where the wetness is running down to her ass. Christ, I love that she's so turned on. It's the greatest fucking thrill of my life to know that I've done that to her. I draw her clit into my mouth, sucking and tonguing her. She's so caught up in what I'm doing to her pussy that she doesn't see the second nipple clamp coming until it bites into her flesh just as I suck harder on her clit. Every one of her muscles tightens into a full-body orgasm that makes her scream.

"I don't recall telling you to come," I whisper against her thigh, taking a nibble of that soft flesh, causing her to startle. "That's grounds for punishment, love."

I can see that she has plenty to say to that, but she wisely bites her tongue and only glares at me.

Laughing, I reach for the bottle of lube on the table next to me and squeeze a generous amount onto my fingers. They slide through her wetness to her anus, which tightens around my fingers. "Let me in, darling. It'll feel better if you push back against me."

She grimaces as I push my fingers past the tight band of muscles, preparing her for the much bigger plug. She's already shown me how much she likes when I play with her ass, so I know she's going to love being plugged. Well, maybe not at first, but I'll bring her around.

When I decide she's ready, I reach for the medium-sized plug that I've already lubed and replace my fingers with it, pressing insistently until her muscles yield to allow it in. I wish I'd thought to film her expressions and the sounds she makes the first time she's plugged. But I don't need the footage, because I'll never forget any of it. I've done this many times before, but it's never felt as intimate or impor-tant as it does with her.

I'm beginning to accept that nothing will ever feel the way it does with her. Having her here at the club, embracing something that's so important to me, is another step on this journey we've been taking together. I've been a fool to think I could do a hit-and-run with her, leaving her to raise my child without me. As I watch her determina-tion, her desire to please me with her submission, I feel a sense of peace come over me.

She's the answer to every question I've ever had about who I am and where I belong. I belong here with her, not in England tending to a legacy I never wanted. There has to be a way out of my obligations to my family so I can stay here and make my own family—with her.

As the plug sinks into her, I watch over her carefully, seeing the first signs of subspace in her almost trancelike expression. I take my cock in hand, stroking myself before I begin to push into her, slowly because she's tighter than usual due to the plug. Grasping her hips, I press forward, and her mouth falls open in a silent scream that travels like an electrical current to my balls.

This is one hell of a time to realize I'm in love with this woman who is bound and clamped and plugged for me and who will soon, I hope, be pregnant with my child.

Ellie

I've lost all sense of time. I have no idea if we've been in this room for an hour or five hours. What does it matter? I've turned myself completely over to Jasper, and he's in charge. I'm floating, or that's how it feels until he removes the clamps on my nipples. The shocking blast of pain draws me out of the detached state I'd slipped into, forcing me back to reality.

Between the pain radiating from my nipples and the tight squeeze of his cock inside me, my senses are overloaded. Tears roll down my cheeks, but I don't feel sad. Actually, I feel elated and overwhelmed, but in the best possible way.

I've never surrendered control like this before, and I would've expected to feel more afraid than I did coming into this room, knowing what was going to happen. But I trust Jasper so completely that fear is the one emotion I haven't experienced in here.

He's seen to my every comfort, from the fur-lined cuffs around my wrists to the velvet bindings that hold my legs open for him. Other than the clamps and plug, which weren't comfortable at all but sent my arousal into the stratosphere, nothing about this has been more than I can handle.

I love the way he watches over me, gauging my every reaction, and that we talked about everything beforehand, so nothing is a surprise. I've been intimate with him for only a few days, and we've already talked more about sex than I have with every other man who came before him combined. Not that there were legions of them, but enough to know that the chemistry between Jasper and me is unusual—and exceptional.

He caresses my clit as he presses into me, and the pressure mounts all over again. I'm not supposed to come without his permission, but he's doing everything he can to make it impossible for me to follow that particular order. And I suspect he's doing it on purpose so he can punish me later. The thought of how he will punish me, combined with his fingers sliding over the tight knot of nerves at my core, sends me flying in a full-body orgasm that's ripped from my very soul.

I must've screamed, because afterward, my throat is achy. He's on top of me, and we're both breathing hard and fast as our bodies throb and tremble in the aftermath. After a long period of silence, he withdraws from me and begins to release my bindings before gathering me into his arms and covering me with a blanket.

"Take a drink," he says, holding a bottle of water to my lips.

My mouth is incredibly dry, and I take greedy sips from the bottle. He brushes the hair back from my face and gazes down at me.

I'm so tired, I can barely keep my eyes open, but I don't want to lose this fragile connection to him.

"Are you okay?"

"Mmmm."

"Words, darling. I need words."

"I'm okay."

"How do you feel?"

"Good. Really good."

"Okay, love," he says with a sigh that might be relief, "you can rest for a bit before we go home."

Letting my eyes close, I mumble, "You forgot something."

His low chuckle is a rumble against the ear I have pressed to his chest. "I haven't forgotten anything."

If I weren't so tired and sated, I might worry about the removal of the plug, but I'm too blissed out to worry about something so trivial.

I'm not sure if I actually sleep or only doze off, but his kisses on my face and lips bring me back to him. "I need to get you home so you can get some sleep."

I'm warm and comfortable, and I don't want to even think about moving. "We should just stay here."

"You won't want to be here in the morning."

"I hate when you're practical."

Smiling, he moves me from his lap to the bed and then kisses a slow path down the front of me. "What if we made a baby here tonight?" he asks.

I've been so taken in by the club, the kink, the atmosphere and the scene with Jasper that I actually forgot about our project for a brief time. That's a testament to his skill, because I didn't think anything could make me forget about that. But now that he mentions the possibility, the yearning comes back with such ferocity, it leaves me reeling. Then he begins to withdraw the plug, and that requires my full attention.

By the time he finishes tormenting me, I'm sweating, my heart is beating fast, and I'm fully aroused once again. Naturally, Jasper can't let that go to waste, and he licks and sucks me to another screaming orgasm.

"This time I swear we're done," he says with a grin as he wipes his face on the back of his hand and helps me sit up. "Get your bearings, love."

I lean against him, not wanting to leave the warm comfort of his embrace, even for a short time. In my right mind, I'd probably be worried about how attached to him I'm getting as one experience after another adds up to so much more than I've ever had with any man. Even though I know he doesn't want the same things I do, I wish I could keep him for a lot longer than it'll take to make our baby.

The thought of letting him go after our project is successfully completed brings new tears to my eyes. Sometimes life can be so exquisitely unfair.

"Are you hurting, love?" he asks, misinterpreting the shine in my eyes.

"Not at all. I feel quite divine, in fact."

"Is that so?"

"Uh-huh."

As if I'm a toddler, he dresses me. Then he dresses himself and offers me a hand to lead me from the room. We run into Devon on the way out.

"How was your evening?" he asks, his gaze trained on me.

"Wonderful," I reply.

Jasper's hand tightens on my shoulder.

I look up to find him watching me with that fierce intensity I'm beginning to expect from him.

"I hope you'll come back to see us again sometime, Ellie."

I accept his outstretched hand. "I'd love to. Thank you for having me."

"Any friend of Jasper's is a friend of mine." He drops a kiss on the back of my hand. "Drive safely."

"Thanks again, Devon," Jasper says.

"Any time, my friend."

The valet has Jasper's car waiting in the carport, and he helps me into the passenger side. It's a good thing I'm not required to drive us home, because I don't think I could if I had to.

"Why do I feel so buzzed when I didn't have anything to drink?"

"That's the comedown," he says. "You went pretty deep into subspace for a while there."

I glance at the clock and am shocked to see that it's 2:10. As in *2:10 a.m.*? How in the hell did that happen? I'm going to be a total disaster —again—tomorrow. "We were in that room a long time."

"A couple of hours."

"It didn't seem that long, but I remember thinking at one point that I had no idea how long we'd been there."

"It's not uncommon for subs to lose track of time and place and to feel almost drunk after the huge rush of endorphins. It's entirely normal."

"Maybe for you, but it's all new to me."

"You were amazing, Ellie. So trusting and accepting. You'll never know what it meant to me to share that part of myself with you. So often I have to keep it hidden from people, and to know I can be myself with you…" He blows out a deep breath. "It's huge."

"I always want you to be yourself with me." His jaw pulses and twitches, and I reach over to stroke his face. "What's this about?"

"So many things. I've told you about my kink, but I've been keeping other secrets, things you should know."

"About your family, you mean?"

He takes his eyes off the road to glance over at me. "What do you know?"

"That you're Henry Kingsley's son and heir to his dynasty."

His hand tightens around the steering wheel. "You looked me up after you saw my real name on the legal documents."

"Are you angry?"

"No, of course not. I knew it was possible you'd be curious when you saw my name."

"You're keeping some pretty big secrets from the people you're closest to."

"Not because I don't want you guys to know. That's not it at all."

"Then why? Did you think we wouldn't understand?"

"No." He draws in a deep breath and releases it in a long sigh. "I guess I keep hoping if I pretend like it isn't happening, my father will find someone better suited to be his heir. So far, no such luck."

"You don't want it."

"Hell, no, I don't want it. I've never wanted it, and he knows that. But it doesn't matter. He's going to saddle me with it anyway. It's my birthright. Lucky me."

The bitterness in his tone is so unlike the happy-go-lucky man I know so well that it's almost shocking. "Where do people in England think Jasper Kingsley is?"

"He's known as a reclusive inventor, working out of his workshop at his father's estate in Cornwall. He hasn't been seen in years. I created the cover story when I went to USC. I leaked it to a few reporters, and it took on a life of its own. Thankfully, there's no interest in reclusive inventors in England."

"Has it ever occurred to you that you don't have to do anything you don't want to do?"

"Only every day of my life, but declaring you don't want something and turning your back on centuries of history and obligation isn't something one does lightly."

"I wouldn't expect you to do it lightly, but you *can* do it. You know that, don't you?"

"I've always known that I could just say no, but I can't, for the bloody life of me, bring myself to actually *do* it. You know? I tried to be a good son, a son he could be proud of. I excelled in school, in sports, in everything except finance, the one thing he actually cares about. It's like none of the other stuff I've accomplished even matters to him. Can you imagine your child winning the top award in his or her field and you not even picking up the phone?"

"No, I can't." My heart breaks for him. He's tried so hard to please his father and has fallen short every time.

"I suppose I shouldn't be surprised. I turned my back on him the day I left for USC to study film. At least that's how he sees it. Why should it matter what he thinks of me?"

I reach for his hand and hold it between both of mine. "It matters because he's your father, and you want him to be proud of you."

"I hate myself for caring about whether or not he's proud. I absolutely *hate* it." After a long pause, he says, "Sometimes I think my need for kink arose from wanting to feel like I was in control of *something* when so many other things are out of my hands. I'm living this fantasy existence here in LA that's going to be yanked away from me someday without warning. In the meantime, I control my career and how I take my pleasure. The rest is up to fate to decide for me."

"I can't imagine living with something like that hanging over my head."

"Welcome to my world, love."

"This is why you signed away custody to our baby before he or she is even conceived."

"You're damned right it is. There's no way in hell I'd ever consign my child to having his fate decided for him before he's even born. No fucking way."

Tears fill my eyes and spill down my cheeks, surprising me with their sudden appearance.

"Don't cry for me, darling. Please don't."

"I can't help it. It makes me so sad that you have to miss out on everything because of something you don't even want."

A few minutes later, he brings the car to a stop outside my house and reaches for me. "I can't bear to see you cry."

"I can't bear to see you so burdened."

Cupping my face, he kisses away my tears before brushing his lips lightly over mine.

"There has to be something you can do, Jasper."

"Not without turning my back on the rest of my family along with hundreds of years of tradition, or at least that's how my father would view the biggest scandal to ever hit Fleet Street."

"So what? You'd weather the storm and then you go on with your life. Your mother and sisters will still love you. Of course they will. How could they not?"

"Don't think I haven't considered it. Of course I have, every day of my bloody life. I lack the courage to put thought into action."

"I wish…"

His thumb wipes away another tear. "What do you wish, my love?"

"That this was real. That you and I might have a chance…" My throat closes around the lump that settles there.

"One thing you must never doubt is that this, you and I, is as *real* as anything has ever been. If things were different—"

I shake my head and place a finger over his lips. "Please don't say it. Please." I can't bear to think of all the things we might've had if only he were free of the legacy that entrapped him the day he was born. It's so blindingly unfair that it's all I can do not to scream from the utter madness of it.

He puts his arms around me and holds me as close as he can within the tight confines of the car. It's not enough. It'll never be enough, and the thought of him being ripped away from me, from our child, from his life in LA, from Quantum...

"Stay," I whisper. "Stay with me tonight. Stay with me every night for as long as you can."

The sound that comes from him is a cross between a groan and a moan. And then he's kissing me with wild desperation, as if I'm his last, great hope, and he's clinging to me in a sea of uncertainty. When we come up for air, many minutes later, the windows are steamed up, which makes me giggle.

My emotions are all over the place—from despair to desire to amusement and right back to despair when I remember that as lovely as this is with him, it comes with an expiration date.

"I like to hear you laugh, love." He runs his finger over my cheek, which is still damp. "And I never want to be responsible for your tears."

"You aren't responsible. The situation is." I look over at him, and when our eyes meet in the murky darkness, the powerful punch of emotion takes my breath away. "Will you stay?"

"All the queen's horses couldn't drag me away." He kisses me again with tenderness that brings new tears to my eyes. "Wait for me."

My heart is heavy as I watch him walk around the front of the car. Under usual circumstances, I'd be out of the car by the time my date tried to be chivalrous. Nothing about this night or this man is "usual." I wait for him because he asked me to, because he needs to be in control of something. If controlling me gives him a measure of comfort, I'm happy to cede that to him. It's the least I can do for him when he's making my greatest dream come true.

In the seconds it takes for him to open my door and reach for my hand, I realize something else. It's *him*. He's the one I've been hoping to find, and he's been right in front of me all this time. That discovery right on top of what we did at the club and learning about his destiny makes me feel unmoored from everything I've known to be true and real.

How will anything ever make sense to me again if I'm given this taste of what *could be* only to have it ripped away? I can't let that happen. I have to fight for him, for us, for our child and the future we should have together, not the one that was determined for him.

No one should have to live like that, least of all Jasper, who has a rare and special talent as a filmmaker. The idea of that talent going to waste, not to mention the life we might have together, is repulsive to me. As suddenly as I was filled with despair, I'm overcome with rage and determination to do something about this untenable situation. There has to be a way for him to have everything he wants. I refuse to consider any alternative.

CHAPTER 14

Jasper

Something changed between us tonight. The feelings I have for her have deepened into something I might describe as magical if I believed in such things. I stopped believing in magic right around the time I figured out that my life had been planned for me. Until this with Ellie, the only place I've found anything that could be described as magic has been behind a camera.

Now I know it can be found in Ellie's arms, too, and it's better than anything I've ever experienced. I'm already addicted to her and the way I feel when I'm with her. Nothing can compare, which makes my uncertain future that much harder to face.

The future is the last thing I want to think about when the present demands my full and undivided attention. While Ellie lets Randy out into the backyard, I pour us each a glass of ice water. Randy comes dashing back inside ahead of her, as if he's afraid he might miss something. I give him some attention and am rewarded with sloppy dog kisses to the face that make me laugh.

"Randy, stop," Ellie says. "Leave Jasper alone."

"He's fine. I miss having a dog." I don't have to tell her that I travel too much to have a pet, because she and her team arrange most of my trips.

"I keep thinking about getting him a companion, but I never seem to get around to it."

I hand her the glass of water and then touch my glass to hers. "Thanks for tonight."

"Thank you for taking me—in more ways than one."

I nearly choke on the water that's halfway down my throat when she says that. "My pleasure."

"What do you suppose it means that I enjoyed what we saw and did at the club so much?"

"I suppose it means that perhaps you've only begun to explore your sexuality, and how lucky am I to be on that journey with you?"

"You feel lucky?"

"That, my love, is very least of what I feel when I'm with you."

"Jasper..."

"What, darling?"

"You have to do something about this situation with your family. You can't give up everything and everyone that matters to you."

"Including you?"

She never blinks when she says, "Including me and our baby. We need you. Surely there has to be some legal step you could take to disengage yourself." She snaps her fingers. "If King What's-his-name could do it when that Wallis Simpson woman came along, you should be able to do it, too. He was the *king*. You're only a marquess!"

Only a marquess. It's all I can do not to laugh out loud. She has no idea what that means in my family. Smiling, I take it all in—the flush remaining in her cheeks from our scene at the club, the lips swollen from our frantic kisses, the hair still mussed from being in bed, and the fierce conviction on my behalf. It's all I can do to contain the three little words that are bursting to break free. I love her. In fact, I'm beginning to accept that it's quite possible I've loved her for as long as I've known her. Hearing her say she and our baby need me made my heart do backflips. "Ah, yes, good old King Edward, and what a rollicking scandal that was."

"They got through it, and they got to be together. Isn't that what matters?"

I place my empty glass on the counter and cross the room to her, placing my hands on her shoulders and leaning my forehead against hers. "It matters, love. You matter. This matters."

"But..."

"No buts." I take her glass from her and put it down before drawing her in closer to me. "We're talking about disrupting my family's primogeniture that dates back centuries, my darling."

"I have no idea what that word means, but what we're talking about is you having the life you want rather than the one that's been predetermined for you."

"The word means the right of succession that usually goes to the firstborn child, or the firstborn male child, depending on the family."

"Wouldn't that happen anyway if you never marry or produce an heir?"

"Yes, but it wouldn't be a scandal like it would be if I said I don't want it. No one does that."

"It's the new millennium, Jasper. Why couldn't it go to your sister, the one who works on Wall Street, who's actually qualified to inherit your father's estate?"

"You've done your research, darling, and you're preaching to the choir. My father is the one who'd need to be convinced, and he's shown no sign of being willing to entertain the conversation. He's even made it so that I'm not able to delegate the responsibilities he's leaving to me at Kingsley Enterprises. I have to see to them myself, which is his own special brand of torture."

"What if you were to force his hand?"

"How so?" I ask, intrigued and aroused by her passion.

"You could go public with the connection between Jasper Kingsley and Jasper Autry and let the world know that Jasper Autry has no desire to inherit the Kingsley dynasty, especially when he has a sister who'd be far better suited than he'll ever be."

"You're suggesting I go around my father."

"Yes."

I try to imagine what would happen if I were to make such a

move. Fleet Street would have a bloody field day with a story like this, especially with my father about to set out on one of his follies.

"What do you think?" she asks, her eyes shining with love and hope.

"It would be the story of the year at home, not to mention what the Hollywood press corps would do with it."

"We could handle that."

"*We* could?"

"Yes, we as in you and me. We could handle it. Together."

"What're you saying, Ellie?"

"I'm saying I want you in my life, in our child's life, and not just as a signature on a monthly check. I want you here, with us, working at Quantum where you belong, not consigned to a role that you were never meant to play. It's all so wrong."

"And this is all so right?"

"It's *so* right. Tell me I'm not the only one who feels—"

I kiss her because I can't not kiss her and touch her and want her and everything she's offering. I want it. I want it so badly, I burn from wanting it. "You're not the only one," I whisper when we finally come up for air. Now that I've started, I never want to stop kissing her. "I want the same things you do. You can't possibly know how badly I want all of it."

"Then have it, Jasper. *Have it.* This is your life, the only one you'll ever get. Do it your way."

Her encouragement fires me with the courage I've lacked in the past. "Tomorrow I'll make some calls and get some advice about how best to proceed."

"You're really going to do it?"

"I really am."

"Jasper..." She places her hands on my face, compelling me to meet her gaze. "No matter what, I'll be right here with you. We all will. We love you."

"*We* do?"

The flush that infuses her cheeks only makes her lovelier than she already is. "Of course we do."

"I love all of you, too. You've become my family." And I adore how we're both saying everything to each other without actually saying *it*.

"Your Quantum family will fight for you, and we'll support you no matter what happens next."

"That means everything to me." After that, there are no more words. None are needed. I take her hand and lead her into her bedroom, where I undress her and then myself. We come down on her bed in a tangle of limbs as our lips meet in a soft, sweet kiss that quickly turns hot and frantic. But I don't want frantic. I want reverent. I want to worship her. I want her to know what her love and support mean to me.

I pepper her neck and throat with kisses before moving down to her breasts, drawing the pointed tip of her nipple into my mouth and biting down just hard enough to pull a sharp gasp from her. She's still so sensitive from the clamps that it doesn't take much to draw a reaction from her. I do the same to the other side, licking and sucking until she is writhing under me, begging me for more with the press of her hips against my hard cock.

I have to stop myself from plunging into her and taking what I want more than my next breath. Though I've had just about every kind of sex a man can have, I've never experienced the kind of craving need she inspires in me. It's like everything is brand-new again with her, and I already know I'll never get enough of her.

We move together like lovers who've been together for years rather than days. Every caress of her hands on my back sets off a wildfire of desire that can't be contained. I don't want to contain it. I feel like I've been numb for most of my life until she showed me how it could be. And now... Now, I'll never survive without her by my side.

I kiss my way down the front of her, taking my own sweet time even as the fire burns so hot inside me, I fear I might combust from the heat that threatens to consume me. She fists a handful of my hair as I open her to my tongue, moaning against her flesh. I want to devour her, to show her what she means to me, to make her so happy she won't ever want or need anything—or anyone—else. I lick and suck and tease her into a series of orgasms that have her crying out from the pleasure. I keep it up until I can't wait another second to be inside her.

She's so hot and so tight that I hold still for a long moment, until I'm sure this won't end too soon.

I look down to find her gazing up at me, her eyes conveying her every emotion, and I realize that I'm making love for the first time in my life.

"Ellie," I whisper as I thrust into her. "You... This..."

"I know," she says. "*I know.*" She wraps her arms and legs around me, holding me close.

I'm at home in her arms, and I never want to leave. I'll do whatever it takes to have her, to have *this*. It's everything. Nothing else matters, and knowing that, I'm free to take the next step, to do what I should've done years ago.

Tomorrow. I'll start the ball rolling, and to hell with the consequences. I'm going to have her and our child. I'm going to have it all. No matter what.

I'M SO exhausted from the amazing night with Ellie that I'm late to the Friday morning partners' meeting. Not by much, but enough to draw the ire of Hayden and Kristian, who greet me with matching glares. I couldn't care less. I'm high on life and love today, and there's just about nothing anyone could say or do to ruin my buzz.

"Thanks for joining us," Hayden says, clearly still pissed at me about last night.

"My pleasure." I help myself to coffee, a muffin and fresh fruit from the spread that Addie arranges for our partner meetings. She says food puts us in a good mood, and the rest of the team benefits from keeping the partners in a good mood. "What's on the agenda today?"

"Flynn has an update on Natalie's project."

Part of me is surprised that Flynn wants to bring his wife's story to the big screen. He's so intensely private, but after her story was made public, they don't have many secrets left—and it is an insane story that will make for one hell of a film.

"We have a screenplay in the works," Flynn reports, updating us on the details of the writer he's hired.

"I feel sort of sorry for this guy, and I haven't even met him yet," Marlowe jokes. "He's got a big job ahead of him."

"Ha-ha," Flynn says, grinning at her. "He's more than up to the task. Nat likes him, which is all I care about. As long as she's comfortable, I'm comfortable."

"I'm sure you're very comfortable these days," Hayden says.

"Likewise, my friend," Flynn says, "which brings me to the next item on the agenda—you monopolizing my assistant."

"I do love to monopolize her," Hayden replies with a dopey, lovesick grin that makes us all laugh. The change in him since he fell for Addie is nothing short of astonishing. He's completely transformed by love, and in the best possible way. No one deserves it more than he does after a childhood marked by nonstop family drama.

"Seriously, though," Flynn says, "you gotta let her work sometimes. I need her."

"Not as much as I do, and you don't get to need her between six p.m. and six a.m. unless it's something arranged in advance. Her days of being your twenty-four-hours-a-day beck-and-call girl are *over*."

"I'm only going to let you get away with calling her that because she's so happy."

"Gee, thanks," Hayden says drolly. "You get twelve hours. I get twelve hours. That's how this is gonna go. Got me?"

"Yeah, yeah, but you'd better play nice. I really, *really* need her."

"So do I."

Having Hayden come right out and say that is huge. Before Addie, he wouldn't have said he needed anything or anyone. I'm humbled by his confession, especially in light of what transpired last night. It gives me the push I need to lay myself bare to my partners.

"I have something for the agenda."

"That's a first," Kristian says dryly, grinning at me.

"First time for everything. And it's kind of a big deal. I don't want any of you to be offended that I haven't told you this before now."

"You've certainly got our attention," Flynn says, sitting back in his chair in a pose that's deceptively casual.

In for a penny... "Have you heard of Henry Kingsley?"

"The British tycoon?" Marlowe asks.

"Yeah, him."

"What about him?" Hayden asks.

"He's... Well, he's my father."

The announcement is met with stunned silence that lasts long enough to become uncomfortable. I break it with a rush of words that lay out the dilemma that is my life. And when I'm done, they stare at me as if they're seeing me for the very first time.

"You gotta be fucking kidding me," Hayden says, breaking a long silence.

"I wish I was."

"Wait, so you wish that you weren't a billionaire heir to a massive fortune?" Marlowe asks.

"Yes, I wish that! I want nothing to do with it. I want this, here, with all of you. This is my life. Quantum is my life. Not that. Never that."

"Jesus, Jasper," Kristian whispers. As my closest friend among the group, I expected him to be the most affected by this news. "How did we never know this?"

"No one knows that Jasper Kingsley and Jasper Autry are the same person. At least no one knew until now. I've gone to enormous lengths to keep my two lives very separate. The British press thinks I'm an eccentric inventor, living on my father's country estate in Cornwall, still trying to pull off my first big patent."

"So you're part of the aristocracy," Marlowe says, her eyes big with wonder. If only she knew that there's nothing wonderful about the reality of it, at least not for me. "Like on *Downton Abbey*!"

"I'm actually a marquess and future duke."

"Shut the fuck up," Hayden says. "Even I know what that means."

"Well, I don't," Flynn says. "Fill in the blanks for me."

"It means that when my father dies, which he's apt to do sooner rather than later thanks to his recent penchant for testing his limits, I'll be required to go home to London and take over the family business as well as the dukedom, whether I want to or not. And I most definitely do not want to."

"Oh jeez," Marlowe says. "We can't let that happen."

"No way," Flynn adds. "We can't lose you."

"I don't want to be lost, but turning my back on my legacy, my responsibilities... If I actually do that, it'd be a huge scandal at home —and probably here, too. It might reflect badly on Quantum, and honestly, that's giving me pause."

"Don't let it," Hayden says fiercely. "You do what you've got to do to get yourself out of this. We're behind you three thousand percent."

The others nod in agreement, which makes my throat feel tight. Hayden's support, in particular, is overwhelming in light of what he witnessed last night at Black Vice. I was afraid things would be weird between us today, but thankfully that hasn't been the case. However, I still hope he doesn't mention to Flynn that I took Ellie to the club. I'd rather not have to explain what we were doing there to her brother. In a perfect world, he'll never know we were there.

"I agree with Hayden," Flynn says. "You're one of us, and you always will be. You let us know what we can do to support you. Anything you need."

Christ, they're going to make me bawl like a wee babe. "Thank you," I say in a hushed tone. "I'm going to talk to some people at home about my options and go from there. I also want to talk to my sister, who'd be the ideal choice to inherit my father's business. Perhaps she and I could share the duties or something. I don't know yet, but there has to be a way, and I'm determined to find it."

I can't tell them the real reason I'm so determined. Not until Ellie is ready to tell her family about us—and the baby we hope to have. For now, I'm keeping the two things separate and dealing with them one at a time.

First on the agenda is contending with my father, a thought that turns my stomach. But then I remember the nearly religious experience of making love to Ellie, and I'm filled with determination. I know now what I need to do, and as soon as this meeting is over, I'll get the ball rolling.

I'm long overdue to take control of my life, and being with Ellie has given me the courage I've lacked in the past. It's given me a *reason* that even my illustrious career couldn't give me to extricate myself from the nightmare I've been saddled with my entire life. If I stay focused on the future I want with her and our child—or *children*—I can do what needs to be done.

"Keep us posted," Flynn says.

"Thank you. I will." That's all I'm capable of saying at the moment.

"And here I thought I'd be the one stirring the pot this morning," Kristian says.

"How so?" Marlowe asks.

"I wanted to talk to you guys about the club. Only a few of us seem to hang out there anymore. We're paying Sebastian to run it for us, and we're not using it."

"I'll admit that I'm guilty of avoiding the club now that Nat and I are married," Flynn says. "She's not a fan of public displays."

"So you're out." Turning to Hayden, Kristian says, "What about you?"

"Addie prefers to keep our private life and her work life separate."

"Can't say I blame her," Marlowe says.

"What's your excuse?" Kristian asks Mo. "You're still single, and I never see you there anymore either."

"I'm not sure exactly," Marlowe replies hesitantly. "Lately, I've been sort of... I don't know... bored with the whole scene."

Astounded by her confession, we stare at her.

"*Bored?*" Flynn asks. "For real?"

I can understand his disbelief. Marlowe has been, without a doubt, the most enthusiastic practitioner of the group. To hear she's *bored* with the lifestyle is shocking, to say the least.

"What's that about?" Hayden asks.

"I don't know," Marlowe replies, looking a little lost. "Lately, they're all the same. There's no challenge to it anymore. They just want to be dominated by the lady movie star. They don't make me work for it the way they used to." She shrugs. "Thus the boredom."

"I understand what you mean, Mo." I empathize with her because I do get it. Before I had Ellie, I too had become somewhat disenchanted with the same-shit-different-night life I'd been living. "It does become less exciting with partners who are a little *too* willing to submit."

"Yeah, that's what I mean. I haven't given up entirely, but I'm taking a break."

"So that leaves us with a very expensive club that none of us are using," Kristian says. "I want to suggest that we make it public." Holding up his hands to ward off the barrage of dissent, he adds, "Exclusive but public. Rather than inviting people to come to the club as our guests, we handpick members, and we continue to make it the best-kept secret in Hollywood."

"I don't know," Hayden says, expressing the same reservations I'm feeling. We've been very lucky up to now that no one has caught wind of the fact that all five of the Quantum principals are BDSM aficionados. Each of us is well aware that as high-profile celebrities, we're playing with fire by partaking in something most people would find scandalous, but we've chosen to do it anyway because we can't *not* partake in a lifestyle that brings us pleasure. Club Quantum in LA and New York has given us a safe place to participate with our closest friends in the lifestyle without fear of being found out. The club in New York has been open to outside members for a while now, but the LA club has been much more locked down.

"Letting in outsiders is definitely a risk," I say, "but with us spending less time there, the risk is also lessened."

Flynn nods in agreement. "That's true. If none of us are regulars anymore, then we have nothing to worry about."

"Other than the fact that the club is housed in our building and named for our company," Hayden says.

"Well, there is that," Marlowe concedes.

"I don't think that should stop us from going forward with a membership program," Flynn says. "Anyone who's admitted should have the same skin in the game that we have. People in this town, for the most part, prefer to keep their personal lives private. They aren't going to talk about us, and we're not going to talk about them."

"Still," Kristian says, "it is a risk that we all need to be aware that we're taking."

"Understood," I say, and the others agree.

"In that case," Kristian proceeds, handing out stapled pages to each of us, "Sebastian has come up with a plan to open up the club to new members. If you guys could take a look at this and get me any feedback by the end of next week, I'd appreciate it."

"Will do." I glance at my watch and see that it's already eleven. I've got stuff to do, and the day is getting away from me. "Is that it?"

"That's all I have," Kristian says.

"Watch for an email update on the project about Nat's story," Flynn says. "We're getting close on a few things."

"I predict this amazing film is going to be another *Camouflage*," Marlowe says, referring to the film we all won Oscars for this year.

"That'd be something, wouldn't it?" Flynn asks with a goofy grin. He's so lovesick over his adorable wife, and her astonishing courage has been an inspiration to us all.

"I can't wait to work on that one," I say as I get up to leave the room. "Sign me up."

Flynn gives me a fist bump as I walk by him on the way out. "Thanks, buddy."

I hope I'll still be his buddy when he finds out that not only am I fucking his sister every chance I get, but I'm trying to make a baby with her, too.

CHAPTER 15

Jasper

In my office, I call my father's longtime assistant, Nathan, to confirm that Henry will be in his London office tomorrow morning. Saturdays have always been my father's favorite day to work when the rest of the office is deserted and quiet, so it doesn't surprise me that he'll be there. Nathan confirms it's his last day in the office before he leaves on his latest quest for publicity and thrills.

Next, I arrange for a private jet to take me to London later today. As an environmental advocate, I'm not a big fan of private planes when it's just me, but in this case, time is of the essence in light of my baby-making plans with Ellie. Calculating the time difference, I make it so I'll be back in time to meet up with her at Flynn's tomorrow night, and then she's all mine for the next week. I can't wait.

Now that I've made a decision I should've made years ago, I feel incredibly serene and determined. Before I had Ellie to encourage and support me, I would've been freaking out at the thought of seeing my father, let alone telling him that he'll have to find someone else to run his business after he dies because it's not going to be me.

"I'm sorry, Father," I say out loud, practicing. "I respect and admire the business you and Grandfather built, but finance is not in my blood. I'd be the worst possible person to take the helm after you're gone, and I'm sure you'd prefer to leave the business to someone who actually knows what he or she is doing. You should talk to Gwen. She'd be fantastic, and I think she might actually want to do it."

I pause to consider that last part. I can't say that about wanting to do it. He's never cared what I *wanted*. Saying that will only open me up to yet another lecture about duty, obligation and responsibility. I can almost hear what he'd have to say to that: *"Do you think Prince William and his pretty wife want to go to all those ribbon cuttings? They do it because he understands his responsibility to history."*

Prince William is a better man than I am. So too is his brother, Prince Harry. No question about it. I couldn't live the way they do, in the giant fishbowl with my every move scrutinized by reporters assigned to cover me. I'd go mad. Though I've enjoyed some fame thanks to my work in the film business and my association with Flynn, Hayden, Marlowe and Kristian, for the most part I'm left alone to live my life, with only the occasional picture showing up in the celebrity rags. I'm a low-level celebrity compared to them, and I like it that way.

I have no earthly idea how they can stand the paparazzi, who pursue them so relentlessly. The firestorm that ensued after Flynn met Natalie is a classic example of the kind of thing that would take me right over the cliff. Her painful past was laid bare for the world to consume, as if they had some sort of right to it. It's a disgusting part of celebrity, one I'm more than happy to avoid.

Hayden carefully managed the announcement of his engagement to Addie, and the betrothal of one of Hollywood's most notorious bachelors was the talk of the town for the last week. But he's gone out of his way to keep her sheltered from the storm, even going so far as to put extra security on duty at the office and at his homes in the city and in Malibu.

With the details of my trip seen to, I turn my attention to work, knowing I'll be out of the office more than in it over the next week. We're gearing up for the shoot of a new action film in Europe this summer, and I've just received the final script and director's notes from Hayden. I spend the rest of the afternoon lost in the new story and thinking about how we'll capture the various scenes on film.

The advance work is one of my favorite parts of the job, even more so than the actual shoot. It's at this stage that my creativity comes into play as I add my suggestions to Hayden's notes. We'll go back and forth a hundred times before we actually shoot, and the collaborative process with him has taken on a recognizable rhythm after working together for so many years.

It's one of many things I love about being part of Quantum. We know each other so well that we can almost finish each other's sentences. They are more than my professional colleagues and my personal friends. They are my family. I'm ready to fight for my family, the one I already have at Quantum and the one I desperately want with Ellie.

I leave my office and go to hers, knocking on the closed door. "Come in."

This is the first time I've seen her since I left her early this morning, and the memories of our incredible night together come rushing back to me. From the club to the confessions to the exquisite magic we created in her bed. I'll never forget a second of it. I close the door behind me and lean against it, drinking her in.

Her face flushes adorably, and I'm completely gobsmacked once again by the fact that she wants me as much as I want her. How did I get so lucky?

"Did you need something?" she asks after a charged moment of silence.

Nodding, I go over to her and draw her chair back from her desk. Turning it to face me, I bend over her, caging her in with my body. "This," I whisper before I kiss her. I was intending a quick kiss until her hand curls around my neck and her mouth opens to my tongue. I'm utterly lost in her, swept up in the madness that takes me over whenever I'm close to her. I can't get enough of that madness. I'll never have enough.

We withdraw from each other slowly, tentatively, until our lips are barely touching.

"I was actually getting something done for a change until you showed up," she says.

Smiling, I rub my lips back and forth over hers, loving the sharp inhale of breath that lets me know she's every bit as affected by this as I am. And thank God for that. "I'm going to London tonight."

"You are?"

"I am. I'm doing it, Ellie. I'm going to tell him that I can't—and won't—be the heir to his business."

She caresses my face, and I turn my lips into the palm of her hand. "How do you feel about it?"

"Determined. I should've done this years ago."

"I'm so happy for you."

"I'm happy for us. Are you?"

"Of course I am. I keep thinking this whole thing has to be a dream, because surely it can't be actually happening."

"It's happening, my darling, and it's the best thing that's ever happened. At least to me."

"Me, too." She gazes up at me with her heart in her eyes, and I can't resist kissing her again. "Could I... maybe... come with you?"

"Do you want to?" I ask, flabbergasted and delighted at the same time.

"I really do."

"I'd love to have you with me, especially because we had plans for this weekend that I haven't forgotten about, but I can't promise I'll get you back in time to watch the kids."

"Flynn will do it if I tell him something's come up. He won't mind."

I drag a finger over her cheek. "You were looking forward to your time with them."

"I can see them any time. You need me, and I want to be with you."

Dropping my forehead to hers, I close my eyes and breathe in her unmistakable scent. "I've never wanted anything more than I want to be free to love you, Ellie."

"I can't believe everything that's happened."

"But you're happy about it?"

"God, yes, I'm happy," she says, laughing. "How is it possible that you've been right here, all this time..."

"I've been right here wanting you and wishing for what we have now. And this is only the beginning, my love."

"What if your father won't let you go? What if—"

I raise my head so I can see her eyes and place my finger over her lips. "Shhh. Don't worry. There is nothing he could say or do that would make me change my mind about you or us. Nothing."

She blinks back a sudden onslaught of tears. Laughing, she brushes them away. "You've turned me into a hot mess in the office again."

"You could never be a hot mess. You're stunning." I tuck a strand of her hair behind her ear and caress her cheek.

"You're rather stunning yourself. I used to close my eyes and just listen to you talk."

"When?"

"At parties, meetings, Christmas Eve at my parents' house. Your voice is right up there at the top of my list of the sexiest things ever."

"Mmm," I say in a low growl, "I'll have to remember that at critical *moments* in the future."

"And your face," she says, cupping my face in her hands, "is tied for first with your voice. I never get tired of looking at this face."

"You'd better cut out the compliments if you don't want to be ravaged at work again."

Her gaze drops down to where J.T. is standing tall and proud, wishing he could be buried inside of her rather than stuck behind a zipper.

She licks her lips, drawing a groan from me.

"Don't do that if I'm expected to behave."

"Jasper..."

"What, darling?"

"Last night was so amazing. It felt..."

"How did it feel?" I'm fairly breathless with the need to know.

"Different. Special."

"For me, too. It was everything."

"What if…" She looks up at me, madly vulnerable and exquisitely beautiful. "What if we made our baby last night?"

"Do you think we did?"

"I don't know, but I've felt sort of tingly all over today and light-headed and…"

I'm instantly alarmed. "Do you need a doctor?"

"No, no," she says, laughing. "Nothing like that. I was going to say I also feel elated in a way I never have before. It's probably too soon, but…" Flashing a goofy smile, she shrugs.

"I hope we made a baby last night. That would be the most amazing thing to ever happen to me."

"Me, too."

"Until this, until you, I never allowed myself to hope for kids or a family of my own or a life that included someone like you. But now…" I have to take a moment to gather myself or run the risk of losing my composure. "Now, everything is possible because of you."

She pushes her chair back a few inches and stands, wrapping her arms around me. "I'm not going to wake up and discover this was all a lovely dream, am I?"

I hold on tight to her, pressing her body against mine and probably leaving no doubt as to what I'd like to be doing right now. "No chance of that." I hold her for a long time. I have no idea how long, and I don't care. We come back to reality when the extension on her desk rings. I let her go, albeit reluctantly.

"This is Ellie." She shifts back into professional mode even as her cheeks remain flushed and her eyes bright with excitement. She listens and then says, "I'll be there in five." After putting the phone down, she gives me a regretful smile. "Duty calls."

"No problem. I'll let you go—for now. I'll pick you up at eight tonight? Is that all right?"

"That's fine."

"What about Randy?"

"I'll take him to my parents'. They're used to last-minute dog-sitting requests from me. I'm always going somewhere to scout locations. They won't think anything of it."

"What'll you tell your team here?"

"I've already scarred poor Dax for life by telling him I'm having 'stuff' done over the next week to try to get pregnant."

I wince. "Ouch."

"I know," she says, sighing. "I felt terrible, but it was the only way I could be sure he wouldn't ask any questions. I'll just tell him I had to leave earlier than expected for my 'appointments.'"

"I'll remember this when he requests hazardous-duty pay."

"I won't blame him if he does." She draws me into another kiss but doesn't let this one get out of hand, much to my dismay. I want to beg for more. I want to plead with her to leave with me, right now, so we can have more of everything. But I've already crossed the line with her at work once before, and I don't want to do that again. Not today anyway.

"I'll see you at eight?"

"I'll be ready. Do I need to pack anything special?"

"Nope. Go for comfort over style. We'll spend most of our time flying."

"I can do comfortable."

"I need to invest in bigger pants if I'm going to be spending all this time with you." To make my point, I adjust J.T.

She giggles at my obvious discomfort. "Don't you dare get bigger pants. I like your pants just the way they are. They leave very little to the imagination, although I now know my imagination needed to think a little bigger."

"Stop. I beg of you. Just stop."

Cupping my cock, she looks up at me. "I'll never stop wanting this."

"I'm shocked to my core to discover that Estelle Godfrey Junior is so *forward*, not to mention cock hungry."

She squeezes me a little too tightly for comfort, which I suspect is her goal. "Call me Estelle, and your parts won't see my parts ever again."

"It's such a sexy name."

"It's my *mother's* name."

"I'm not thinking about your mother right now." I'm literally about to say fuck it all to hell and take her right here and now, when her extension rings again.

She picks it up. "I'm coming. Right now." She puts down the phone and kisses my cheek. "See you later."

I watch her walk out of the office, knowing there's no way I can follow her. Not for a few minutes anyway. So I take a seat at her desk and study the family photos she has framed. One set of dark-haired children whom I recognize as her sister Aimee's kids and a group of blond boys who belong to Annie. There's a photo of Max and Stella Godfrey with their youngest daughter between them, all three wearing big smiles, and another of Ellie with Flynn on his wedding day.

I love the Godfrey family, more so than my own, if I'm being honest. There's something so warm and welcoming about them. After being raised with stiff British reserve, I much prefer the Godfreys' way of doing business. Will they still treat me like one of their own when they find out that Ellie and I are trying to have a baby together? I know how I would feel if she were my daughter, but anyone who knows Ellie well—and they know her better than anyone—understands that she only does exactly what she wants.

I'm still trying to believe that I'm what she wants. I'll have to make sure her parents and siblings know how much I love her and how I'll take care of her and our child for the rest of my life.

Her phone, which is lying on her desk, dings with a new text. I glance at it and see it's from someone named Serenity about the dating service she talked about joining. That's all it takes to remind me that Ellie and I are a long way from having everything sorted. The good news is that the text takes care of what's left of my ardor.

I'm about to get up to leave her office, when a knock on the door precedes Hayden's entrance. He stops short when he sees me where Ellie should be.

"What's up?" he asks.

"I was just leaving a note for Ellie." The moment the words are out of my mouth, I wish I could take them back. Who leaves actual notes for anyone these days?

Hayden steps into the room and closes the door behind him. Uh-oh. "Are we gonna talk about what happened last night?"

"What happened last night?"

"Don't play dumb with me, Jasper. You took Flynn's sister to a sex club. You don't think you need to explain that?"

"I took *Ellie* to a sex club—at her request, I might add—and no, I don't feel any obligation to explain myself to you or anyone else."

His gaze turns stormy. "Flynn would fucking flip his lid if he knew you'd taken her there."

"Did he flip his lid about you taking his assistant there?"

"That's not the same thing! She's my *fiancée!*"

"Was she your fiancée the first time you took her there?" I have no idea whether they've been there before last night, but judging from the way his eyes narrow with annoyance, I've hit a nerve.

"That's none of your business."

"Just like it's none of yours what Ellie and I were doing there. Leave it alone, Hayden. It doesn't concern you."

"What're you doing with her?" he asks in a more conciliatory tone.

"Also none of your business."

"It's my business if it's going to cause trouble in *my* business." He waves his hand to gesture to the Quantum offices.

"Pulling rank, partner?" While Kristian, Marlowe and I are partners in the business, Flynn and Hayden are the founders and managing partners.

"If I have to."

"What does that mean?"

"That if you don't talk to Flynn about whatever's going on with you and Ellie, I will."

"You're *threatening* me? Did I threaten you when you were spending time with Addie without telling him?"

"Addie isn't his sister."

"She may as well be."

"Look, Jasper, I don't want any trouble here, and I don't want any trouble with Flynn. I have information that I'm now keeping from my best friend and business partner. That's a problem for me, so it's a problem for you, too."

"Believe it or not, I understand where you're coming from, and all I'll say is Ellie and I are working things out. When there's something to tell, Flynn will be among the first to know."

He stares at me for a long moment before he says, "Fair enough. Just don't wait too long." Without another word, he exits the room, leaving me fuming in his wake. I really do understand where he's coming from, but I don't appreciate being threatened by a man I've always considered a close friend. Nice to know where I stand with him, although I shouldn't be surprised. He and Flynn are closer than brothers, and he's just proven that he'll put his brother ahead of me any day.

I leave Ellie's office feeling dejected after the conversation with Hayden, but my spirits lift considerably when I think about the trip I have planned with Ellie—the trip that's going to set me free to live the life I want rather than the one that was planned for me.

CHAPTER 16

Ellie

After getting stuck at work later than expected, I'm running around throwing clothes into a bag ten minutes before Jasper is due to pick me up. Thankfully, Flynn and Natalie agreed to take over my babysitting gig tomorrow after I told him I had a conflict. I'm free and clear to go with Jasper on this important trip, and I'm so excited about the time away with him that my usually formidable packing skills aren't up to par. Thankfully, I don't need anything fancy. At this rate, I'm apt to end up without a toothbrush.

Randy rubs up against me, letting me know he's worried about where I'm going. Suitcases always freak him out, the poor guy. My dad is coming to pick him up after we leave, so I take a moment to reassure him. "I won't be gone long this time, buddy, and Pappy is coming to get you in a little while."

He whines and licks my cheek, and I give him a hug. Whoever said dogs don't like to be hugged hasn't met mine. He burrows into my embrace and lets me hold him for as long as I want, which is far longer than I have time for, but hey, he's my baby.

I'm still snuggling Randy when Jasper comes through the door looking ridiculously sexy in khakis and a white shirt rolled up to expose his forearms. Even his forearms are sexy.

"Am I interrupting something, darling?"

I sigh. The voice. It just does it for me. "Randy's feeling a little sad about Mama going away again."

"He can come along. We're flying private. He won't be able to get off the plane when we get there, though. The UK is freaky about keeping rabies off our pristine shores."

"I think my baby would be better off with Grammy and Pappy than cooped up on a plane for so many hours." I kiss Randy's sweet face. "I just need a couple minutes." I leave Randy in his favorite spot on the sofa and go into my bedroom to finish packing. I'm in the bathroom gathering essential cosmetics when Jasper joins me, molding his body to the back of mine, his arms encircling my waist and his lips finding my neck. That's all it takes to make me weak in the knees.

"Today was the single longest day of my entire life." The soft caress of his breath on my neck sends goose bumps scurrying down my back.

"Mine, too."

"I'm so glad you're coming with me. You'll help me keep my mind off the reason for this mission."

"And how will I do that?" I ask, meeting his gaze in the mirror.

"That's for me to know and you to find out."

A shudder ripples through my body, converging in an almost painful throb between my legs.

Jasper's hands drop to the hem of my dress that falls to mid-thigh. He drags it up, slowly, his fingertips light on my sensitive skin. "Are you wet for me, Ellie?"

"Always."

His low growl is like gas thrown on my already out-of-control fire.

I push my ass into his hard cock, letting him know what I want.

"Is someone feeling impatient?"

"You're the one who said it's been a long day."

He slides his fingers up my inner thigh to press against my core. Only the thin silk of my panties separates his skin from mine. A sound escapes from my tightly clenched jaw that's not quite a moan and not quite a groan. It's a needy, desperate sound I've never made before in my life. I'm about to come, and he's barely touched me. Then he withdraws, and I cry out in despair.

"Easy, darling."

I look over my shoulder to find him quickly unbuckling his belt and freeing his cock. My skirt is raised and my panties pulled aside as he moves my legs farther apart. All this happens in the span of seconds, making me feel like I'm on the most thrilling of rides at the best of amusement parks. I'm breathless, and my heart is beating so fast, I'd be worried about a heart attack if I didn't know for sure that he is the cause.

Then he's inside me, hammering into me while his fingers tightly grip my hips, holding me still for the wildest of wild rides. I come so hard I see stars, but still he doesn't let up. When I installed this pedestal sink, I never could've imagined being fucked to within an inch of my life while bent over it. The thought has me squeaking out a giggle.

"What the hell is funny?" he asks, sounding so supremely British.

"I'm hoping I installed the sink properly."

That draws a gasp of laughter from him, too, and he slows the pace ever so slightly. His arms wrap tight around my body and his teeth clamp down on my earlobe. I had no idea until that very second that my earlobe is wired to my clit.

"You're so fucking hot," he whispers gruffly. "I want to spend my entire life inside you."

If there have ever been sexier words uttered in the history of mankind, I'd like to know what they are. Certainly no such words have ever been said to me. I grasp his hand that's flat against my breast and hold on for dear life as he drives into me again and again. I can hear Randy barking, but I can't be bothered to do anything about it. Until I hear my dad's voice and freeze.

"No, no, *no*," Jasper whispers, echoing my panic. He withdraws from me so suddenly I nearly fall over. Only his arms around my middle keep me upright. I push down my skirt, adjust my panties and run my fingers through my hair before I call to Dad. "Be right out!"

"Take your time."

Jasper grimaces as he tries to zip his pants over a huge erection. "This is *not* happening."

I cover my mouth to contain my laughter.

His scowl only makes the need to laugh even worse.

"Do I look awful?" I ask, whispering.

"You look beautiful and very well fucked, if I do say so myself."

"Stop!" The thought of my father overhearing such a comment makes me break into a sweat. "Stay here. He'll be gone in a minute."

"No choice but to stay put."

I glance down at the "problem" in his pants.

"You looking at it doesn't help," he says between gritted teeth.

I choke back another laugh, and, as if my father didn't just nearly catch me having sex, I go breezing into the living room where Dad is sitting next to Randy on the sofa. Randy, that traitor, has his head in Dad's lap and is enjoying a thorough ear scratching. "Sorry! Just got out of the shower." I hope that might explain my red face.

"No problem," Dad says, thankfully keeping his attention on Randy and not me. "This trip came up awfully sudden."

"I know! They need me to look at a property in England before they can decide on a location shoot. I'll be back tomorrow. Flynn agreed to take the hoodlums for me until I can get there."

"He told me." Dad continues to stroke Randy, who's totally blissed out. "He hadn't heard you were leaving town, though."

"Oh, well, it was something for Jasper and Kristian. I don't think Flynn is involved in this one." Why am I lying? Why don't I just tell him the truth? Because I'm not ready to go public with our news, even if my dad isn't exactly "public." I want Jasper to have his situation resolved before I tell my family about us.

And, selfishly, I want to keep what's happening with Jasper between us for a little while longer. It's so new and exciting, and I like that no one knows. For now, it only belongs to us. As soon as we tell someone, it's not just ours anymore. I'm sure Hayden and Addie have their suspicions after last night, but that's all they are—suspicions. They don't know anything for certain.

I make a big show out of checking my watch. "Oh damn! I've got to go! Plane to catch."

"You need a ride to the airport?"

"No, I'm good. Jasper is picking me up. He's going with me."

"I thought I saw his new car out front," he says as he stands. "Come on, Randolph. Let's go see what Grammy is up to." Dad stops to kiss my cheek, which has to be the deepest shade of scarlet ever invented. "Have a safe trip, honey. Send us a text to let us know you got there okay."

"Oh, um, yes, I will! Thanks for having Randy."

"Any time. Love you."

"Love you, too."

Dad calls for Randy, and he trots along behind him, with nary a look back at his mortified mommy. I sense Jasper behind me before I feel him press up against me. "Shoot me right now," I groan. "Please, just make it fast and painless."

"Only if I can go with you, darling."

"How did I think I would get away with that? He raised four kids. He knows everything!"

"Do you think he heard us having a hump? If he did, I'm never showing my face at your parents' home again."

I turn to face him. "*Having a hump?* Is that what we were doing?"

"That's most definitely what we were doing, and only one of us got to finish—twice. I'd say that puts you deep in debt, my love. How ever shall I collect my payment?"

"So this means you're over my dad possibly catching us 'having a hump'?"

He caresses my cheek with his finger. "I'll be over it the minute my cock bumps up against the back of your throat on the plane."

I'M BUCKLED into my seat on the private jet, and we've just taken off from Burbank for our twelve-hour flight to London. Normally, I take something to knock me out on long flights, but I want to be alert for this one. I still can't believe what he said to me before we left my house. Picturing myself on my knees, his cock in my mouth bumping up against my throat makes me hot for more of what we were doing before my father showed up.

Never before has the thought of giving a man a blow job turned me on, but I can't wait to see if Jasper follows through on his "threat."

A chime dings, and the pilot lets us know we've reached our cruising altitude. We're free to move around the cabin, but he recommends keeping our seat belts on when we're seated.

"I want you to go into the bedroom. Get naked. Stretch out on the bed with your arms over your head and your eyes closed. Your legs should be spread as far apart as you can get them. I'll be in shortly. Any questions?"

Remember that accent I've told you about a time or two? Yeah, well… I'll have to ask him if he would mind recording what he just said so I can listen to it on playback every day for the rest of my life. In addition to my reaction to *how* he said it, I'm so stunned by *what* he said, I can barely breathe, let alone speak. He honestly expects me to do all that just because he told me to?

A quick glance at his unyielding expression tells me he does, in fact, expect me to follow his instructions.

"The choice is always yours," he reminds me, his tone softer, more conciliatory. "Say the word."

He's referring to the word "baby" that we agreed upon last night. It occurs to me that I'd *be* a baby if I used it before I know what he has planned. His orders alone have me so turned on I can't see straight. I release the clasp on my seat belt and get up slowly, testing my legs to ensure they'll hold me up before I begin moving toward the back of the plane where the bedroom is located.

This is utter decadence. Flying on a private jet with a sexy man who wants to dominate me at thirty-five thousand feet. How has this become my life? Only a few weeks ago, my idea of an exciting evening might've been a run on the boardwalk with Randy, followed by a movie in bed with him snuggled up to me. As much as I love Randy, and I love him irrationally, this is a whole other level of excitement.

I'm so excited, in fact, that my hands are shaking as I freshen up in the tiny bathroom before removing my dress. The cool air pumping through the plane's vents feels extra chilled against my heated skin as I step into the bedroom completely naked.

I stretch out on the bed, arms over my head, eyes closed, legs spread. My muscles are trembling from anticipation and desire and a kind of elation I've never experienced before. How long will he make me wait? What will he do to me? How will it feel? Will I be scared?

No. I won't be scared. Not with Jasper. I can't conceive of doing something like this with anyone but him. I trust him completely, and that trust frees me to enjoy whatever is about to happen.

Will we make a baby on this plane? Did we already make a baby last night? How soon can I find out? I need to ask Dr. Breslow about that.

With my eyes closed, I sense Jasper before I'm fully aware that he's quietly joined me. Without my vision, my other senses are heightened. I can hear his fingers sliding over the fine fabric of his shirt as he unbuttons it. I distinctly hear the metallic clink of his belt buckle, the snick of his zipper, the rustle of his pants sliding down over his legs.

The heat of his body next to mine tells me he's near. Not knowing what he's going to do makes my nipples so tight, they ache as the cool air flows over them. I feel his hands on my hair as he slides something over my face. A blindfold. I experience a moment of sheer panic when I realize I can't escape the darkness.

"Shhh," he says. "Relax, my love. I'm right here."

The sound of his voice soothes and calms me. As long as he's there, I'm safe. I may not be entirely comfortable, but I'm always safe. He continues to soothe me by running his hands over my body in a soft caress, beginning at my shoulders, to my breasts, belly, legs, feet and then back up the insides of my legs, pressing them farther apart as he goes.

I feel him shift his weight to the middle of the bed, between my obscenely spread legs and then a stream of air hits my core, making me squirm.

"Stay still, darling."

"Don't do that if you want me to stay still."

"No more talking unless you need your safe word. Tell me again what it is?"

"Baby."

"And you know that if you say that, it stops everything, right?"

"Yes."

Right when I think he's going to focus on my core, my wrists are captured in fur-lined cuffs that are then attached to the headboard, rendering me trapped in his sensual web. That he's brought the cuffs along on the trip tells me he's planned this in advance, and knowing that feeds the wildfire that burns inside me.

I sense him moving about the tiny space, and it's a struggle to remain still while I wait to see what he'll do next. My body is wound so tightly, I fear I'll implode before we get to the main event—whatever that may entail.

Apparently, Jasper is in no particular rush. Minutes pass without his touch, and I begin to feel abandoned. I've been reduced to nothing more than nerve endings that are on fire for his touch. I ache for him, and I'm on the verge of begging him to do something, anything, when I feel his tongue on my left nipple.

The sensations are so heightened that I cry out from the shock that ripples through my body. Then he's gone again, leaving me bereft. This is the sweetest torture I've ever experienced, and I realize it's only just begun. His lips are now on the inside of my lower left leg, sliding upward at an excruciatingly slow pace. My hips rise up to meet him, but he's gone before he reaches the place where I need him most.

I strain against the cuffs, moving restlessly on the bed, on the verge of a complete meltdown or the biggest orgasm of my life. I'm not sure which will happen first at this rate.

"I want to film you like this," he whispers.

I turn toward his voice, seeking the comfort of his nearness.

"Would you let me?"

Right now, I'd give him anything he wants if it means relief from the ache that grows sharper by the second. "Yes," I whisper through parched lips.

"Soon, love. I want you to see how exquisitely beautiful you are when you submit to me."

I need to come so badly I can barely process what he's suggesting. All I know is I'd give him anything he asked of me to continue feeling the way I do when I'm with him. It's as if all the emotion I've experienced in my life up to now has been rebuilt into a nuclear bomb that has the power to obliterate me. And I've given him that power willingly, freely, happily. This, finally, is what it feels like to be in love.

"Jasper." His name is a sob on my lips.

"What, love?"

"I need…"

"What do you need?"

"More. Something. *Anything.*"

His low chuckle makes me want to punch him—and I would if my hands weren't shackled to the bed. "Patience, darling."

"I have no patience left."

"Shhh. You don't want to earn a punishment by speaking out of turn, do you?"

There's no other word to describe the squeak that comes from me than inelegant. "*Punishment?* What the hell are you talking about?"

"Did we forget to talk about what happens when you don't follow my directions?" His fingertip makes a path from my throat down the front of me, between my breasts, over my quivering belly, halting just above my clit, which burns for him.

"You know we didn't talk about that," I say through gritted teeth.

"Allow me to correct that egregious oversight on my part."

He's loving the hell out of this. I can hear it in his lighthearted tone.

"Should you happen to disobey me during one of our scenes, I'd have no choice but to administer a punishment that can be anything from a sound spanking of your sweet arse to requiring you to wear a plug in public to standing naked in the corner for a period of time until I'm certain you've learned your lesson. I tend to be almost as creative when it comes to punishments as I am when it comes to pleasure."

His fingertip finds my clit in a quick, glancing stroke that's gone before I even register that it's happening. But it's enough to trigger the release that's been building for what feels like forever at this point. I scream from the power of it, and when I come back to reality, tears are streaming down my face.

"Mmm, so beautiful," he says, "and so very naughty. Did I say you were allowed to come?"

"N-no."

"Then you know what that means?"

"W-what?"

"You must be punished. The question is, however, shall we take care of that now or wait until later? I think I'll let you decide what you prefer. What'll it be? Now or later?"

I'm furious about the thought of being punished—and painfully aroused at the same time. How is that possible? "Never?"

"Ahhh, my sweet love. I don't recall offering 'never' as an option."

When my team at work presents me with good-news-bad-news situations, I always want the bad news first to get it out of the way. "Now," I say on a growl. I can't believe that I actually want him to punish me. Who have I become with this man?

"Turn over." His voice has taken on a huskier tone that tells me he's as turned on as I am. The blindfold makes me more aware of these sorts of nuances.

I'm surprised to discover I can easily turn over even with my wrists shackled. My arms are now crossed, however.

"Arse up, legs apart, head down."

As I haltingly position myself to his liking, I begin to feel disconnected from what's happening in this small room. It's like I'm floating above it, looking down at the woman shamelessly arranged, waiting to be punished by her lover.

He leans over me, his body pressed against mine, his lips brushing against my ear. "I'm going to plug you and then spank you."

"That's two punishments!"

"No, it's one punishment."

"That's not fair."

"Shall we go for two punishments?"

"No!"

"I thought that's what you'd say."

CHAPTER 17

Ellie

*H*e withdraws from me, and I immediately feel the loss of his body heat. I begin to tremble from the cool air and the anticipation and the powerful desire for anything and everything he wants to do to me. I'm floating above it all, imagining how I must look to him and wondering if he's on fire, too. If he is, he's got a lot more patience than I do.

I hear the sound of a cap opening, like one that might be found on a bottle, and then I feel the cold smear of lubricant being applied to my bottom. Oh my God. Am I really going to allow him to do this to me again? My safe word is on the very tip of my tongue, ready to burst free if or when this gets to be too much for me. And as two of his fingers breach my most private place, it's all I can do to refrain from saying it. I shouldn't like this as much as I do. I should stop him. I should—

His fingers are removed and immediately replaced with something much bigger, which forces its way past the tight ring of muscle, stretching me to the point of pain before the pain morphs into unlikely pleasure as the plug moves into place. "I wish you could see how sexy you look with your sweet arse plugged for me." He runs his hands over my bottom, fanning the wildfire.

That's when I become aware of the fact that my inner thighs are wet from the power of my arousal. That has certainly never happened before.

We're interrupted, jarringly, by an announcement from the pilot warning of some turbulent air ahead. Normally, the turbulence warning would frighten me, but I have much greater things to be afraid of at the moment. Such as the hand that Jasper brings down on my ass. It echoes through the room in a loud, resounding crack that hurts more than I expect it to.

Then he soothes the ache by rubbing the spot until pain turns to pleasure.

I'm aware of the plane bouncing somewhat violently as Jasper's hand continues to rain down on my ass, moving from side to side, from the place where my cheek meets my leg to the fleshier middle. By the time he finishes, I'm a drooling, sobbing mess of need and want and excruciating desire that is stoked to nearly unbearable levels when he shoves his hard cock into me without warning. Thanks to the plug, the fit is so incredibly tight that his first deep thrust triggers a second epic orgasm.

I've probably earned another punishment, but I can't find the wherewithal to care as he pounds into me, harder and deeper than he ever has before. With each hard thrust, his body strokes against my ass, which is still hot and sensitive from the spanking. The combination is overwhelming.

"Don't come until I say you can," he says, going deep again. "Don't you dare come."

Holding back is going to kill me. I have no doubt about that as I clench my teeth so hard, I worry my jaw will break under the pressure of trying to hold off the inevitable. He reaches under me to fill his hands with my breasts as he pushes my legs farther apart. The move sends him even deeper into me and triggers the orgasm that can't be stopped no matter how hard I try.

I come harder the third time than the other two combined, and he's right there with me, surging into me again and again until we collapse into a heaving pile of flesh on the bed. Though I'm still floating, I have the presence of mind to hope once again that we've made a baby.

"Such a naughty, disobedient sub," he whispers after long minutes of silence, other than the heavy breathing that follows exertion.

"It's not my fault."

He runs his fingers through my hair, providing soft, easy comfort in the wake of tumultuous emotion. "Whose fault is it?"

"Yours! You knew exactly what would happen when you did all that."

The low rumble of his laughter makes me smile. I love to hear him laugh.

"I have no idea what you're talking about."

"Sure you don't. You've turned me into a brazen hussy sex fiend."

"And this is a bad thing, darling?"

He sounds so very British and so very, *very* sexy. "Well, I'm still not sure how I feel about being plugged, but the rest wasn't so bad."

"By the rest you mean the three screaming orgasms?"

I elbow him and receive a grunt of laughter in response.

"Speaking of your third screaming orgasm, that happened without permission, so that has earned you another punishment."

I groan dramatically. "My poor tortured bum can't take anymore."

Rubbing his hand over my ass, he chuckles. "No more spanking, but I do think we'll keep the plug in place until we get to the hotel."

"How long will that be?" My voice rises in protest.

"Only a few more hours."

"*Hours?* I'll never survive that."

"I guess we'll find out, won't we?"

He withdraws from me slowly, which is far more arousing than you might think, given that he's still half-hard and I'm compressed by the plug. Next he removes the cuffs and rubs my wrists until the tingling stops. The removal of the blindfold has me blinking furiously to bring him into focus in the soft glow of the bedside light.

"There you are," he says, cupping my cheek and leaning in to kiss me. He has a bottle of water ready, and I take greedy sips of the cold liquid.

"Why do I get so thirsty?"

"Probably because you're breathing differently and exerting yourself the way you would during a workout."

"Sex with you is definitely a workout."

He studies me with those golden-brown eyes that *see* me in a way no other man ever has. "Do you like it, darling?"

"You couldn't tell?"

"I could tell you had good orgasms, but did you *like* being blindfolded, cuffed, plugged, spanked, dominated?"

"I liked it," I confess, feeling my face heat with embarrassment and arousal.

He caresses my face. "What did you like best?"

"I have to pick one thing?"

"You can pick more than one."

"The blindfold made me more aware of everything else that was happening."

"Losing the use of one sense heightens the others."

"I lost two senses because I couldn't touch you either."

"True. What did you think of the punishment?" As he speaks, his finger makes circles on my breast, round and round without quite touching my nipple. That's all it takes to start the low hum of desire all over again.

"I won't say that I *liked* it, but it wasn't awful."

"Not awful. I suppose it could be worse. And the plug?"

"Uncomfortable at first, but not so bad once it was in place—until you took up the rest of the room inside me." I flatten my hand on his chest and drag it down to encircle his reawakened erection.

His sharp gasp of surprise pleases me inordinately.

"Was it good for you, too?"

His eyes, which had closed while I stroked him, pop open, his gaze locking on mine. "Do you honestly have to ask?"

"I guess I do."

"Darling... My sweet, sexy Ellie... Nothing has ever been better for me than being completely myself with you."

"I always want you to be yourself with me."

"You have no idea what an amazing, incredible gift that is to me. Not every woman would be strong enough to give herself over to me the way you just did."

"I liked giving myself over to you. I was a little scared at the beginning, but I kept reminding myself that I was with you and that you'd keep me safe."

"I'll always keep you safe, my love. You can count on that."

"I'm starting to believe I can."

"Believe it. Now that I have you in my arms and in my bed, I'm not going anywhere."

"I still can't believe you wanted me and never said so."

"And how would I have gone about saying so? At work? In the midst of our group of friends?"

"You could've called me."

"Like on the *phone*? Do people still do that?"

I laugh at his scandalized expression. "I think some people do."

"You want to know the truth, darling?"

"Always."

"I didn't tell you because I wasn't sure you'd want me the way I wanted you, and because of who you are to me, who your brother is to me and who your family is to me, I didn't want to risk making things awkward between us if you didn't feel the same way I do. We spend too much time together to take that risk."

I drag a finger through his chest hair, loving the soft texture and the moan that escapes from him when I touch his nipple. "I'm sorry you never said anything."

He draws me in closer, kissing the top of my head. "Trust me, so am I."

"I'd listen to you in meetings at work or when you tell a funny story when we're all together somewhere. Afterward, I wouldn't be able to tell you what you said. I was so dazzled by *how* you said it. I'd fantasize about being in bed with you while you said filthy things to me in that beautiful voice."

He slides his leg between mine, the friction of his hairy leg against my skin electrifying. "I wish I'd known you had those thoughts. I could've been saying filthy things to you for years now."

"We might not have been ready before now."

"Probably not."

"Are you nervous about seeing your father?"

"I'm more resigned than nervous. It's way past time that I dealt with this situation once and for all."

"What do you think he'll say?"

"He'll be bloody furious. He'll rant about me shirking my obligations. The usual tirade. But I'm not backing down." He tightens his arms around me. "This is what I want. My life in LA is what I want. I'm never going back to London, and it's time he knew that."

"I'm so proud of you for standing up for what you want, Jasper."

"That means so much to me, love. I should've done it years ago, but you've given me the best reason I've ever had, not to mention the courage I've lacked."

"How can you say you've lacked courage? You stood up to him at eighteen and fought to attend the school of your choice, to pursue the career of your choice. That took incredible courage—and balls."

"I guess, but what does it say about me that I've let him cast a shadow over my entire life by making it clear that I'm expected to step up when the time comes? I swear his latest daredevil stage is all about making me sweat. Every time he climbs a mountain or goes off on some quest for a record in an experimental aircraft, he knows I'm holding my breath the whole time. I bet he fucking loves that, the sadistic bastard."

"After this, you never have to see him again if you don't want to."

"I definitely don't want to, and he's not going to want to see me either."

"I'm sorry you've had such a difficult relationship with your father. It makes me feel extra lucky to have had Max Godfrey as my dad."

"You're so lucky. He's the best dad I know."

"You're going to be a wonderful father, too."

"I hope so. I have no earthly idea how to do it."

"You know how *not* to do it. That's a good place to start."

"I suppose that's true."

"Try not to worry too much," I whisper when I can't keep my eyes open any longer. "No matter what happens, I'll be right here to help you through it."

"That means everything to me, darling."

We arrive at Heathrow late in the morning local time. A car service whisks us into town, where I've booked a room at Claridge's, located in the exclusive Mayfair neighborhood and a short walk to my father's office. We worked extra hard on the baby-making project on the flight, and other than a few catnaps, we haven't slept.

I can tell that Ellie is stimulated by the ride into town as the plug is still in place and every bump on the road draws a gasp of shock from her. I love watching her reactions, and judging from the glow of her cheeks, she's living in a perpetual state of arousal. I can't wait to get my business done so I can get back to her and pick up where we left off on the plane. She's yawning continuously by the time we reach our room. I help her out of her clothes, tuck her into bed and sit next to her, gazing down at her lovely face and drawing energy from the adoring way in which she looks at me.

"Shall we remove the plug now that you've taken your punishment like a champ?"

"After you get back."

"Ahhh, something to look forward to."

"For you, maybe," she retorts.

Laughing, I say, "Get some rest, darling. I'll take you to afternoon tea when I return. You'll love it."

She takes hold of my hand. "I love *you*, and I'm so proud of you for fighting for your freedom. I'll be right here waiting for you when you get back."

"I have no words to tell you what that means to me. And PS, I love you, too. I can't wait to have everything with you."

She reaches for me, drawing me into a sensual kiss that immediately fires me up. I'm amazed that J.T. has any gas left in his tank after the fuck-fest on the plane, but he is a resilient bugger. I reluctantly withdraw from the kiss. There's nothing I'd rather do than dive into bed with her and pick up where we left off. But I can't procrastinate on this errand from hell. My appointment is at noon, and Nathan has given me exactly fifteen minutes with His Grace. I hope it takes less than five minutes to conduct our business.

"I'll be back soon." I kiss Ellie one more time and pull the covers over her shoulders. I have to force myself to leave her, to take the lift to the lobby, to walk out of the hotel when everything in me wants to go running back to her and avoid this confrontation nearly twenty years in the making. The thought of seeing my father makes me feel sick in the gut and the heart that he has broken too many times to count. I swear to God that no child of mine will ever feel that way about me. I wouldn't be able to bear it.

My father's London office hasn't changed much in the nearly two decades since I was last here. It's a huge blue glass spire that juts into the sky like a rocket ship, which was his intent when he designed the monstrosity that was completed the year I was born. He wanted the world to know that Kingsley Enterprises was heading in one direction and one direction only. My father sits atop his kingdom in the building's penthouse suite that includes a luxury apartment where he spends most of his time these days.

My parents have never had what I would call a traditional marriage. How could they when his primary goal in life is adding to the family fortune and keeping up the family traditions? Where is there room amidst all that ambition for a wife or family? My mum spends most of her time in Cornwall, far from the hustle and bustle of my father's life in London. She says she's happy there, but I have my doubts.

My father waxes poetic in the media about his love for her, but I'd be surprised if he spends even two months a year with her. I suspect she'd love to be free to pursue the kind of relationship she reads about in her romance novels, but he'd never let her go. Divorce smacks of failure, a word that isn't in Henry Kingsley's vocabulary. Despite the fact that he leaves her alone for long periods of time, if he has a weak spot, it's her. My sisters and I agree that he has an odd way of showing his love for her.

Their kind of marriage would never work for me. After I take care of things with my father, I'll ask Ellie to marry me. We're going to do this the right way, with a big white wedding followed by as many babies as she wants to have, none of them burdened by an inheritance they never signed on for. I'm counting the seconds until I can get back to her and start our life together, free from the encumbrances that have weighted me down from the day I was born.

Nathan, my father's longtime assistant and majordomo, meets me as I step off the elevator on the thirtieth floor of the Kingsley building. I contacted the man I've known all my life to arrange the meeting. If he was surprised to hear from me, he never said so. Nathan is everything to my father that I am not—faithful, devoted, available. I have often joked to my sisters that Nathan is the son my father never had.

With his perfectly groomed dark hair and intense eyes, Nathan is the picture of British elegance in a gray bespoke suit that fits his trim frame like a glove. He shakes my hand. "It's nice to see you, Jasper. You're looking well."

"Likewise." Beyond a starched dress shirt and perfectly pressed pants, I haven't dressed for this meeting, which I know will irritate my father. However, in light of what I've come to say, I expect that my lack of a jacket and tie will be the least of his concerns.

"Things seem to be going well for you in Hollywood," Nathan says with typical understatement.

"You could say that." Most people would agree that winning the Oscar, the Golden Globe and the BAFTA in the same year counts for much more than doing "well" in my career. However, the people in my father's world don't think like "most people." I'm at the top of my game, and Nathan knows it. So does my father. I'm as good at my chosen career as he is at his, and that must chap his arse more than any of the many other things I've done to enrage him, such as live my own life. "Does he know I'm coming?"

"I told him ten minutes ago."

I hold back a smile and refrain from acknowledging that Nathan has played this as well as I could've hoped by not giving my father enough time to work up a head of steam ahead of my arrival. "I appreciate your assistance."

"I serve at the pleasure of the Kingsley family, which includes you, my lord."

Not for much longer. I don't share that thought with the man who is only trying to do his job—a job I've made more difficult than it already is with my presence here today.

As much as I'd like to think I'm as courageous as Ellie believes me to be, my stomach is tight with anxiety and my hands are unusually moist. Because he's too well-bred not to, my father will shake my hand, and he will view my sweaty palms as a sign of weakness. I rub them on my pants, wishing I were anywhere but standing at the door to Henry Kingsley's domain.

Nathan gives me a look to ask if I'm ready.

As ready as I'll ever be, I nod.

He knocks once, and when he opens the door, a thousand memories assail me all at once as I follow him. Years of Saturdays spent imprisoned in this room being force-fed the Kingsley family credo, though it was obvious to anyone who knew me that I couldn't have possibly cared less about credos or finance or legacies. My father was the only one who couldn't seem to see that, and he kept up my "lessons" even when it meant schlepping into the city from Berkshire while I boarded at Eton. Recalling those years of pure torture does nothing to elevate my mood.

Three walls of glass overlook the financial center of London, as well as some of the most recognizable landmarks, including the Tower of London and St. Paul's Cathedral. The fourth wall is covered with plaques, mementos and photos of Henry with everyone who is anyone. My sisters and I refer to the office as the center of the universe.

"Your Grace," Nathan says, formal as always, "the Marquess of Andover to see you, sir."

"Thank you, Nathan."

With military precision, Nathan turns and leaves the room, closing the door behind him.

My father's voice is exactly as I remember—deep, authoritative and formidable—but his hair is now snow white and his face has aged considerably in the decade since I last saw him. Photos of him in the media haven't properly conveyed the ravages of time that are readily apparent to me as I approach his desk and lean across it to shake his outstretched hand. My father is the atypical Brit, tanned year-round from his many outdoor pursuits.

"Hello, Father."

"This is an unexpected surprise."

"Surprises are often unexpected." The moment I say the words, I regret them. My father has never appreciated what he calls my "cheeky" sense of humor.

Right on cue, his dark blue eyes narrow with predictable displeasure. "To what do I owe the honor?"

"I've come because it's time we talked about the future."

"What about the future?"

Though he hasn't invited me to, I take a seat in one of his visitor's chairs, inhale a deep breath and let it out slowly. "I'm not coming back to London. Ever."

"Of course you are. You have an obligation to this family—"

"Which I am officially relinquishing to whomever you choose to replace me. My life and my career are in Los Angeles, and that's where I'll be staying."

"Is that what you think?" he asks with a nasty little smirk that sends a chill up my spine. I've seen that smirk many times before. Nothing good has ever come of it.

"That's what I know." I force myself to use a tone as authoritative and formidable as his.

"I was afraid it would come to this one day," he says with what sounds like weary resignation.

"Come to what?" I ask as my heart begins to beat faster. What the hell does that mean?

He gets up from his desk and goes over to the credenza that sits low against a glass wall. God forbid anything as common as furniture block his view of the universe. Using a key that he produces from his pocket, he unlocks one of the drawers, opens it and withdraws a packet that he brings back to the desk with him. His every movement is deliberate and calculated, as if he's rehearsed this performance for years in anticipation of this day.

A sick sense of dread begins to work its way through me as I try to anticipate what's about to happen.

CHAPTER 18

Jasper

Remaining standing, my father withdraws a file folder from an envelope and begins to place eight-by-ten photographs on the massive glass desk that had nothing more than a pen on it before he lays out one photo after another, each of them more damning than the last. Beginning with my college years, there are compromising photos of me in bed with women, lots of women, sometimes multiple women at the same time. He even has photos of me with the woman who taught me everything I know about BDSM.

Dear God, she'll have me killed if those photos get out.

Before I can begin to figure out how he would've gained access to my most private spaces, he builds his case slowly, methodically. You know that feeling you get when you watch a bad accident unfurl before you and you know what's coming, but you can't do a thing to stop it?

Yeah, there I am in my first BDSM club, flogger in hand, giddy smile on my face as I dominate the pale, skinny woman bent before me on the spanking bench. Next I'm in a dungeon, fucking a woman I don't remember up the arse, then at Club Quantum in New York, double-teaming a woman with Kristian—him in her mouth, me in her pussy. The scenes unfold before me like a porn movie of my life over the last twenty years. I should've known he'd have me followed, even into places I considered private.

I should have fucking known.

"You'll never do anything with them," I say with more bravado than I feel. "You'd never bring that sort of scandal down on yourself."

"No, I wouldn't."

I'm about to ask him to cut to the chase when he lays a photo of me with Ellie on the desk, and my heart skips a beat. My body goes cold with fear and regret and rage like I've never felt before. The photo is from the night we had pizza outside in Venice Beach. We're holding hands and talking with our heads bent together. Anyone looking at that photo in the context of the others would see that *this* woman is different. There's another of me kissing her on her front porch, my arms around her, hers around me, the two of us fully enthralled with each other. And then he produces a photo of us at Black Vice, with scenes happening on the stages behind us. There would be no question to anyone who saw the photo that we were in a sex club. The rage that overtakes me is so hot and so potent I can't get air to my lungs.

"I wonder," my son-of-a-bitch father says, "if you've told your business partner that you took his sister to a sex club? Does your Ellie know that her brother is also an active practitioner in your sick lifestyle?" He produces a photo of the first night Flynn brought Natalie to Club Quantum, and I fear for a terrifying second that I'm going to vomit on my father's priceless Turkish rug.

"Does your Ellie know that she works for and with a bunch of deviant perverts?"

One by one, he produces pictures of Hayden, Kristian, Marlowe, Flynn, Emmett and Sebastian participating in various BDSM scenes at our clubs in New York and Los Angeles. Bile stings my throat, forcing me to swallow furiously to keep from vomiting. How in the fuck did he get someone in there when we vet the living shit out of everyone who walks through the door?

He produces a photo of me with Max and Stella that was taken at Flynn and Natalie's wedding in their backyard. "What would your good friends Max Godfrey and Estelle Flynn think of you if your self-ishness ruined their son's career and their daughter's reputation?"

All I can do is stare at the photos that would ruin everyone I love if they were made public. The fact they even exist is enough to make my chest constrict so tightly, I fear I might be having a heart attack.

"So you see, son, your choice is very clear—honor your obligations to your family, or I'll make the photos of your friends public. It's that simple."

I stare at the photo of Flynn in a sensual embrace with his beautiful wife, remembering the guts it had taken for her to come to the club in the first place. Having that image made public would destroy her, and Flynn would never forgive me. None of them would ever forgive me.

It takes a full minute before I find the wherewithal to speak. "How is it possible that a father could hate his son so much that he would do something like this to him?"

"I don't hate you. I've never hated you."

"If you don't hate me, I can't imagine how you'd treat someone you *do* hate."

"What you fail to understand, what you have *always* failed to understand, is that I was once in your place, burdened by obligations I never signed on for, that I never wanted, and yet, I did the honorable thing and put my family and my heritage ahead of my own selfish desires. I did what was *expected* of me, and you will, too."

Though I can't take my eyes off the horror show laid out before me, I shake my head. "No."

"Excuse me?"

"You heard me. No, no, no, *no*." The thought of a life trapped in this glass prison is so revolting to me that even the possibility of ruination for me and my closest friends and loved ones isn't enough to convince me to bow to his will. My brain is racing. The others would tell me to tell *him* to take his threats and shove them up his arse. Emmett will know of legal action we can take to stop him from releasing the photos. Surely there are things that can be done.

"You're obviously not thinking clearly. What will Flynn Godfrey think of you when you launch another media firestorm aimed at him and his wife after the last one only just died down? What will Hayden Roth's future father-in-law think of him when pictures of his precious Addison in a sex club go public? From what I heard, Simon York only recently accepted his daughter's choice of a husband. How awful would it be for the happy couple if he took back his approval of their marriage?"

I have to give him credit for being thorough, but now I'm wondering if someone in our tight-knit group is actually on his payroll. If that turns out to be true, I pity the person when the wrath of Quantum comes down upon them.

I get up to leave, hoping my legs will support the weight of my body. "As always, Father, it's been a joy to see you."

"I'm sorry that it's come to this, Jasper, but I expect you to do the right thing."

"I fear, Father, that once again I will fail to meet your many expectations. In the meantime, I'd suggest you find someone who actually *wants* to be your heir before you succeed in actually killing yourself on one of your grand follies."

His lips tighten in anger and his face turns an unhealthy shade of red, which pleases me greatly except for the fear that he might actually drop dead. "You have twenty-four hours to tell Nathan you've seen the error of your ways. Otherwise, these photos will be released to the media around the world."

"How sad that you're so desperate that you have to stoop to blackmailing your only son to get him to fall in line." I gather the photos into a pile that I'll take with me. "I'll be certain to give your regards to Mother and the girls when I tell them about our meeting."

I'm gratified to see a brief crack in his veneer when I let him know I'll be telling the rest of the family about his blackmail. But the crack lasts only a second.

"I'm sure your mother will be very proud to learn how you've been spending your time since you left home."

"She's very proud of me, as are my sisters, all of whom called me after I won the biggest awards in my field earlier this year. I'm sure you meant to call, too, but now I know you were so busy with your blackmail schemes that it probably never crossed your mind."

I'm not sure where my bravado is coming from, because I have no doubt in my mind that he will make good on his threats if I fail to comply. One thing I know for certain is that I will never see him again in person after today, so my parting shots matter more than they ever have before.

Parting shots aside, however, the thought of the scandal that will consume my partners, Ellie and me is truly terrifying. But I'm not the scared, meek little eighteen-year-old I was the last time I stood up to him. I'm a man with considerable resources of my own, resources I will fully employ to beat my father at his own game.

"Always a pleasure to see you, Father. Be careful on your upcoming jaunt. I'd hate to see anything happen to you when your estate is in such disarray."

I'm gratified to have the last word and to know that his nasty smirk has been replaced by something that looks an awful lot like fear. Good. A little fear is the least of what he deserves. With the damning photos tucked under my arm, I walk out of the office, past Nathan's desk. He stands as if to say something to me, but I leave without a word. I'm actually afraid that if I open my mouth, the only thing that will come out is a howl of rage.

The lift ride to the lobby seems to take forever, and when I finally burst through the main doors into the cold winter air, my lungs are about to explode from holding my breath. I take in greedy gulps of oxygen as I try to calm my rapidly beating heart. *Oh my God. What am I going to do?* Despite my audacity with my father, I'm terrified of the photos becoming public. That they even *exist* is horrifying.

I'm too wound up to go straight back to the hotel, where Ellie is waiting to hear that I've cleared the path to happily ever after for us. What she doesn't know is I've opened the gates to hell for her, her brother, her family and her closest friends. If my father makes good on his threats, she'll regret agreeing to let me father her child, not to mention every second we've spent together.

"Fucking hell," I mutter, drawing a glare from a woman walking hand in hand with a young boy. "Sorry." I'm not sure if she hears my apology, and frankly, I don't much care. I've got far bigger problems. Though the last thing I want to do is tell anyone about what just happened, I've got a looming deadline to consider. I pull my cell out of my pocket and place a call to Emmett, realizing after it rings the first time that it's four thirty in the morning in Los Angeles.

"Yeah," he says when he answers. Clearing the sleep from his throat, he adds, "This is Emmett."

"Em, it's Jasper. I'm sorry to wake you up."

"Jasper? I thought you were in London."

"I am. I just met with my father, Henry Kingsley."

"Your father is..."

"Henry Kingsley. Yes."

"Holy shit," he says in a whisper. "I knew that was your legal name, but you never said you were part of *that* Kingsley family, so I never suspected. Are you kidding me right now?"

"You have no earthly idea how much I wish I were joking."

"You're Henry Kingsley's son."

"Yes."

"How in the motherfucking hell have you managed to keep that a secret?"

"I use my mother's maiden name professionally, and my father has gone along with the story that Jasper Kingsley is a reclusive inventor, toiling away in his workshop in Cornwall. Until now." After a long pause, I continue, filled with dread and shame over the potential scandal. "I saw him today for the first time in years. I told him I have no plans to return to London to be his heir and that he needs to find someone else to carry on the family dynasty. Suffice to say, he didn't take it well."

"How so?"

"He's been having me followed, since I left for USC at eighteen. He has pictures."

After a brief but significant pause, Emmett asks, "What kind of pictures?"

"The worst kind imaginable. And not just of me. All of us. He's had someone in our clubs, Devon's club. It's bad, Em. As bad as it gets."

"How... I mean... Oh my God, Jasper."

The rare note of panic in Emmett's tone only fuels my own out-of-control anxiety. "He's given me twenty-four hours to change my mind about being his heir, or he's releasing the photos to the media."

"We'll get an injunction. We can stop him."

"We can stop him with only twenty-four hours to work with and an international situation on our hands?"

"You bet we can."

"Or I could sell out my partnership in Quantum and give him what he wants to protect us all."

"No. You know Flynn and Hayden as well as I do. They don't do blackmail, Jasper. They'd stand beside you and fight him every step of the way. You know they would."

My throat closes, and my eyes sting with tears that make me feel worse than I already do, as if that's possible. "I do know that, but I can't and won't ask them to risk their careers and reputations on my behalf."

"You won't be asking them. I will. Get your ass back to LA. I'm on it, and we'll do everything we can to keep this from going public."

"Flynn doesn't even know about me and Ellie."

"It might be time to tell him."

"As long as those photos exist somewhere in this world, the people I care most about are in peril. I'll give him what he wants before I'll take you all down with me."

"Listen to me, Jasper. I know you and your partners better than I know my own siblings, and I speak for the others when I tell you they'd *want* you to bring this to them. They'd want to try to help you. And Flynn and Hayden will be so pissed off about someone infiltrating our clubs that they'll be out for blood and vengeance. Hell, so will Devon Black. Your father isn't the only one with resources, and he has no idea who he's tangling with. How about we give him the four-one-one on how Quantum rolls?"

"God, I'm so tempted, but the thought of those photos going

public makes me sick. I couldn't give a shit less about myself, but Flynn and Natalie and Hayden, Addie, Marlowe, everyone else... They'd be collateral damage in my war with my father."

"What would you say if one of them was being blackmailed? Would you want them to roll over and take it, or would you want to fight with everything we've got to protect one of our own?"

"I'd want to fight, but—"

"No buts. Let us do for you what you'd do for any of us."

I realize defeat when I'm staring it in the face—or hearing it in my attorney's voice. "Give me a couple of hours to talk to Flynn, and do me a favor. Draw up the partnership dissolution paperwork and have it ready for me when I get back in case we decide that's the best course of action. I'll come straight to the office from the airport."

"I'll draw up the papers if you insist, but—"

"I do insist. My partners need to know all their options, up to and including severing ties with me."

"What good will that do if your father releases the photos anyway?"

"I could tell him that I'm no longer associated with them, so he can keep his vitriol focused on me rather than on them."

"And how does Ellie figure into that, Jasper? If she gets hurt, Flynn gets hurt. You know how they are."

I do know, and the thought of either of them hurt because of me is excruciating. "Let me talk to her." I dread having to tell her that there's photographic proof of her visit to Black Vice, and I have no idea how I'll handle the threat to the other Quantum partners. One step at a time, I suppose.

"Keep me posted, and I'll do the same for you."

"Thank you, Emmett. I'm sorry to wake you up, but I didn't know who else to call."

"You made the most important call first. I'll do everything I can to get you free of this situation. You can count on that."

"Thanks again."

"You got it. Safe travels."

The line goes dead, and I picture him bounding out of bed to hit the shower before he goes to the office to wage war. Knowing he's on my side is huge, but he faces a formidable foe in my father.

I make my way back to Claridge's, and I'm almost to the main doors when a photographer waylays me, the flash from his camera temporarily blinding me.

"Jasper, what're you doing in London? Are you shooting a new film? Is Flynn with you?"

I scowl at him and go into the hotel where the security working the door will keep him from following me. Fantastic, now my sisters and mother will know I was in England but didn't call them. This day keeps getting better.

In the lift, I try to think about what I'll say to Ellie. In the short time we've been together, she's become as essential to me as oxygen, and there's a very good chance she's already pregnant with my child. I'll take care of her and the baby. Of course I will. But there's every possibility now that we won't get to have the life we'd hoped for if she's in LA and I'm in London. She's far too close to her family to follow me into an uncertain future half a world away from everyone else she loves.

This must be what it's like to stare down an executioner, knowing life as you know it is over. I am dead inside at the thought of disappointing the woman I love.

She thought I was courageous for coming here to face off with my father, but now I have to tell her I was outplayed by a master. I'm ashamed to have to face her, to have to tell her nothing is going to be like we planned. For the first time ever, I'm also ashamed of the lifestyle that has always brought me such pleasure. I'm furious with myself for naively thinking I could go about my life without a worry about how my choices would catch up to me one day.

Now that day has come, and I'm faced with an impossible choice. Fight for the life I want so desperately, or do what has always been expected of me. If I wage war against my father, people I love will be harmed, perhaps irreparably, and I can't live with that possibility, no matter how much it hurts to picture a life without Ellie and the child I've come to want so desperately.

I return to the room defeated, laid low and humiliated. I've never felt like more of a failure in my life. Before I go in to see Ellie, I stash the photos in my messenger bag. I hope she never sees them. I hope no one ever sees them.

In the bedroom, I sit on the edge of the bed and stare down at her lovely face for a long time before I lean over to kiss her awake. "Ellie, my love," I whisper. "Wake up."

Her eyes flutter open and sparkle with joy when she sees that I'm back. "How'd it go?"

"Not so great."

That's all it takes to dim her joy. "What happened?"

CHAPTER 19

Ellie

With one look at him, I can tell that something is very wrong. His face, which was relaxed after our lovemaking on the plane, is now tight with tension, and his brows are drawn together in a frown that's so contrary to his normally upbeat and amused expression, I barely recognize him.

I push myself up against the pillows and take hold of his hands. "Tell me. Whatever it is, just tell me, and we'll face it together."

"He has photos." He swallows hard and diverts his gaze as if he's ashamed. "Of me and us."

"W-what kind of photos?"

"Me in every sort of compromising position you can imagine, and us at Black Vice as well as the pizza place in Venice and kissing on your front porch."

As if I've been gut-punched, the air leaves my body in a whoosh.

"I've talked to Emmett," he says quickly, perhaps trying to keep me from totally freaking out, "and he's working it from his end and seeing what our options are. My father has been having me followed since I left home."

I think about my parents, my sisters, my brother, my nieces and nephews seeing photos of me in a sex club online, and I'm suddenly and viciously nauseated. "Oh my God, Jasper. *Oh my God!*"

"Ellie, darling, listen. I'll give him what he wants before I'll let him or anyone hurt you. No one will see those photos. I swear to you. I'll do whatever it takes to protect you."

"*At what expense?*" The words are ripped from my soul. "You being forced to live a life that's all about obligation and nothing to do with love or joy or passion?"

He draws me into his embrace. "I'll figure it out. One way or the other, I'll figure it out, and I will protect you and our child."

"No!" I push him away, even though that's the last thing I want to do. I'm just so furious, I feel like I could commit murder on his behalf. "You're *not* going to give in to him. I don't care what we have to do, but you are *not* giving in."

"Darling, it's not that simple."

I meet his gaze, and I hope he can see every bit of what I feel for him in my determination. "It is absolutely that simple."

"He's not screwing around, El. If I call his bluff, he'll come out swinging. If the pictures of us at Black Vice become public, it'll devastate you and your family."

"How did he get someone in there?"

"Believe me, that's one of many questions we'll be trying to answer in the coming days. In the meantime, I need to get back to LA. Can I take a rain check on high tea?" His sweet smile is in stark contrast to the weariness I see in his eyes.

I don't tell him that I've been to high tea at Claridge's—many times, in fact, when we spent the summer I was thirteen in London while my father shot a film here. I don't tell him because I've never been to high tea at Claridge's with *him*. "Yes, you can, but I'm going to cash in that rain check the next time we're here."

"Of course, love." He says the words I want to hear, but I can tell his heart is not in them. Not like it was before he saw his father.

"We *will* be back here again. Many times, probably, for London premieres and the many more BAFTAs you and the Quantum team will win. We'll be here to see your sisters and your mother. We'll be back, and you'll take me to high tea at Claridge's, damn it." Before he can say anything, I put my arms around his neck and draw him into a kiss. I'm throwing everything I have at him, my words, my body, my heart and my soul. I can only hope it'll be enough.

He withdraws slowly from the kiss, leaning his forehead against mine. "There's one thing we need to do right away, my love."

I'm comforted by the fact that he still calls me that. Perhaps that means he still loves me as much as I love him. "What's that?"

"We need to tell Flynn about us."

"Oh. We do? Right now?"

"I'm afraid so. I know you wanted to wait and keep it private for a while longer, but if we're to put up a fight against my father, Flynn will need to be involved. I don't want him to stumble upon the news that we've been trying to make a baby. We should tell him that ourselves. Don't you agree?"

Nodding, I say, "Yes, I agree, and I don't care if he knows. I don't care if the whole world knows. Let's call him."

"It's five in the morning in LA. You'll scare the hell out of him if you call him now."

"Will we be able to call him from the plane?"

"Probably not. We'll be too high up and over the ocean for the first half of the trip."

"Then let's call him now." I make sure all the important parts of me are covered by the sheet, reach for my phone, click on the Face-Time app and call my brother.

He answers with a grunt, and I'm treated to the sight of him and his wife wrapped around each other like human pretzels. Okay, so maybe FaceTime wasn't the best idea. I show the phone to Jasper, and he smiles.

"Flynn, wake up."

"I'm awake. What's wrong? Why are you calling me in the middle of the night, El?"

"It's not the middle of the night where I am."

"Where are you?"

"In London with Jasper."

After a long pause, he says, "Why are you in London with Jasper?"

"Because I'm in love with him, and we're having a baby together."

"*You're pregnant?*" Natalie lets out a squeal, pops up and the covers drop to nearly expose her bare breasts. Thankfully, she catches the sheet before we see her assets.

I smile at Jasper, who watches me with an unreadable expression. "I don't know. Maybe. I hope so."

"This is huge news!" Natalie says. "You dirty dogs! How did you manage to keep this hidden from all of us?"

"It's a relatively new development."

"Where is he?" Flynn asks in a clipped tone that puts me on edge.

"Right here with me."

"Put him on."

"Flynn..."

"Put him on, Ellie."

Grimacing at Jasper, I turn my phone toward him.

"Flynn."

"Jasper. Are you in love with my sister?"

He takes hold of my hand. "I am. I have been for a long time."

My heart does backflips and cartwheels as I listen to him profess his love for me in that accent I could listen to all damned day and never grow tired of. Jasper Autry is in love with me. I need a fan because it's getting warm in here.

There's another long pause as we wait to hear what Flynn will say. "Well, why the hell didn't you say so before now?"

"That's complicated and between your sister and me."

"Fair enough, but there are things we need to talk about."

"Yes, there are. In fact, you'll be hearing from Emmett about some of them this morning."

"What does he have to do with anything?"

"I'll let him tell you. We're on our way back to LA shortly. We'll talk when I get to the office."

"You're goddamned right we will."

I take the phone from Jasper and stare at the face looking back at me. He may be world-famous, but he'll always be my baby brother. "Be nice, Flynn."

"You woke me up at five on a Saturday morning to tell me you're hooking up with my partner and making a baby. How nice do you expect me to be?"

"Don't worry, Ellie," Natalie says. "I'll take care of him."

Flynn waggles his brows. "Mmm, yes, you will."

"I'm outta here. See you later." I press the End button before I see something that can't be unseen. To Jasper, I say, "That went as well as could be expected."

"I know he's your baby brother, darling, but he's an awful pain in the arse sometimes."

"You're telling me? Believe me, I know, but his heart is in the right place."

"Usually."

"Thank God for Natalie. She keeps him under control."

"I have to say, I'm still surprised by how hard and fast he fell for her. I never thought I'd see the day."

"But you're happy for him, right?"

"Of course I am. I'm thrilled for both of them. No one deserves it more than they do."

"You do. You deserve to be happy, too."

He shrugs. "We don't always get what we want in this life. I've been resigned to that reality for as long as I can remember." Filled with restless energy, he gets up and crosses the room to look out the window. I can see the tension in the set of his shoulders.

Though I'm naked, I get up and go to him, wrapping my arms around his waist. At first he tenses, but then he relaxes ever so slightly. "That's bullshit. You're in charge of your own destiny, Jasper. We all are. No one can make you do anything you don't want to do."

"I wish that were entirely true, darling. You have no idea how much I wish that were true. Everything feels so out of control all of a sudden."

"Not everything. If it's control you need, control me."

"I'd be afraid to touch you right now. I'm too filled with rage and a million other unpleasant emotions."

"I'm not afraid of you or your rage. You would never hurt me."

"I can't be sure of that right now."

"I'm sure of it—now and always." I raise my hands to his shoulders and run them down his arms to grasp his hands. "Come to bed with me, Jasper. Be with me."

"We don't have time. I have to get back to LA to deal with this nightmare he's unleashed on me."

"We have time, and Emmett is already working on a solution. You're not in this alone. Not anymore." I urge him to turn to face me, and the yearning I see in his expression goes straight to my overcommitted heart. Raising my hands to his face, I draw him into a kiss that goes from sweet to smoking hot in about two seconds. He devours me. There's no other word for it. His obvious hunger for me is incredibly arousing. I wrap my arms around him, offering him everything I have to give. "Take me, Jasper. I'm yours."

"You don't know what you do to me. You have no fucking idea."

I swallow hard. "I think I might."

Then he kisses me, harder and more desperately than he ever has before. In some ways, I feel like I'm infusing him with my strength and determination to get through this challenge. Maybe if I'm strong enough for both of us, we can come out on the other side together. Other than the baby I hope we've already created, the only thing I want is a chance at a life with him.

We come down on the bed in a tangle of limbs, and he continues to kiss me as if his life depends upon it. After more heated kisses, he moves from my lips to my neck, kissing a path down the front of me.

"As I recall," he says gruffly, "we have a pesky plug to deal with before we can be on our way back to LA."

The intense control I hear in his tone is all it takes to set me on fire for him. He's back in charge, and I wouldn't have it any other way.

"Hands over your head, love."

While complying with his instruction, I break out in goose bumps as the cool air caresses my heated skin.

He is effortlessly sexy in the way he touches me, looks at me, teases me. Everything he does is with the ultimate purpose of making me crazy with lust. I've never been like this with any other man. I'm usually bored or distracted or making my grocery list while enduring a man's touch. I had bigger and better orgasms by myself than with any of them.

With *this* man, however, there's no room in my brain for anything other than him and the way he makes me feel. The orgasms I have with him are nothing less than life changing.

Of course he can't just remove the plug and get on with our day. No, he has to make a production out of it, kissing a path up the inside of my leg while he tugs and releases the plug so many times, I'm about to come from the sheer power of the anticipation he arouses in me. No matter how anxious I get waiting to see what he will do, I know now that whatever happens will be amazing.

Kneeling between my legs, he drags his tongue from the base of the plug to my clit, sucking it into his mouth and then releasing it in time with the push-pull of the plug. "Don't come."

The reminder that he controls my pleasure draws a choppy-sounding sob from me. It's sheer torture to try to control my body's natural responses to what he's doing.

"You can do it, love." He continues to lick and suck and tease me by putting pressure on the plug before withdrawing it almost completely and then reseating it.

I'm writhing on the bed, wanting to get closer to him, but needing relief, too. "Please..."

"What do you want? Tell me what you need."

"You know!"

"Tell me anyway."

"You're enjoying this too much." When I go to push back my hair from my face, I realize my body is bathed in perspiration.

"Is there such a thing as enjoying this *too* much?"

"Yes! When you're torturing your partner."

"Ahhh, my love, this is not torture. If you want to experience torture, I'd be happy to show you if you'd like."

I moan in frustration. I can't imagine anything more torturous than trying not to come while he sucks hard on my clit and tugs on the plug in my ass. My legs are shaking violently from the effort to hold back.

"Does my darling want relief?" he whispers as he pushes two fingers into me, curling them to reach the place that always makes me detonate.

"Yes!"

"Not yet." He withdraws his fingers and continues to torment me for so long that I lose track of time and place and reality. I'm just one big nerve ending on the verge of cataclysmic explosion. He plays me like a maestro, seeming to know the exact second when I'm about to reach the point of no return. That's when he backs off and starts over again.

Tears stain my face, my nose is running, and I might've been concerned about how unhinged I must look to him if all my concentration wasn't required to follow his orders.

"Do you love me?" he asks.

"Yes," I cry, hiccupping on a sob. "You know I do."

"Tell me."

"I love you, Jasper. I love you so much. I'd do anything for you."

"Will you come for me?"

"Yes, *yes!*"

"Soon, darling."

I dissolve into tears, not because I'm sad but because the emotional overload is too much to contain. I hear the click and the sound of liquid. Through my tears I can see he's stroking his long, thick cock as he looks down at me with eyes gone dark with desire.

He pulls gently on the plug. "I want you here, my love. Tell me you want me, too."

"I want you, Jasper. I want you so bad."

CHAPTER 20

Ellie

A low groan rumbles from his chest as he withdraws the plug and tosses it aside. He immediately presses his cock against my ass, pushing insistently until my body yields to allow him in. "Relax, love. Push back. Let me in."

I want to laugh at him telling me to relax, but I can't laugh or breathe or speak.

His fingers press against my clit, and just that quickly, I'm right back on the edge of release.

I grasp the rails of the headboard so tightly, my fingers feel like they could break from the strain.

"Easy, my darling. Breathe."

I suck in a deep, restorative breath.

"That's it. That's my girl."

"Jasper." His name is ripped from my chest, a plea, a pledge, a promise.

"I'm right here. You feel so good. So hot and so tight." He grasps my ass cheeks and angles my body toward him. He's staring down at the sight of his cock buried in my ass. "I wish you could see how amazing we look together."

"Please, please, *please*..." I think I might be drooling now, too, but I can't let go of the headboard out of fear I might lose complete control.

He presses hard against my clit. "Come, love."

The orgasm rocks my entire body as my muscles strain and seize. It goes on for what seems like forever, and I'm aware of him fucking me harder now, hammering into me in deep strokes until he's coming, too, thrusting into me one last time before coming down on top of me, his cock throbbing in my ass.

Oh my God. Oh my God. Oh my God.

When he kisses me softly, wipes away my tears and whispers sweet words of comfort, I realize I said the words out loud. I'm floating in this odd state of suspended animation. I know where I am and who I'm with, but I can't seem to move or think or do anything more involved than breathe.

After a long moment of silence, Jasper begins to withdraw from me, and I cry out from the friction against my abused flesh. "Easy... Nice and easy." He gets off the bed and goes into the bathroom.

My eyes close when I hear water running, and then he's back with a warm towel that he uses to wipe my face and then my body. I whimper when the terrycloth drags against my sensitive nipples and again when he wipes between my legs.

Tossing the towel aside, he reaches for my hands and brings them back by my sides. "You were amazing, my love. *That* was incredible."

"I've never, I didn't... I didn't know..."

"Shhh," he says, brushing his lips over mine. "I didn't know it could be like that either. It's never been like this for me." He continues to kiss my lips, my face, even my chin. "Are you hurting?"

I shake my head. I'm so blissed out that I doubt I'd even know if something hurt.

He offers me a bottle of water, and once again I take deep sips of the cold liquid.

"Just so you know," he says after we share most of the water, "I'd planned to come back here and pack you up to head home."

"Well, *I* certainly didn't plan *that*."

"It's you. You make me crazy. You make me forget all about my father blackmailing me and the urgent need to get home to figure this out. I take one look at you, and I forget about everything else."

"You seem to have the same effect on me."

He makes soothing circles on my back as we lie in bed, pretending we have nothing better to do.

"Do you ever worry…" I'm not sure how to ask what I want to know.

"Do I worry about what?"

"That you'll be bored if you only have one woman for the rest of your life."

"If that one woman is you, I'll never be bored."

"How you can know that for certain? We've been together only a short time, and you were with so many women before."

"And none of them was to me what you are. None of them even came close. I was just killing time until you asked me to father your baby."

"I did not ask you to father my baby. You volunteered."

His low chuckle makes me smile. "I was afraid afterward that maybe I seemed a little *too* willing."

"You were just willing enough to make me believe you were sincere."

He cups my ass cheek and squeezes gently. "I'm extremely sincere where you're concerned."

I cling to him, nuzzling my nose into his neck to breathe in the clean, crisp smell of his cologne. "We're going to fight for this, Jasper. We're going to fight with everything we have. I've waited my whole life for you. I'm not letting you go."

"I'm terrified of my father doing something to cause you or your family harm. I wouldn't be able to bear that."

"My family and I are stronger than he could ever imagine. Don't worry about us. We've weathered lots of storms with three members of our family in the public eye. This isn't our first rodeo. Do you remember the starlet that accused my father of attacking her on a film set about fifteen years ago?"

"What? No! I've never heard a bad word said about your dad—or your mum."

"It was awful. My parents were enraged, and the Hollywood press was relentless until it was proven that my father wasn't even there the day she said it happened. She was completely discredited and run out of town, but the scandal took a toll. It took months for my parents to laugh and smile again. I'll never forget it. That's when I realized that an accusation, even an unfounded accusation, can ruin a life."

"I don't want my crap to rain down on you and your family, Ellie. That would be the worst thing that could happen."

"No, the worst thing would be you having to be anywhere other than with me."

He releases a deep sigh. "I hate to say that we really do need to go home."

"I know." But rather than release him, I hold on tighter while I still can. An awful feeling of dread fills me as we hold each other. Now that I've had this amazing time with him, what would I ever do without him?

Jasper

We sleep most of the flight back to LA and arrive rested in the early evening, refreshed and ready to do battle. I hope to God that Emmett has come up with a plan while we were in the air. I'm so intent on getting to the office, that I don't take the time to check my phone. Whatever Emmett has told my partners, I want to wait to talk to them in person rather than by text or email.

I realize my mistake when reporters and photographers swarm us in the Burbank airport. *What the fuck?*

"Jasper, is it true? Are you Henry Kingsley's son and heir?"

"Are you leaving Quantum to run Kingsley Enterprises?"

"How have you kept that secret all these years?"

"Do Flynn and Hayden know about your bloodline and your billions?"

A thousand scenarios cycle through my mind as I cling to Ellie, who's tucked up against my side, her head down and her face, hopefully, shielded from the photographers.

"Hey!" one of them shouts. "That's Flynn's sister! What's her name? She works for them!"

"Jasper, are you with Flynn's sister? How long have you been together?"

I tighten my hold on her and power through the scrum. We're nearly to the main door when I see Gordon Yates, our director of security in LA, come running in with a few of his guys. I've never been so happy to see anyone. Like a military unit, they surround and escort us into an SUV that's waiting at the curb. I'll deal with my car later. Apparently, I have much bigger concerns at the moment.

"What the fuck is going on?" I ask when Gordon has us sealed off from the melee. As the SUV pulls away from the curb, they follow us, banging on the windows. "How do they know everything?"

"Your father gave an interview about his upcoming jaunt," Gordon says in a clipped tone. A former Marine, Gordon carries his tall, muscular frame with military bearing, and he still wears his blond hair in a boot-camp buzz. "He was asked if he's concerned about the future of his company if something should happen to him. He waxed poetic about his son and heir, Academy Award-winning cinematographer Jasper Autry, who works under his mother's maiden name so as not to capitalize on the Kingsley name." Gordon withdraws his phone from his pocket and reads from his screen. "'Everything my son has accomplished, he's done entirely on his own, and I couldn't be more chuffed. But he's also well aware of what's expected of him in the future. I can pursue my passions in peace knowing my family and business will be properly cared for should the worst happen.'"

"That son of a bitch," I whisper. I'm stunned but not as surprised as I should be that he's found a way to let me know he fully intends to deliver on his threats unless I fall in line.

Ellie takes my hand and holds it between both of hers. "So what if people know who you really are? That doesn't change anything."

"It's a firestorm, though," Gordon says grimly. "The swarm at the airport is only the start. The offices are surrounded, and they're staking out your homes in the city and at the beach."

"We'll go to my place, then," Ellie says.

"I'm sure that by the time you get there, they'll be waiting for you," Gordon says.

I sense her panic and want nothing more than to reassure her.

"We're taking you to Kristian's place in the city," Gordon tells us. "It has underground parking, and he's made the apartment available to you both for as long as you need it."

That tells me they think we're in for a siege.

"The others are meeting you there to figure out next steps," Gordon says.

I watch the city go by in a blur outside the SUV's darkened windows. "He's blackmailing me." I can hear the weariness in my own tone. I wonder if they can, too.

"Excuse me?" Gordon says, his brows narrowing.

"My father is blackmailing me. He has pictures of me from the time I left home right up to this week, pictures that would ruin my career and reputation as well as Ellie's." I can't add that he has pictures of the other Quantum principals, too. Not in front of Ellie.

"How... What..."

"I have no idea, but he has them, and it's bad, Gordon. As bad as it gets." I look him directly in the eye, hoping to convey that it's far worse than I'm able to say in mixed company.

His mouth falls open before he snaps it shut. As our director of security, he's going to take this breach harder than anyone. I also have no doubt that he'll work harder than anyone to ferret out the mole in our midst. We're quiet the rest of the way to Kristian's place on the top floor of a high-rise in Hollywood, which has undergone a renaissance of sorts in recent years.

While it's not the most exclusive neighborhood in the city, Kristian likes the easy access to the office, downtown and his place at the beach. Thinking about things such as why Kristian chooses to live here rather than the more obvious choices of Silver Lake, Beverly Hills or Los Feliz gives me something to think about other than the potential disaster hanging over our heads.

My cell phone rings, and I glance at the caller ID. Mother. I take the call, because I always take her calls, no matter what. "Hello, Mother."

"Jasper, I'm appalled that your father would do this to you," she says without preamble. Her anger is palpable even with almost six thousand miles between us.

And she has no idea what else he's trying to do to me. "It is appalling, but sadly not surprising. I went to see him."

"When?"

"Yesterday, or was it today? I've lost track of the time zones. I'm back in LA now."

"You didn't mention you were coming."

"It was a last-minute thing. I wanted to see him before he takes off on his latest quest for world domination."

"He's a fool."

"On that we agree."

"I take it the visit didn't go well?"

My bark of laughter is filled with irony.

She sighs. "And now he's lashing out."

"You could say that. He's actually blackmailing me with photographs that would be extremely embarrassing to me and others if they were to be released."

"*Blackmailing you?* Over what?"

"Over my resignation as his heir."

"You told him..."

"That I'm not coming back to London. Ever. My career and my life are in Los Angeles." I smile at Ellie as I say that. "I want to have a wife and children who are not burdened by the weight of obligation from the day they are born. I want *my* life. Not his."

"Finally," she says. "I've been hoping for years that you'd take a stand."

Her confession shocks me. "You never said so."

"You had to get there on your own. I couldn't and wouldn't suggest it. I'm walking a fine line between the two of you. I always have."

"He's out to ruin me, Mother." *And others I care about, my closest mates, my partners, my family.*

"That's not going to happen. You leave him to me."

"I'm not sure anyone can change his mind about this, even you."

"Don't be so certain. I'm on my way to London today to see him before he leaves. I'll take care of it."

"While I'd never doubt your ability to influence him, I hope you'll understand that his threats are serious enough that I feel compelled to take my own action to protect myself and the people I love."

"You do whatever you feel you must. And when you're ready, bring your lady love to see me."

Her support and kindness restore my faith somewhat. "I will. Thank you, Mother."

"No thanks needed. Be well, Jasper. I'll be in touch."

After the line goes dead, I glance at Ellie, who is smiling.

"Am I allowed to say that I love your mum?"

"She's the bee's knees. Always has been, and thank God for that. Without her to give some balance, he would've driven me completely off my trolley." I've never told my mother, my sisters, or anyone for that matter, about some of the tactics my father employed to keep me in line. Those "tactics" left scars on my soul that I carry with me to this day.

"Off your trolley?" she asks, her brow raised.

"Crazy. Mad. Nuts."

"Ahhh, gotcha. I can't wait to meet her."

Ellie's unwavering conviction along with my mother's determination have given me something I've been sorely lacking since the meeting with my father—hope.

CHAPTER 21

Jasper

We arrive to chaos at Kristian's. Apparently, a pipe has broken in his kitchen, and he's desperately trying to contain a flood.

"Let me." Ellie runs toward the kitchen, grabs a wrench that Kristian left on the counter, drops to the floor and shimmies under the sink. Watching her, I'm incredibly aroused by how sexy she looks as she cranks the wrench and gets the water to stop, but not before she gets completely soaked in the process.

"That was amazing," Kristian says, stunned by her competence.

I'm ridiculously proud—and randy—as she emerges from under the sink, her white T-shirt clinging to her lovely breasts.

Kristian hands her a towel and looks away from her wet T-shirt while I continue to stare.

"How'd you learn to do that?" he asks.

Ellie wipes her face with the towel. "Saturday mornings at Home Depot. You'd be amazed what you can learn how to do in a couple of hours."

"I'm seriously impressed," Kristian says. "And extremely grateful. A flood on the top floor doesn't bode well for friendly relations with the neighbors below."

"Our stuff is in Gordon's car," I say. "Could you loan her something dry?"

"Of course." Kristian disappears into his bedroom, leaving us alone in the kitchen.

"That was rather brilliant, my love. I'm also very impressed."

She shrugs off the praise. "I like knowing how to do stuff."

This woman can afford to hire someone to do anything she needs done, but she'd rather do it herself. If I weren't already gobsmacked by her, I would be now.

Kristian returns with a T-shirt for Ellie, and she ducks into the half bath off the kitchen to change. "How bad is it?" he asks, cutting right to the chase when we're alone.

"Worst case."

To his credit, my closest friend doesn't seem angry with me, though he has every good reason to be. I'm not sure how I'd feel if my sexual preferences were being used to blackmail one of my partners.

"Whatever you're thinking," he says as he uses a couple of beach towels to mop up the water on the floor, "stuff it. You didn't cause this. You're a victim just like the rest of us."

"I dragged you all into it."

He looks up at me, his brow raised. "By being born?"

The utter ridiculousness of it all hits me then, and I release an uneasy laugh. "Something like that."

His dark hair is mussed when he stands upright, his blue eyes heated with what might be rage, but it's not directed at me. "Whoever sold us out is going to regret the day they ever tangled with the Quantum partners."

His show of support means more to me than I'll ever be able to tell him. "I haven't said anything to Ellie about the rest of you being dragged in. That's not up to me."

"Understood."

Flynn arrives a short time later, with two nieces and three nephews in tow. Kristian invites them to check out his game room while Flynn gives me a wary look that, knowing him, probably has more to do with my relationship with his sister than the threat of his secrets being made public. "Jasper."

"Flynn."

We circle each other like rabid dogs. "Where's my sister?"

"In the loo getting changed after saving Kris from catastrophe."

Kristian brings him up to speed on the near-flood. "Your sister is Wonder Woman."

"Not sure I'd go that far," Ellie says when she joins us wearing a much bigger shirt than the one that got wet. I miss the wet one. She greets her brother with a kiss to his cheek. "Behave yourself, or I'll beat the shit out of you."

"As if you could," Flynn says with a huff of indignation.

"I wouldn't mess with her after what we just witnessed," Kristian says.

I nod in agreement. "Seriously. She's amazing."

Ellie rolls her eyes at our effusiveness, but I can tell she's enjoying the well-deserved praise. "You need to get a plumber in here to replace that pipe."

"The super called the emergency line, and someone is on their way. I hate to think about what might've happened if you hadn't gotten here when you did."

"No problem." To Flynn, she says, "Where's Nat?"

"She's picking up Aileen and the kids at the airport."

I notice Kristian perks right up at the mention of Natalie's friend from New York, who'd been fighting breast cancer when Flynn met Natalie. He used his connections to get her in with some of the best doctors in New York, and she's been doing much better. We're looking forward to seeing her and her kids for the first time since Flynn and Nat's wedding last month. I realize that no one is looking forward to seeing her more than Kristian is.

Interesting.

Hayden and Addie arrive with Emmett, Marlowe and her assistant, Leah, in tow. Now that they're all here, I can no longer postpone the inevitable meeting with my partners.

"We need a few minutes alone," Kristian says. His meaning is clear—partners only. Ellie and Addie have worked for us long enough to know that occasionally we have to tend to business that is confidential. Leah, who has been with Marlowe for more than a month now, is starting to catch on, too.

Ellie gives my arm a squeeze before she joins Addie and Leah on the sofa in the living room. The rest of us follow Kristian into his home office.

I pull the photos out of my satchel and hand them over to Emmett, who studies each one before passing it on.

"Motherfucker," Hayden whispers when he sees the one of himself and Addie at Black Vice. Their embrace is relatively innocent, but behind them, a sub is bent over a spanking bench while her master wields a flogger. "You really think your father would actually release these photos if you don't fall in line?"

"I really do."

"Jesus. And I thought my family was fucked up."

Flynn stares down at the photo of Ellie and me that was taken at Black Vice. The muscle pulsing in his jaw ramps up my anxiety. "What're our options, Em?"

Emmett runs through the series of actions he's already taken, including requesting an injunction in London that would prohibit Henry Kingsley from releasing the damaging photos. Due to the international element at play here, it's tricky but not impossible, Emmett reports.

"I appreciate what you all are doing and how well you're taking this serious breach of your privacy, but I'm not willing to risk it. I'll give him what he wants. I'll resign my partnership at Quantum—"

"No," Marlowe says, "you won't." With her red hair contained in a ponytail and her face devoid of makeup, you'd never know she's one of the top box office draws in Hollywood. However, right now, right here, she's my friend and partner, and her green eyes are ablaze with anger. "You won't make that kind of sacrifice on my behalf. I'm a big girl. If those photos get out, I'll deal with it, but I don't expect you to abandon your life and career to protect me."

"Neither do I," Kristian says, his gaze steely and determined.

Hayden hesitates, and I know he's thinking of Addie and not himself. "I don't want that either. I can't imagine this job or life without you smack in the middle of it. You've got to fight him."

All eyes turn to Flynn, who is staring at a photo of him and Natalie taken at Club Quantum. He looks at me. "Is my sister pregnant?"

"I hope so."

"*Whoa*," Marlowe says. "How about bringing me up to speed?"

"Seriously," Kristian says. "What the hell?"

"Jasper?" Flynn says with a smirk that makes me want to punch him—except that maybe, if we can get through this nightmare, he might one day be my brother-in-law. I contain the urge.

"When we were in Mexico, Ellie told me she wants to have a baby. She said she's tired of waiting for Mr. Right to come along, and time is running out. I offered to help her. One thing led to another, and we've both confessed to having had feelings for each other for a long time."

"Holy shit," Marlowe says. "How'd we miss this?"

"I always sort of suspected," Flynn says.

I scoff at him. "You did not."

"I did, too! She looks at you a lot when you're not aware, and you do the same. If you don't believe me, ask Natalie. I told her there was something brewing long before you woke me in the middle of the night to confirm it."

Now I'm gobsmacked for a whole other reason. I thought I'd been so subtle about my affection for her. Apparently not so much if Flynn picked up on it.

"So she's already pregnant?" Marlowe asks.

"We hope so. We've been giving the project a tremendous amount of effort."

"Not another word," Flynn says, holding up his hand, "or I won't be responsible for my actions."

Though I'm still heavily burdened by anxiety and the fear of what might happen if the photos are made public, I can't help but laugh at the face he makes.

"The way I see it," Flynn says, "the only place you belong is right here with my sister and my future niece or nephew."

"I couldn't agree more," I tell him, thankful for his support and friendship.

"Then we'll fight," Flynn says. "We'll fight with everything we've got, and if the worst happens, we'll deal with it. But no one is going anywhere."

"I can't tell you what it means to me…" My throat closes around a lump. I look down at the floor while I try to get my emotions under control.

"You're one of us, Jasper," Hayden says. "And when one of us is threatened, we all are. The far bigger issue, in my opinion, is who the fuck took those photos and how the fuck did they get into our club and Devon's?"

"Sebastian and I are already working that angle, and we're going to loop Gordon in, too," Emmett says. "Believe me, Sebastian is as enraged as you are to hear we've had a breach, and he doesn't even know the full extent."

"There's no chance…" Kristian shakes his head. "Never mind."

"What were you going to say, Kris?" Marlowe asks.

"Nothing. Doesn't matter."

"You're wondering about Sebastian, aren't you?" Hayden addresses the question to Kristian, who winces. "Let me assure you, there's no fucking way he'd ever roll on us. Not after everything we've done for him."

"And I know that," Kris says. "That's why I didn't say it."

"Despite his past, he's one of us," Hayden says of his childhood friend. "He'd never have anything to do with harming us."

"I'm sorry to have even had the thought," Kristian says.

"Everyone is suspect until they aren't," Flynn says.

"Not Sebastian," Hayden says, glaring at Flynn.

"We'll get Gordon on it," Emmett says. "Let's give his people a chance to fully investigate before we start tossing around accusations."

"Agreed," Kristian says.

"Someone needs to talk to Devon and give him a heads-up," I say. "If his security teams up with ours, we might figure this out sooner rather than later."

"I'll talk to him," Hayden says.

We adjourn to join the others, who now include Natalie, Aileen and her children Logan and Maddie, both of whom have grown since they were last here. They immediately run off with Ellie's nieces and nephews who want to show them Kristian's game room.

Aileen looks a thousand times better than she did a month ago, and I'm not the only one who notices. Kristian goes to her, as if he can't *not* go to her. With everyone watching, he kisses her cheek and gives her a hug that leaves her flustered and flushed.

"It's so good to see you," he says.

Aileen offers him a shy smile. "You, too."

"You look fantastic," Marlowe says, pushing Kristian aside to hug Aileen.

"I feel fantastic." Her blonde hair is still thin after a recent round of chemo, but her brown eyes are alive with excitement, which is a marked improvement.

"Do you want to take the kids to the pool on the roof?" Kris asks.

"They'd love that," Aileen replies, glancing quickly at him before redirecting her gaze. "They're full of energy after the long flight."

"Let's all go up," Natalie says.

"I brought all the food and booze we were going to have at their house," Addie says, using her thumb to point to Flynn and Natalie. "We're overrun with reporters outside the gate, so we moved the party."

"Oh good," I say, "thanks for arranging everything."

"That's my job!"

Ellie comes over to me, begins to put her arm around me, and then appears to think better of it. "Everything okay?" she asks, looking up at me with a crease in her brow that lets me know she's worried. I hate that she's worried. I hate that my father has given her reason to be.

I put my arm around her and kiss the top of her head. "It's all right, darling. They all know now."

"Oh," she says, adorably flustered.

"He calls you *dahhling*," Leah says, fanning her face. "How do you not spontaneously come every time he says that?"

Her question is met with stunned silence followed by screaming laughter.

"Crap." Leah covers her mouth with her hand. "I can't believe I said that out loud."

"I can." Natalie shakes her head in amusement.

"PS," Ellie says with a wink for Leah, "it's all I can do not to."

Now it's my turn to be mortified as the others howl with laughter. But the embarrassment quickly fades, replaced by elation that Ellie and I have now officially gone public as a couple. The rousing support of my partners has also helped to improve my dour mood. We're far from out of the woods, but between Emmett's efforts and my mother's, the kernel of hope continues to burn bright within me.

The gathering at Kristian's pool turns into a party that's made raucous by seven excited kids. My nieces and nephews pick right up where they left off with Logan and Maddie after Flynn and Natalie's wedding.

While Flynn plays lifeguard for the kids, Marlowe, Natalie, Addie, Aileen and Leah corner me at one of the tables. "What?" I ask between bites of corn chips and delicious pineapple salsa.

"You've been holding out on us," Marlowe says. "You and Jasper? Making plans *and* a baby?"

I look over at him, sitting next to the pool with Emmett and Kristian. Hayden is actually in the pool with the kids, leading a loud game of basketball. Though Jasper is with his friends, I can see he's a million miles away, the weight of his worries heavy upon his shoulders.

"It's, um, well, still very new."

"Not according to Flynn," Natalie says. "He claims it's been coming on for a while now."

"And of course he'd know better than Jasper and me."

She laughs. "He thinks he knows better, but I've sort of noticed a vibe, if you will... Call me crazy..."

"You're not crazy." I feel my face get warm with embarrassment, which is funny because I'm never embarrassed when talking to my friends about guys. Until this guy. "There's been a vibe for a while now."

"I *love* you two together," Marlowe says.

"Really?"

"God, yes. It's a perfect match."

"It feels sort of perfect, or it did until he saw his father and now... It feels sort of tenuous." My stomach hurts at the thought of what could still happen if his father makes good on his threats. I'd gotten sort of used to the idea of raising our child with Jasper.

"He'll figure something out." Marlowe's confidence gives me a badly needed boost. She is rarely ever wrong about anything. "Here he comes now with Flynn. They're coming in hot."

While the others laugh, I notice a new pep to Jasper's step and a renewed sense of determination in the way he carries himself.

"Flynn has an idea we want to run by you," he says when they stop next to the table where I'm sitting with the girls.

"I'm listening."

Jasper's gaze darts from me to the others.

"It's okay," I tell him. "We're all in this together."

"You bet your ass we are," Marlowe says. "Let's hear it."

"An interview with Carolyn Justice," Flynn says. "We'll give her a huge exclusive on why Jasper kept his pedigree a secret for all this time, how no one ever found out, why his father spilled the beans, and how Jasper has no plans to return to London now or ever."

"It sounds like a good idea." I look up at Jasper. "What do you think?"

"It's a great idea, and it would knock the legs right out of my father's plan to blackmail me. But Flynn thinks it would be more powerful if you did the interview with me. How would you feel about that?"

"I told you I'd do anything I could to help you, up to and including doing an interview on national TV." As I say the words, a flurry of nerves attacks my belly. I can go on TV. Of course I can.

"It needs to happen fast," Flynn says. "Henry is due to leave on his trip in two days. If we want him to hear about it before he goes, we need to move."

"What about the deadline?" I ask.

"We talked about that," Jasper says. "I'll call my father's assistant, Nathan, and tell him what they want to hear to buy us the time we need to get the interview done and on the air."

"Will they be able to do it in two days?" I ask.

"When I offer it to Carolyn, I'll tell her that's the condition," Flynn says. From the fierce look in his eyes, I can see that my brother is entirely focused on the challenge at hand, and willing to do whatever it takes to help his friend—and me. "Shall I make the call?" He holds up his cell.

Jasper looks to me, and I nod. "Do it," he says.

I reach for his hand and hold on tight to what I want as much as I want the child I hope we've created together.

"Before you go on TV," Flynn says to me, "you need to talk to Mom and Dad about what's going on." His gaze shifts to include Jasper.

"I know."

"They're coming here later. They had another party to go to, but they said they'd come by."

"I'll talk to them then."

"*We'll* talk to them then," Jasper says, smiling down at me.

My heart flutters from the way he looks at me with so much warmth and affection and love. I've waited my whole life for a man to look at me the way he's looking at me now, and I never want this feeling of joyful elation to stop.

"I'll make the call," Flynn says, heading for a quiet corner of the deck.

Jasper sits next to me on my lounge and puts his arms around me. "Are you okay?"

"I'm good. You?"

"I'll feel better when we manage to neutralize this threat."

"I like Flynn's idea. How do you feel about it?"

"Well, I'm not him, so the idea of being on TV makes me nervous."

I lean my head against his shoulder. "Me, too."

"I'm sorry to put you through this, darling, but I think it's our best chance."

"Could you say that again?" Leah asks.

"Say what?" Jasper replies, sounding perplexed.

"*Dahhhhling.*" She fans her face. "Do you really get to listen to that every day?"

"I really do," I say, smiling at Jasper, who rolls his eyes at the two of us.

Flynn comes back. "We got lucky. Carolyn is in LA. She's coming here with a team at nine."

I blink up at him. "As in *tonight*?"

"As in tonight."

"You ready to go public, *darling*?" He puts extra emphasis on the last word for Leah's sake, and she fans her face again.

"As ready as I'll ever be."

CHAPTER 22

Ellie

My parents arrive at Kristian's about thirty minutes before Carolyn is due. After they say their hellos, Jasper and I ask for a moment alone with them. I can see that Mom is baffled as to why we'd both need to talk to them, but Dad seems less so after nearly catching us together the other night. They come with us into Kristian's office.

"Is everything all right?" Mom asks the second the door closes behind us.

"Everything is fine. In fact," I say, glancing at Jasper, "everything is great. Jasper and I... We, well..."

"We're together now."

I want to kiss him for saying the words for me.

"Oh, well, this is a wonderful development," Dad says, grinning from ear to ear. "How long have you been seeing each other?"

"It's been years now," Jasper's mouth twists into a sly smile as he reaches for my hand. "We've been friends a long time, as you know, and only recently have we both confessed to wanting to be more than friends."

"When we were in Mexico, I told Jasper that I'm tired of waiting for Mr. Right to come along and that I want to have a baby. He offered to help me out with that, and one thing led to another, and..."

"And, we're together."

"You, you're... You're having a baby?"

My mother's unusual stammer makes me want to giggle. "We don't know that yet, but we're hoping so."

"I assume this means you're going to marry my daughter," Dad says in his sternest Dad voice.

"Dad! Stop. This is the new millennium. We don't have to be married to have a baby."

"Now wait just a minute—"

"Max," Jasper says, "I fully intend to marry your daughter, and I'd love to have your blessing."

He does? He would? This is news to me. Not bad news, but news just the same.

"But before I get down on one knee, I have a few things to take care of so I'm free to be what she needs."

"This business with your family," Dad says, nodding.

"Yes." Jasper's sexy mouth is set in a grim expression that I hope to never see again after we get this situation sorted out. I want to see him laughing and smiling and happy and hopeful about the future the way he was before we went to London.

"We were so surprised to hear about your lineage," Mom says. "A future duke, of all things!"

"He's a marquess," I interject, earning a scowl from my beloved.

"Very impressive," Dad says.

"I'm sure it must seem impressive, but it's been mostly *oppressive* to me. I'm not well suited for the role that was predetermined for me before I was born. If I were being asked to tend to only the title and the holdings that come with it, I could handle that. But taking on Kingsley Enterprises, too?" He shakes his head. "It's just not for me."

"Surely something can be worked out with your father."

Of course my dad would think that. He's never been anything other than completely supportive of whatever his four children wished to do with their lives. He has no ability to understand any other sort of father.

"I wish that were the case," Jasper says, "but it's always been all or nothing with him. No gray area whatsoever. In fact," he says, glancing at me, "my father has resorted to blackmail to try to get me to march to his beat."

My parents are shocked speechless by this news.

"We're dealing with it on a number of fronts," Jasper assures them. "Flynn had the brilliant idea for me to do an interview with Carolyn Justice about what's happening to try to cut my father off at the knees." He puts his arm around me. "Ellie and I are doing the interview tonight, and we wanted you to know what's going on before we go public."

"He's *blackmailing* his own *son*?" Dad asks, stupefied.

"I'm afraid so."

"And whatever it is he's holding over you—"

"Would be embarrassing to me and others I care very much about."

"Dear God," Mom says for all of us. "This is an outrage!"

"Welcome to my world," Jasper says ruefully.

"I'm almost ashamed to admit that at times I've envied Henry Kingsley for his daring approach to life and business and adventure," Dad says. "But after hearing all this, any admiration I might've had has been replaced with revulsion." He places a hand on Jasper's shoulder. "You were an honorary member of the Godfrey family long before I knew you love my daughter, and of course you have our blessing to ask her to marry you. You'll always be one of us, Jasper. You fight that son of a bitch with everything you've got, you hear me?"

While I blink back tears, Jasper nods. "I appreciate your support, Max," he says gruffly. "It means the world."

Mom goes up on tiptoes to kiss Jasper's cheek. "We love you, and I'm thrilled to know that you and that yummy accent will be available to read *The Night Before Christmas* to us every year from now on."

Jasper barks out a laugh. "It would be my honor, Stella."

Mom turns to me, smiling widely, and hugs me tight. "Someone has been keeping secrets from her mama."

"I was going to tell you soon. I promise."

"How do I go to Vegas six months a year when there may be a new baby coming?"

"That was one reason why I didn't say anything. I didn't want to influence your decision."

"Why in the world would you do something foolish like that? Max, this is the sign I've been waiting for."

"She has been waiting for a sign," Dad confirms.

"It's not the time for Vegas. There'll be time for that when the grandkids are awful teenagers and we need a break from them."

We share a laugh and more hugs before they leave me alone with Jasper. He puts his arms around me and gathers me into his embrace. I breathe in the intoxicating scent of his cologne as we take comfort from each other.

"That went well, don't you think, darling?"

"It went very well. They already loved you as our friend and Flynn's business partner."

"It's quite something else when a man is telling his lady's parents that he intends to marry their daughter."

"About that…"

His laughter makes me smile. "Did I catch you by surprise?"

"You could say that."

"How can you be surprised that I want it all with you, Estelle Godfrey Junior?"

I playfully scowl at him. "Don't call me that."

"How about just Junior, then?"

"How about just Ellie?"

"How about love of my life, mother of my children, every beat of my heart?"

"Jasper," I whisper, "is this really happening? Do you really feel those things for me?"

"I love you desperately, Ellie. I suspect that I have for quite some time, long before I knew what it was like to hold you and kiss you and make love to you. And now that I've held you in my arms, I can't imagine a time that I'll ever want anything other than more of you."

I raise my hands to his face and draw him into a kiss that's all about the overwhelming love I feel for this man, who's risking everything to be with me. Unlike every man who came before him, I haven't a single doubt about his sincerity. This one is as real as it gets, and I know that my heart will be safe in his hands and my life with him will be filled with love and family and friends and excitement.

He withdraws slowly from the kiss, but keeps his lips close to mine. "I feel guilty for talking about the future before I've taken care of the present. If I ever had to disappoint you—"

I cover his lips with my fingers. "The only way you could disappoint me is if you stopped loving me."

"That's not going to happen."

"No matter where you are, I'll be there with you, whether it's here or in London or Cornwall or whatever. I'm with you, mate."

His eyes dance with love and amusement as he looks down at me. "Spoken by a Los Angeles-born-and-bred woman who's never been to Cornwall."

"Spoken by the woman who loves you no matter where in the world you are."

"Thank you, darling," he whispers, his lips brushing against my neck and setting off a reaction I feel everywhere. "Do you suppose we'd be missed if we take a few more minutes alone?"

"I'm sure we'll be missed and razzed upon our return, but I'm willing to put up with that if you are."

"I'm very, very willing." He grabs hold of my hand and tugs me along behind him into the bathroom that adjoins Kristian's office, kicking the door closed behind us and locking it.

Oh my...

Jasper

My emotions are all over the place—soaring highs, crushing lows and everything in between. The overwhelming support of my partners and Ellie's parents has cemented my resolve to fight my father with every tool in our considerable arsenal. Flynn's idea to do the interview, to steal my father's thunder, is brilliant.

If there's anything Henry hates more than negative publicity, I don't know what it is. Well, he probably hates me most of all right about now, but I can live with that if it means freeing myself from the shackles he's had me in my whole life.

But with my lovely Ellie in my arms, the last thing I want to think about is my father, his threats or those bloody shackles. I'd much prefer to think of shackles of a different kind, the sort in which Ellie is bound to my bed and submitting to me. Since that's not possible right now, I turn her to face the mirror and hold her from behind, running my hands over her sexy body while watching her reactions play out on her expressive face.

I cup her breasts and drag my thumbs over her nipples, watching as her mouth falls open and her eyes widen with desire. I fucking love her sweet face and how it gives away every thought and emotion she experiences. She hides nothing from me, which only makes me love her more than I already do. Lifting her top up and over her head, I fixate on the sight of her breasts contained by the sheer, sexy bra that leaves very little to my fertile imagination.

I release the front clasp and slide the straps down her arms, leaving her bare from the waist up. Her nipples tighten before my eyes, making J.T. so hard he could pound nails.

"Put your hands on the vanity and lean forward."

As she follows my command, she meets my gaze in the mirror, and the slight hint of apprehension I see in her eyes only makes me harder. She knows I would never, ever hurt her, but she's uncertain about what's about to happen. Judging from the glow in her cheeks and the tight buds of her nipples, the apprehension is feeding her arousal.

I drop to my knees behind her and run my hands up the backs of her legs, raising her skirt up and over her bottom. Ah, God, look at that sweet arse with the thong disappearing between her supple cheeks. I could die right now and I'd go happier than I've ever been in my life. I touch my lips to cheeks that are still pink from the spanking on the plane and revel in her gasp.

"Does it hurt?" I ask her.

"No. Just very sensitive."

"I like very sensitive." I drag my finger from the waistband of her thong down into the valley between her cheeks, pressing lightly against her back door. "How about here? Does it hurt?"

"It aches, but in a good way."

I groan at the husky tone in her voice. "So that's something we'll do again?"

"Mmm, maybe not every day, but once in a while."

"I can live with that." I can live with anything as long as I get to live with her. My fingers continue their journey to the front of her, which is hot and wet and swollen. I press against her clit through silk panties that are soaked from her desire. "How about here?"

"Also aching in a good way," she says breathlessly.

Suddenly ravenous for a taste of her, I roughly remove the strings she calls panties and bury my face between her legs. I spread her arse cheeks and leave no part of her unexplored with my tongue. She goes crazy, bucking up against me and crying out every time my tongue circles around her clit.

"Oh God," she says, "I need to come. Please, Jasper..."

Because torturing her is so fun, I don't give in. Not yet. By the time I'm ready to burst myself, her legs are trembling madly and sweat is rolling down her back. I love how real and raw it is with her. I never have a single doubt that she's as into me as I am with her.

It's time to give her what she wants so I can have what I want—my cock, balls-deep in her. I press the flat of my tongue against her clit and drive two fingers into her from behind. Letting my tongue vibrate against her throbbing flesh, I tell her to come.

She explodes, screaming so loud I wonder if they'll hear her up on the roof. Hopefully, the kids are making too much of a racket, and hopefully, no one chose that moment to come looking for us. I bring her down softly, gently, calming her until she sags against the vanity, her legs still shaking violently.

"Jesus, Jasper," she says, gasping for air.

Smiling at her in the mirror, I grab a towel off the counter and wipe my face, tossing it aside in my haste to free J.T., to drive deep into her, to start her climbing all over again.

I reach around to fill my hands with her breasts, pinching her nipples between my fingers. Her inner muscles clamp down upon my cock, and I have to bite my lip—hard—to keep from coming too soon. God, it's never been like this before. I've never had to fight so hard to maintain control with any other woman.

Later we'll have time to spend hours in bed, but right now we're on a schedule. That's the only reason I give in to the powerful need to let go, to join with her in another combustible moment of unity. Our eyes meet in the mirror in the second before we hit the peak simultaneously. I've never felt closer or more in tune with another human being than I do with her right here and now.

I keep my arms wrapped around her and my face pressed to her back while her muscles continue to contract around my cock. Christ have mercy... I'm never going to survive her. What I'd consider "vanilla" sex with anyone else is almost too hot to handle with her. I love that it's as exciting to bend her over a bathroom vanity as it is to tie her to a bed. It doesn't matter what we do or how we do it, as long as we do it together.

"They'll be relentless," she says after a long period of silence.

"I'm not finding the will to care."

"Me either, but now I've got a heck of a job to do to put myself back together for TV."

"You could go out there starkers and be the most beautiful woman she's ever had on that show."

"*Starkers?*"

"Naked."

"That's not happening." She nudges me with her elbow. "Let me up, you sex-crazed beast."

I stand upright and zip my pants. "Ouch. That hurts my feelings."

"No, it doesn't. You can't fool me."

With her hair disheveled and her face flushed from two orgasms, she turns to face me. I've never seen anything more stunning than she is after we make love. I caress her face with my thumb.

"Is there a dictionary I can get my hands on?" she asks.

"Pardon?"

"Of all these British terms you toss around. I need a translator."

"I'll be your translator." I kiss her nose and then her lips. "How about we borrow Kris's shower and make ourselves presentable for this interview?"

"I need my bag to be presentable."

I kiss her again. "I'll go find it. Be right back." At the door, I look back to see her shimmying out of her skirt, and I have to remind myself that I was supposed to be doing something. Now that I'm allowed to touch her any time I want, that's all I want to do.

I leave the bathroom and cut through Kris's office to the hallway that leads to the foyer where Gordon left our bags. I'm on my way back with both bags when Flynn waylays me in the hallway. He stares at me but doesn't say anything, which puts me on edge.

"Everything all right, mate?"

"You tell me. You talked to my parents?"

"We did. They were very supportive." I pause and try to interpret his unreadable expression. "Flynn, I'm sorry if my relationship with Ellie has upset you—"

"It's not that. I actually think you two will be great together."

"Then what is it?"

"The rest of it. Did you think we would tell anyone?"

I exhale a long sigh when I realize his feelings are hurt by the secrets I kept from him and the others. "It wasn't that."

"Then what? I want to understand how I could work side by side with you for all this time and not know the first thing about who you really are."

"That's not true." The words come out far more sharply than I intended. "The Jasper you know is exactly who I really am. The man I've been here, with all of you, is the only person I've ever wanted to be. I'm sorry if you're hurt by the secrets I kept, but I kept them out of self-preservation, not because I didn't want you to know. It was never that."

"Fair enough." He looks up at me, and asks, "Does she know? About me? And the club..."

"No. I'd never tell her that. It's not my place, and I doubt she'd want that info anyway."

"You... You're being careful with her, right?"

"I love her, Flynn. I'll always be careful with her."

That seems to satisfy him. "Good enough, I suppose."

"I need to get ready for Carolyn."

He moves to step aside to let me pass. "You'll take care of her, right?"

I know he's not talking about Carolyn. "Always."

With a curt nod, he turns and walks away, leaving me to feel like I've just passed a huge test I wasn't expecting to take right then, but I suppose that conversation was inevitable from the moment I set my sights on his sister. When I open the door to join Ellie in the bathroom, I'm greeted with a cloud of steam.

I shed my clothes and step in to join her, wrapping an arm around her waist and propping my chin on her shoulder.

"I wondered if you were coming back."

"Flynn found me."

"Oh jeez. I hope he didn't say anything ridiculous."

"Not at all. We had a good chat."

"You'd tell me if he was an arse, as you would say, wouldn't you?"

"I'd take great pleasure in telling you that, but he wasn't."

"Is everything okay?"

"Everything is better than okay, and once we get this interview out of the way, I'll feel a thousand times better."

"Then let's get it out of the way."

CHAPTER 23

Jasper

Carolyn Justice is lovely and gracious and down to earth. After a few minutes in her presence, I see why Flynn chose her for the one interview he did when Natalie's painful past was made public. She puts Ellie and me at ease by first speaking to us off camera about what we'd like to say and what we won't talk about. Not surprisingly, she has a lot of questions about how a British aristocrat became one of Hollywood's most successful cinematographers.

I realize as I tell her the quick version of my story that it's a huge relief not to have to keep it secret anymore. My father did me a favor by spilling the beans, not that I'll ever let him know that.

And then it's show time. Ellie and I are seated next to each other with cameras pointed at us, and I discover how much I prefer being on the other side of the cameras. Being interviewed doesn't come naturally to me, not like it does to Flynn, Marlowe and Hayden.

As if she knows I need the reinforcement, Ellie reaches for my hand and holds on tight. After we pass the welcome-thanks-for-having-us pleasantries, Carolyn begins with my father's bombshell announcement.

"What can you tell us about why you chose to keep your title a secret for all these years?"

"At first it was about wanting to separate myself from the Kingsley name and everything it stands for. I was eighteen, venturing out on my own for the first time, and I was interested in a career that had nothing at all to do with my title, my legacy, my inheritance. I just wanted to make films, and that's what I've done for the last fifteen years."

"Very successfully, I might add," Carolyn says, launching into a list of the awards I've won over the years, culminating with the recent Oscar for *Camouflage*. "Why do you suppose your father decided now was the time to go public with the truth?"

"I don't pretend to understand much of what my father says or does, but I suspect the timing had to do with my recent visit to London during which I let him know that I won't be available to take over Kingsley Enterprises, as he's always planned for me to do."

"How did he take that?"

I glance at Ellie, who's watching me closely. "Not well. In the time it took me to fly home from London, he told the world who I really am, and here we are."

"What I don't understand is how it was possible to keep such a secret for all this time, especially in the digital age when everything is on the Internet."

"At home, Jasper Kingsley is known as an eccentric inventor, squirreled away in his Cornwall workshop. Here, I'm a lowly cine-matographer, made famous by osmosis thanks to the company I keep. I was extremely fortunate that no one ever dug into my background. I guess I'm just not that interesting."

"I'd argue with that," Ellie says, drawing smiles from Carolyn and me.

"As I understand, you went to see your father because you've decided to get married and have a family here in LA."

"That's right." I squeeze Ellie's hand as I look over at her. "Ellie and I are making plans that don't jibe with the plans my father has made for me all my life. I figured it was time to let him know that I won't be joining him at Kingsley Enterprises. I felt it was only fair to give him time to make other plans for his business."

"Ellie, how did you feel when you learned the truth about Jasper's background?"

"First of all," she says, "I already knew when it went public. I respect and admire Jasper's family history, but I don't believe that he or anyone should be forced to live any life but the one they choose for themselves. In this day and age, he can certainly uphold his responsibilities to his title while continuing to pursue a career that means the world to him at the same time. Not to mention, he's insanely talented, and the world of film would be lesser without his contributions."

"You sound like a woman in love, Ellie," Carolyn says.

Though my heart is full to overflowing, I say, "I paid her to say all that."

Both women laugh at my comment.

"What does your brother think of your relationship with his business partner?" Carolyn asks Ellie.

"He's been very supportive of us both, and I wouldn't expect anything less from him. Jasper has been our close friend for many years, so it's not like he's a stranger."

"And your parents?"

"The same. They're big fans of Jasper's, and they've always wanted the best for me. They're thrilled that I've found that with someone they already love."

"First Flynn, then Hayden and now you, Jasper. Love is in the air in the Quantum building."

"So it seems," Jasper says.

"Some of our viewers may not understand the role of the cinematographer. Can you explain it for us?"

"Simply put, I'm the director of photography on a film shoot. I work very closely with the director, usually Hayden, whose vision I bring to life through light and film. I'm in charge of the camera and how a scene is shot."

"How does one become a cinematographer?"

"Many of us get our start as photographers first. For me, it all began when my grandfather, ironically my father's father, gave me a thirty-five millimeter Leica Rangefinder and then taught me how to develop the film in his darkroom. I was instantly hooked. I progressed into tormenting my sisters with an eight-millimeter film camera. Being accepted to film school at USC was one of the best days of my life, and I've never looked back."

"When your father passes away, you'll become a duke, which is the highest rank below the royal family in Britain. How do you plan to balance your responsibilities to your family in Britain with your family here in LA?"

"I'll find a way to do both, but I don't see any reason to walk away from a life and a career I love here in order to fulfill my responsibilities there. As long as my father's company isn't in the mix, I see no reason why I can't have it all."

"Here's to having it all," Carolyn says. "Thank you both for being here, for the exclusive opportunity to hear your story. I wish you nothing but the best."

"Thank you so much."

"And we're out." Carolyn immediately removes the microphone from her lapel. "What an amazing story, Jasper. Thank you for sharing it with me."

"Liza explained that the timing of this interview is critical?" I ask, referring to our publicist.

"She did. We plan to air it tomorrow during my prime-time show. Will that suffice?"

"That'd be ideal. Thank you again."

She shakes my hand and then Ellie's. "Thank you both. I appreciate the exclusive."

"Flynn thinks the world of you," Ellie says.

"Likewise."

When we're alone, Ellie looks up at me. "That went well, don't you think?"

"It went very well, and you were brilliant, my love."

"Listening to you talk about your work... It would be so wrong for you to be anywhere but here where you belong."

I wrap my arms around her. "I know, darling." I hold her for a few minutes, taking some badly needed comfort from her. "I have to make a phone call, and then we can rejoin the others."

"Are you calling your father?"

I shake my head. "No, his assistant."

"Do you want me to stay close?"

"Always, but go have a drink. I'll be right along."

She kisses me before she leaves me alone in the room that was full of people and lights and activity a few minutes ago. Carolyn's film crew has packed up and moved on with a kind of efficiency I admire. Left alone with my thoughts of Ellie, the things she said about me in the interview and a fierce determination to chart my own course, I place the call to Nathan.

Even though it's early Sunday morning in London, he answers on the second ring. "Jasper."

"Nathan."

"I've been expecting your call."

"So he told you about how he's blackmailing me with embarrassing photos of me and people I love that he's going to release to the media unless I yield to his demands?"

"Yes."

"How do you do it, Nathan? How do you continue to work for a man who would blackmail his own flesh and blood?"

"I've begun to ask myself that more often lately."

That's the first crack I've ever seen in Nathan's armor when it comes to my father. "You should come to LA. I could find a job for you in a second."

"Don't tempt me."

"He's gone off on his jaunt having given you the photos and orders to release them, hasn't he?"

"Perhaps."

"Nathan, please don't do it. You're a decent sort of bloke. Will you be able to live with yourself if you're part of something like this?"

"You should know your mother was here before he left. There was a lot of yelling."

I'm still stunned that she actually left Cornwall to go to London, a place she hates. But I'm even more stunned by the idea of my father yelling at her. For that alone, I want to kill him.

"I've never heard her yell at him like that before."

"Wait... So *she* was yelling at *him*?"

"She was, and from what I heard, she let him know there will be dire consequences if he does anything to harm you."

"Well, I'll be damned." I've never once, in my entire life, heard my gently bred mother raise her voice to anyone, least of all her husband the duke.

"Despite your mother's best efforts, he hasn't withdrawn the order he gave me before he left."

"I can only ask you to look into your heart and think about whether you're willing to cross a line like this on his behalf. Whatever he pays you, I'd double your salary if you came to work for me. In fact, you might very well be the answer to my prayers about how to handle a dukedom and a film career at the same time. And I'd never ask you to do anything like this—ever."

"I'm sorely tempted. I've been very conflicted over this assignment."

"Make the leap, Nathan. I'll make sure that you're never sorry."

"Your faith in me is humbling, my lord."

"Call me Jasper."

"Give me some time to think over your kind offer?"

"Take all the time you need, but don't release those photos. Please don't."

"I'd already decided not to release them, but your call only cemented my resolve. Your father wanted to be the only one in possession of the photos, so I have the only flash drive that exists with the photos on it. I assure you it will be completely destroyed."

"Thank you, Nathan." Relief floods my system, leaving me light-headed. "Now tell me, what do you know about the person who infiltrated my life to get those photos?"

Ellie

I've never been so anxious. Waiting to see what's going to happen with Jasper's father, the photos, the possible scandal, the interview… It's all too much for me to process, and the only thing I want—to be completely alone with Jasper—isn't possible right now. The Quantum team is circling the wagons, working with the information Nathan gave them to contend with the mole.

Devon Black arrived an hour ago, along with his girlfriend, Tenley, one of the top stylists in Hollywood and a friend of ours. With one look at Devon's stormy expression, I'm thankful to be on his good side. God help the person who infiltrated his club to collect dirt on Jasper.

The thought of that photo of us at Black Vice being made public makes me feel ill, but only because it would embarrass my parents, not because I'm ashamed of being there. That's not it at all. It's none of anyone's business, and knowing we were photographed there to support a blackmail plot is infuriating.

Jasper comes up behind me and begins massaging my shoulders. "I can see how tense you are from across the room, darling."

"I just want to hear some good news."

"We've already heard the best news—Nathan won't release the photos."

"True, but I won't relax entirely until we know where they came from and that they've been destroyed."

"Don't worry—we'll get to the bottom of it."

I look over to the dining room, where Hayden, Kristian, Marlowe, Flynn, Sebastian, Gordon and Devon are conferring. "It's amazing of them to step up for us this way."

"It's not just for us, love." That's all he says, but it's enough to open my eyes to the fact that we're not the only ones featured in the photos. Dear God… That's more information than I wanted about my friends, but it helps to explain Jasper's full-on panic over the fact that they exist in the first place.

"I have so many questions."

"I'm sure you do, but you'll have to understand that there are some things I can't and won't talk about, even to you."

"I do understand, and part of me doesn't want to know."

We're interrupted by a shout from Devon. "I'll fucking kill him!" He gets up and charges for the front door with Tenley in hot pursuit.

Hayden chases after him. "I'll make sure he doesn't actually commit murder."

"I'll come with you," Addie says, running for the door.

Jasper and I go over to the table, where those remaining slump in their chairs, exhausted. "What'd you find?" Nathan had only told us that we'd find the source of the photos at Black Vice.

Flynn runs his fingers through his hair until it's standing on end. "Devon's director of security, Greg Thompson, a frequent guest at Club Quantum, too, sold out to Kingsley. There're multiple deposits in his account for amounts ranging from twenty-five thousand to half a million. Thompson would've had the know-how and equipment to do covert surveillance."

"Apparently, he was going through a bad divorce and needed the money," Kristian adds.

"Thank God it wasn't one of our people," Sebastian says.

"No kidding." Gordon stands and stretches before packing up his laptop. "I'm glad I don't have to resign."

"Thank you all so much," Jasper says.

I can hear the exhaustion in his voice and see it in the slump of his shoulders.

"I'm so sorry to have brought this down on us."

"Don't you dare apologize," Marlowe says sharply. "This was done *to* you. It's not your fault."

Jasper sends her a weak smile, but I know it'll be a long time before he forgives himself for what his father put everyone through.

"The goal now," Gordon adds, "is getting to the source of the photos and destroying them."

"I have full confidence in Devon being able to get that done," Flynn says. "Until then, I'm going to try to get some sleep, and you all should do the same."

With all our homes currently surrounded by photographers, Kristian is putting up Jasper and me, Flynn and Natalie, Aileen and her kids and my nieces and nephews, who are asleep with Aileen's kids on air mattresses in the game room.

"Flynn," Jasper calls to his retreating back.

My brother turns to him.

"Thank you again for your support."

"Of course. Try not to worry. I think the worst is behind us on this."

"I really hope you're right."

"When have you ever known me not to be?" He flashes the cocky grin that made him an international superstar and heads upstairs to his sleeping wife.

"I walked right into that, didn't I?" Jasper asks me.

"You certainly did." I take hold of his hand. "Let's go to bed." I need him to wrap his arms around me and make me feel the way that only he can.

"Are you going to bed, Kris?" he asks.

"I'm going to have a drink with Aileen." He nods to her, sitting on one of the lounge chairs on the expansive deck that overlooks the city.

I hadn't noticed that she was still up.

Jasper shakes his friend's hand. "Thank you for everything today. I appreciate you opening your home to us, feeding us, everything."

"It's nothing you wouldn't do for me. Am I right, mate?"

Jasper smiles at Kristian's use of British terminology. "You are indeed. We'll see you in the morning."

"Bright and early," I add. "The hooligans don't sleep in."

Kristian winces. "Better you than me."

As we make our way upstairs, I see Kristian take a bottle of wine and two glasses to the deck. It makes my heart happy to witness his obvious interest in Aileen, who deserves a love story for the ages after everything she's been through.

"What's got you smiling like that, my love?"

"Kristian and Aileen."

"He does seem rather besotted."

"Imagine that... A single mom with two kids who's fought such a difficult and valiant battle with breast cancer catching the eye of one of the most eligible men in Hollywood. It's a story right out of the movies."

"My darling is a romantic at heart."

"I never used to be, but now I want everyone to be as happy as I am."

He ushers me into our room and closes the door. "Are you happy, darling? Even with all the insanity—"

I kiss the words right off his lips. "I'm thrilled. Ecstatic. Over the moon."

His phone rings, and he groans. "I fear I must take this, as much as I'd rather not."

"Go ahead."

He withdraws the phone from his pocket and looks at the screen. "It's my mother." He accepts the call and puts it on speaker so I can hear it, too. "Hello, Mother."

"Jasper, I've just left your father."

"For good?"

"Of course not. He's leaving in a couple of hours for Greenland, where his flight will set off. When he returns, he's going to announce that Gwendolyn will become the heir-apparent to his business interests."

Jasper sits on the bed. "He really agreed to that?"

"He really did. He was, however, unmovable about the succession of his title. I'm afraid that's still all yours, my dear."

"That's fine. That's... That's more than fine. How can I ever thank you, Mother?"

"No thanks necessary. It's the right thing for everyone involved."

"And Gwen agreed to this?"

"She was thrilled to be asked. Apparently, it's what she's always wanted."

"I feel like I've been set free."

"You have, and you should use your freedom to live the life that best suits you, Jasper."

I slip my arm around him and rest my head on his shoulder, needing to share in this momentous occasion.

"And please bring your Ellie to Cornwall very soon, will you?"

"I will," he says softly. "Thank you, Mum."

"Be well, Jasper."

The phone goes dead, and he sags against me. "Did that just happen?"

"It did. How do you feel?"

"Stunned. I can't believe he let me go. I never thought he would."

"You didn't give him much choice. You stood up for yourself and made it clear that you wouldn't be blackmailed or strong-armed."

"It didn't hurt that my mother probably threatened to divorce him if he did anything to harm me."

"Probably not, but the first step was yours, and I'm so proud of you for taking a stand for the life you want."

"And this, right here with you, is the life I want. It's the only life I want." He kisses me and then pulls back to look at me. "You asked how I feel. What about you?"

"I feel relieved and giddy and excited for the future and so, *so* happy for you."

"For *us*."

"For us."

"And how would you feel about your son being the eleventh Duke of Wethersby?"

"Will he have his father's love and support as he learns how to tend to his family's history while also pursuing his own dreams?"

"He'll have his father's whole heart and soul and all the support he needs to be anything he wants."

"In that case, I'd be honored to raise the eleventh Duke of Wethersby."

Smiling, he gazes into my eyes and tips up my chin to receive his kiss. It's a soft, sweet kiss that's full of love and hope. The desire burns as hot as ever between us, but we take it slow, undressing each other with unusual patience, touching with reverence. Now that the road to forever has opened up before us, we have the freedom to take our time, to savor each moment.

He stretches out on top of me and looks at me with awe and amazement etched into his expression, as if he, too, is wondering what he did to get so lucky. Taking my hands, he places them over my head. "Keep them there," he says gruffly.

"Why?"

Raising his head, he meets my gaze, lifting a brow in inquiry.

"Why do you always want my hands out of the way? I want to touch you."

"I, um... I don't always want them out of the way."

"Yes, you do. Nearly every time."

"Oh, ah, well, you don't have to if you don't want to."

I bring one of my hands to his face to caress his cheek. "Tell me why it matters to you."

He exhales a ragged sigh and drops his head to my chest. "He would hit me. Any time I failed to properly answer his questions, any time I was unable to fake enthusiasm for the things he wanted to teach me, any time I was less than what he wanted in a son."

I wrap my arms around him and cradle his head to my chest, all the while blinking back tears for the boy who'd tried so hard to be what his father wanted him to be.

"The worst was when I told him I'd turned down all the schools he made me apply to, and the only one left was USC film school. He broke my jaw that day."

"God, Jasper." A sob hiccups through me, and tears fall from my eyes. "What about your mother? Where was she?"

"She never knew about it. She was in Cornwall when that happened. I showed up at school with my jaw wired shut and my face so bruised I was barely recognizable to myself. But I refused to let him take that away from me. I told people I'd been in a car accident.

Until now, the only way I could really let go with a lover was to ensure her hands were out of the equation."

I comb my fingers through his hair, wishing I could crawl inside him and personally eradicate every scar on his soul. "I'm so sorry."

"I don't want you to pity me, Ellie. I would hate that."

"Pity is the least of what I feel for you. I'm so damned proud of you for standing up to him when you were so young, for following your dream no matter what it cost you. Look at where that dream has taken you—to the very top of your profession."

"And it's brought me right here to you."

"That, too. I'll never touch you with anything other than love on my mind."

Raising his head from my chest, he kisses away my tears. "Don't cry for me, sweet Ellie."

"Only happy tears from now on." I keep my arms around him as he settles between my legs, his cock hard and hot against my core.

"Remember the project that brought us together in the first place?"

"How could I forget?"

"We've gotten a little sidetracked in the last couple of days, and I believe there was a schedule we were to keep to."

"I'm feeling *very* sick and *very* fertile."

"Mmm, I do so love when you talk dirty to me, darling."

In keeping with the slow theme of the day, he enters me in teasing increments, going deep before retreating over and over again, leaving me desperate for more, which I suspect is his intention. The next time, I keep him from escaping by curling my legs around his hips.

Chuckling, he brushes his lips over mine. "It seems you've completely trapped me, my love."

I smile up at him. "That was my evil plan all along."

"I've never been so happy to be trapped in all my life."

EPILOGUE

Ellie

Jasper and I stand together in the bathroom, looking down upon the array of plastic sticks on the vanity. My heart is beating so hard and so fast that I fear I may hyperventilate. Per Dr. Breslow's advice, we made ourselves wait until my period was officially a week late before we took the tests, and now that the moment is upon us, I can't bear to look.

I close my eyes and say a silent prayer. I've waited too long to try to have a baby. It would've been easier when I was younger. But back then, I didn't have Jasper standing by my side, his arm around my shoulders, the heat of his body warming the chill that's taken me over as the fears multiply with every second it takes for the tests to do their thing.

I turn my face into his chest. "I can't stand it."

"My poor darling." I want that voice to be the last thing I hear before I leave this life. "How could you *not* be pregnant with the effort we've put forth over the last few weeks?"

How could I not love a man who makes me laugh when I'm more nervous than I've ever been in my life? But that's how it is with Jasper. He knows just what to say to me to calm my fears, soothe my hurts and set me on fire with the kind of desire I never knew existed until I had him.

We're in Cornwall visiting his mother for a week, and we've had the best time exploring his childhood home, going on long hikes and having picnics in remote corners of the estate where we've made love outdoors more times than I can count. It's been a peaceful, restful escape from the madness that overtook us in LA after our interview with Carolyn aired.

The revelations of Jasper's pedigree, his new relationship with Flynn Godfrey's sister and the timing of his father's latest folly combined to set off a feeding frenzy during an otherwise slow news week. I now have a much better understanding of what Flynn deals with on a regular basis, although how he can stand it is a mystery to me.

Jasper suggested we escape to Cornwall, so here we are. I received the warmest possible welcome from his mother, and I've met two of his sisters and their families. I already feel right at home with the Kingsleys. We haven't heard a word from Jasper's father, and he's said he doesn't expect to hear from him, especially after Jasper managed to lure Nathan away. It's probably better if I don't meet Henry, as I'd probably make one hell of a scene letting him know what I think of a man who would treat his own son the way he has treated Jasper. Greg Thompson turned over the original images and video from the clubs to Devon Black, who pressed charges against his former security chief.

We finally relaxed somewhat when Devon let us know that the images had been destroyed. We're still trying to track down the private investigator who followed Jasper, and Gordon is making headway there, too. We won't completely relax until all the images of Jasper in compromising situations have been located and destroyed.

"Let's talk about something else while we wait," Jasper suggests. "Such as the news from home about Aileen and the kids moving to LA. How about that?"

"I'm so glad they're coming."

"I've never heard Kris so excited about anything."

"Do you have the scoop on how it came about?"

"He said that when Maddie and Logan cried when it was time to go home, Nat suggested that Aileen move to LA, and the kids begged her to do it. Hayden offered her the receptionist job that's open at Quantum. Flynn promised to help her find a place to live, and Kris said he'd do whatever he could to help them get settled."

"They put on the full-court press, huh?"

"They certainly did, and it worked. She's letting the kids finish the school year in New York, and then they'll be relocating."

"Such great news."

"Kris is crazy about her, not that he'll admit it to me, but it's obvious to anyone who knows him."

"I'd say it's quite mutual. She lights up in his presence."

"I can't wait to see what happens with them," Jasper says. "You know who else lights up around a man?"

"Who?"

"Leah whenever Emmett is in the room."

"That'd be an interesting pairing. She'd keep him on his toes."

"Indeed, she would," he says with a chuckle. "Shall we take a look, my love?"

I groan and press my face deeper into his chest. "You do it. I can't."

"We're looking for two lines, right?"

"Muh-huh." His shirt muffles my voice. I close my eyes as tight as I can and hold my breath.

"Darling... Take a look."

"I can't."

"You're going to want to see this."

Still holding my breath, I turn slowly, preparing myself for any possibility. I open my eyes and blink the strips of plastic into focus. There're double lines everywhere I look. "Oh my God! *Oh my God, Jasper!* We did it! *We really did it!*"

"We did it and we did it and we did it some more, and you're thoroughly and completely preggers, my love."

I bring both hands to my mouth, as if that could possibly contain the sob that erupts from the deepest part of me. We did it.

He holds me tight as the emotions tumble out of me in a mess of tears and sobs and probably some not-so-attractive snot. I've never been this happy. Ever.

Then he drops to his knees before me, and I gasp.

"My dear darling, Ellie, who gave me the courage to fight for the life I want more than I've ever wanted anything, will you please do me the honor of becoming my wife now that I've thoroughly and completely knocked you up?"

I'm laughing. I'm crying. I'm beside myself with joy as I nod and whisper, "*Yes,*" in response to his adorable proposal. Then he tops himself by sliding a purple pacifier on the third finger of my left hand, and I lose it all over again, realizing he planned this so perfectly.

He stands and gathers my soggy self into his arms. "Mother gave me my grandmother's ring to give to you. I hope you love it, but if you don't, we'll get you one you do love."

"That's so lovely of your mum, but I don't care about the ring. That doesn't matter. This... *Us*... This is what matters."

He tightens his hold on me. "I love you desperately, Estelle Godfrey Junior. Only you. Forever."

"I love you, too, my lord." I love to tease him by calling him that. "Thank you for making all my dreams come true."

"Trust me, my darling. It was entirely my pleasure."

~

KEEP READING *for a sneak peek at Delirious, Kristian & Aileen's story!*

DELIRIOUS

QUANTUM SERIES BOOK 6

CHAPTER 1

Kristian

I counted the days. I can't remember the last time I was so excited for something to happen that I counted the fucking days. I did that leading up to today, the day Aileen and her kids, Logan and Maddie, officially move to LA. I first met them in January when they came for Flynn and Natalie's wedding. Before Natalie's life blew up after she got together with Flynn, she was Logan's teacher. Aileen was sick with breast cancer then, and Natalie was a good friend to her and her kids.

The first time I saw Aileen at the wedding, she was painfully thin with deep, dark circles under her eyes and the shortest hair I'd ever seen on a woman. I found out later that was because she'd lost her hair during chemo, and it had started to grow back. I remember wondering about the odd haircut and then feeling guilty when I found out why her hair was so short.

But the signs of her illness aren't what I remember most about my friend's wedding day. No, it was Aileen's joyfulness that stood out. I'd never met a woman who had such incandescent light about her, even during what had to be some of the darkest and most difficult days of her life. She was, even in the throes of illness, so beautifully *alive*.

I was drawn to her like the proverbial moth to flame, and like a moth that doesn't know enough not to fly directly into the heat, I was unable to resist talking to her, getting to know her and nurturing an immediate and unprecedented attraction. The heat of that attraction swallowed me whole, and I was powerless to walk away. I let the attraction grow and flourish into friendship over subsequent visits, including the one in which I helped to convince her that she and the kids ought to move from New York to LA to live near us. Hayden offered her a job at Quantum, and we all encouraged her to take the leap.

And then I counted the fucking days.

So, what am I doing sitting on the floor of the game room closet in my Hollywood penthouse apartment, ignoring one call after another from my business partners, who are also my closest friends and the only family I've ever had? They want to know where I am, if I'm all right and why I'm out of touch on a day we've all been looking forward to.

We have plans. Flynn and Nat are picking up Aileen and the kids at LAX while the rest of us—Jasper, Ellie, Hayden, Addie, Leah, Emmett, Marlowe, Sebastian and I are supposed to be waiting for them at the house Ellie used to call home in Venice Beach. Since she's moved in with Jasper, Ellie is renting the house to Aileen. I'm sure the others are already there as the airport contingent is due home within the hour. Everyone is excited for them to get here.

We have surprises waiting for them. Two days ago, Natalie, Marlowe, Addie and Leah accepted the shipment from the company that moved Aileen's stuff from New York. Flynn, Hayden and I spent an entire evening putting beds together while the women unpacked their kitchen stuff. Aileen thinks she has all that to contend with when she arrives, but when they walk into the house today, their things will be waiting for them along with a black Audi sedan in the driveway.

I check my watch to confirm the car is being delivered right about now. The car will be in the company's name, but I bought it for her. I knew she'd never accept such an extravagant gift unless I billed it as a company car. I'm not sure why I felt the need to do such a thing, but I was at the dealership finalizing the purchase when it occurred to me that buying her a car might be too much too soon. By then it was too late to take it back, and besides, I didn't want to. She needs a car, so I got her one.

Natalie stocked the kitchen with groceries and filled the house with vases full of Aileen's favorite white hydrangeas.

Imagining her reaction to everything we've done has me yearning for something I simply have no right to. If she is an angel sent straight from heaven, I'm the devil himself in comparison.

I grew up mostly on the streets in the meanest part of Los Angeles, clawed my way into the film business, catching a couple of lucky breaks that brought me to where I am today. I'm one of Hollywood's most influential and powerful producers, a partner in the Quantum Production Company with some of the biggest names in the business. I'm on top of the world—literally—in my penthouse apartment right in the heart of Hollywood, which is suddenly trendy again.

Despite my many successes, despite the Oscar and Golden Globe that sit on a shelf in my office at work, and despite the fortune I've accumulated through hard work and determination, I'm still the homeless, rootless boy I once was. Crippled by fear, I'm sitting in the corner of a closet, ignoring calls and texts from the people closest to me and telling myself it's the right thing to do.

I'm a piece of shit compared to her. The things I've done to survive and thrive in this harsh world would horrify her. I'm wealthy beyond my wildest dreams—and I had some fairly wild dreams as a kid running the wicked streets of LA—but all the money in the world can't scrub the darkness from my soul.

I shudder in revulsion when I think about the things I did to stay alive. I don't believe in regrets as a matter of principle. You can't change the past, so why waste the present with regrets, or at least that's always been my philosophy. But for the first time in my life, I wallow in a vast sea of regret. I wish I were someone different so I'd be good enough for a beautiful, unspoiled angel like her. Bile stings my throat, bringing tears to my eyes. I have to stay away from her and her precious children, even if everything inside me calls out for her, wishing I could let her fix what's wrong with me, wishing she could be the one to chase away the darkness and fill me with her light.

She's finally here. I could see her *right now*. All I've got to do is get up off the fucking floor, get in the car and point it toward Venice Beach. Everyone I care about is there. They're looking for me, wondering where I am.

Moaning, I drop my head into my hands and rock back and forth as my phone rings again.

I can't. I just can't.

Aileen

I've never been this excited about anything, except my babies, who are now nine and five and out of their minds with excitement. I couldn't believe it when Flynn insisted on sending the Quantum jet to pick us up.

The Flynn Godfrey, who is now my *friend*. I still can't believe that!

Even though he's now happily married to one of my best friends, I have the biggest celebrity crush on him. I've seen every movie he's ever been in at least five times. I've watched *Camouflage* a dozen or more times. He won the Oscar and every other major acting award for that film this year, and having met and spent time with him, I know firsthand that he's as good of a person as he is an actor.

I'll never forget the first day Natalie brought him to my apartment. That was last winter when I was so frightfully ill and fearful of what was going to become of me and my children. Then Flynn made a humongous donation to the fund that the kids' school started for us, alleviating so many of my worries. Then he went a step further, hiring a housekeeper and nanny to help me with the kids. He single-handedly saved my life in every possible way, especially by getting me in to see the top breast cancer doctor in the city, who took over my care and made a few tweaks to my treatment program. Within weeks, I was feeling better than I had in a miserable year of surgery, chemo and radiation.

I'm not out of the woods yet. It'll be years before I can consider myself "cured," but I'm doing much better than I was, and I have Flynn to thank for that, too.

The entire Quantum team has become like family to the kids and me during our trips to LA for Flynn and Nat's wedding and later for school vacation. They took us in and made us part of their tribe, and when they teasingly suggested we relocate, the kids begged me to do it. They love California and the people we've come to know there. With nothing much holding us in New York, they prevailed, and I agreed to the move, but only after they finished the school year.

School ended yesterday, and today we're on the Quantum jet about to land in Los Angeles, our new home. If there's one person among our new friends I'm looking forward to seeing more than anyone else, well, that's my little secret.

I don't know what you'd call the flirtation or whatever it is between Kristian and me, but it's *something*, and I can't wait to find out if it might turn into something *more*. It's been years since I've dated anyone or been interested in a man, and I've never been attracted to anyone the way I am to him. He makes me feel so special by listening to every word I say like they're the most important words he's ever heard. The last time we were in LA, when we all stayed at his place in the city to avoid the reporters who'd swarmed around a scandal in Jasper's family, Kristian and I sat on his patio and talked until four in the morning while everyone else was asleep.

With wavy dark hair, intense cobalt-blue eyes and sexy dimples that appear only when he's truly happy or amused, he's so gorgeous that I often find myself staring at him like a lovesick puppy.

I'm *dying* to see him again, to find out if the attraction is still there and to see what might come of it. I'll never admit that he was one of the primary reasons I wanted to move here, but I'd be lying if I tried to deny it.

"How much longer, Mom?" Logan's question interrupts my delightful thoughts of Kristian Bowen.

I check the time on my phone. "About twenty minutes."

The kids are so excited to see our new home, to get settled and to spend the summer in LA. I'm starting my job at Quantum in two weeks, part-time for the summer while the kids attend camp and then full-time when they go back to school. I can't believe I'm going to work for the company that produced *Camouflage* and counts among its partners Flynn Godfrey, Hayden Roth and Marlowe Sloane. Talk about being starstruck! And I haven't even mentioned the other two Quantum partners, Jasper Autry and Kristian Bowen.

Kristian Bowen.

His name makes me want to sigh in anticipation, knowing I'm going to see him again *today*. If I were to let out my inner high school girl, I'd be writing his name next to mine on the cocktail napkin the steward gave me with the glass of wine I ordered and then drawing hearts around our names. But I'm not a high school girl. I'm a mature woman of thirty-two with two incredible kids who are my whole world and a brand-new life in a dynamic city to look forward to.

With maybe a brand-new man, too. *God, I hope so.* He's so beautiful and sexy and intense, and I haven't had sex since the dinosaurs were roaming the earth, or at least that's how it seems. The last time was when I was pregnant with Maddie, who just finished kindergarten. There are dry spells and then there's my life, a barren sexless wasteland. I'm ready to get my groove on again, and Kristian Bowen is the one I want.

He's the *only* one I want.

But does he want me like that? Or are we stuck firmly in the dreaded friend zone? Why in the world would a man like him who could have—*literally*—any woman in the world want to be with one who's fighting an ongoing battle with breast cancer while raising two young kids alone? There's baggage and then there's my two-ton trunk, a heavy load for me, let alone a man who can have any woman he wants.

Ugh. Do yourself a big favor, girlfriend, and don't put the proverbial cart in front of the sexy horse. He's apt to run for his life away from you and all your luggage.

Before I can let that depressing thought derail my excitement, a crackling sound comes from the speaker system ahead of the pilot's voice. "Hello from the cockpit, Gifford family."

The kids bounce in their seats, their excitement palpable.

"We've begun our final descent into LAX, and we'll have you on the ground in about ten minutes. We ask you to fasten your seat belts and prepare for arrival. Welcome home, folks."

The pilot's sweet words of welcome bring tears to my eyes. After what I've been through, I'm so grateful for every day and determined to make this move the best thing that's ever happened to my little family. My primary concern is making sure the kids are happy and healthy. They will miss their friends in New York, but they're excited about moving to California, especially Logan, who missed Natalie terribly after she left in the middle of the school year.

A few minutes later, the plane descends through the clouds to reveal the sprawling city of Los Angeles below. "Look, guys." I point to the window. "There it is."

"Move your head," Logan says to his sister. "I want to see, too." She insisted he sit with her, and she allowed him to have the window seat, even though he wanted it for himself. He's so good to Maddie and often stepped up to help with her when I was too sick to care for them. He's far too mature for his nine years, and I hope this move will allow him to be a kid again and not a kid with a sick mother and a little sister who needs him more than she should.

They cheer when the plane touches down with a thud and the roar of the thrusters, which they're used to from our earlier flights to LA.

After taxiing for quite a few minutes, the plane finally comes to a stop.

I supervise the kids, making sure they have everything and ushering them to the door, which opens right onto a tarmac where Natalie waits with her movie star husband, who is now our friend. Pinch me, please. *Flynn Godfrey* is *my friend!* It's taken some practice to get used to saying that sentence, but he's made it easy by being so amazing from the first time I met him. He's done so much to help make this move happen, and I'll never be able to repay him for his astonishing generosity. It's easy to forget just how beautiful they both are until I'm with them, and then it hits me all over again that my lovely, wonderful friend Natalie hit the husband jackpot with her gorgeous, generous husband. They both have dark hair, and while her eyes are green, his are brown. I can't imagine how stunning their future children will be. It'll be unfair to the rest of the average-looking world.

Logan and Maddie run to Natalie, who embraces them both at the same time while Flynn looks on, grinning widely. He and Natalie are so in love that being around them gives me hope for myself. Maybe someday I'll find someone who looks at me the way he looks at her. I'm mildly disappointed to realize that Kristian didn't come to the airport, but then I check myself. *Why* would he come to the airport? I'm Natalie's friend, after all.

Flynn hugs and kisses me. "Welcome to LA."

"Thank you so much for everything. The plane, the movers, all of it."

"Anything for you."

He'll do anything for Natalie—and her friends—and has proven that many times in the months since we met.

They load us and our suitcases into a silver Mercedes SUV, one of sixty cars that Flynn owns. Natalie mentioned that once, and I thought she was kidding until she told me she was dead serious. *Sixty* cars! It boggles the mind. But like he says, he could be addicted to worse things than cars.

On the way to our new home in Venice Beach, Natalie and Flynn point out landmarks and other points of interest, none of it registering with me because all I can think about is whether Kristian will be there when we get to the house. Now that I'm finally here, I want to get to know him better. I want to find out if the attraction that burned so brightly between us is still there or if it will fade now that we're going to see each other more often.

I hope that doesn't happen. I'll be so disappointed. I've allowed my crush on him to get totally out of control, blowing it up in my mind into a romance with epic potential. In reality, he was probably being nice to me because he feels sorry for the single mom with cancer.

I'm appalled by the tears that fill my eyes. I stare out the window at the passing scenery as I try to get myself under control. With everything else I've got to deal with, including a new home, a new job and two kids who've been uprooted from the only life they've ever known, I simply don't have time to obsess about a man.

But then we arrive in Venice Beach and pull up to the bungalow that now belongs to us, thanks to Flynn's sister Ellie. The street is lined with some of the nicest cars I've ever seen, including a black Range Rover, a gray Jaguar, a Porsche and something else I don't recognize, but it looks expensive. I begin to feel hopeful again. Does one of those fancy cars belong to Kristian? I have no idea what he drives, but it's probably something amazing.

In the driveway is a black Audi sedan that looks new. The porch is decked out in balloons, and the yard is full of friends waiting to greet us. My heart pounds with excitement as I take in the familiar faces—Marlowe, Leah, Emmett, Sebastian, Addie, Hayden, Ellie and Jasper.

Everyone is here. Everyone, except Kristian.

Delirious is available in print from *Amazon.com* and other online retailers, or you can purchase a signed copy from Marie's store at *marieforce.com/store*

ALSO BY MARIE FORCE

The Quantum Series

Book 1: Virtuous *(Flynn & Natalie)*

Book 2: Valorous *(Flynn & Natalie)*

Book 3: Victorious *(Flynn & Natalie)*

Book 4: Rapturous *(Addie & Hayden)*

Book 5: Ravenous *(Jasper & Ellie)*

Book 6: Delirious *(Kristian & Aileen)*

Book 7: Outrageous *(Emmett & Leah)*

Book 8: Famous *(Marlowe)*

Contemporary Romances Available from Marie Force

The Gansett Island Series

Book 1: Maid for Love *(Maddie & Mac)*

Book 2: Fool for Love *(Joe & Janey)*

Book 3: Ready for Love *(Luke & Sydney)*

Book 4: Falling for Love *(Grant & Stephanie)*

Book 5: Hoping for Love *(Evan & Grace)*

Book 6: Season for Love *(Owen & Laura)*

Book 7: Longing for Love *(Blaine & Tiffany)*

Book 8: Waiting for Love *(Adam & Abby)*

Book 9: Time for Love *(David & Daisy)*

Book 10: Meant for Love *(Jenny & Alex)*

Book 10.5: Chance for Love, A Gansett Island Novella
(Jared & Lizzie)

Book 5: All My Loving *(Landon & Amanda)*

The Treading Water Series

Book 1: Treading Water

Book 2: Marking Time

Book 3: Starting Over

Book 4: Coming Home

Book 5: Finding Forever

Single Titles

How Much I Feel

Five Years Gone

One Year Home

Sex Machine

Sex God

Georgia on My Mind

True North

The Fall

The Wreck

Everyone Loves a Hero

Love at First Flight

Line of Scrimmage

Romantic Suspense Novels Available from Marie Force

The Fatal Series

One Night With You, *A Fatal Series Prequel Novella*

Book 1: Fatal Affair

Book 2: Fatal Justice

Book 3: Fatal Consequences

Book 3.5: Fatal Destiny *The Wedding Novella*

Book 4: Fatal Flaw

Book 5: Fatal Deception

Book 6: Fatal Mistake

Book 7: Fatal Jeopardy

Book 8: Fatal Scandal

Book 9: Fatal Frenzy

Book 10: Fatal Identity

Book 11: Fatal Threat

Book 12: Fatal Chaos

Book 13: Fatal Invasion

Book 14: Fatal Reckoning

Book 15: Fatal Accusation

Book 16: Fatal Fraud

Historical Romance Available from Marie Force

The Gilded Series

Book 1: Duchess by Deception

Book 2: Deceived by Desire

ABOUT THE AUTHOR

Marie Force is the *New York Times* best-
selling author of contemporary romance,
romantic suspense and erotic romance. Her
series include Gansett Island, Fatal, Treading
Water, Butler Vermont and Quantum.

Her books have sold nearly 10 million
copies worldwide, have been translated into
more than a dozen languages and have appeared on the *New York
Times* bestseller more than 30 times. She is also a *USA Today* and *Wall
Street Journal* bestseller, as well as a Speigel bestseller in Germany.

Her goals in life are simple—to finish raising two happy, healthy,
productive young adults, to keep writing books for as long as she
possibly can and to never be on a flight that makes the news.

Join Marie's mailing list on her website at marieforce.com for
news about new books and upcoming appearances in your area.
Follow her on Facebook at www.Facebook.com/MarieForceAuthor
and on Instagram at www.instagram.com/marieforceauthor/. Contact
Marie at marie@marieforce.com.

Made in the USA
Middletown, DE
10 September 2020

19429561R00156